THE LUCKLESS

SECOND AGE OF RETHA BOOK 1

A. M. SOHMA

For the real Napert family,
Thank you for all the memories.
(Though I'm not sure my family would thank you for intro-
ducing me to Lotro.)

CHOOSE YOUR CHARACTER

KIT LOGGED into her gaming session peacefully, keeping her eyes closed as the game integrated her consciousness with its system.

She felt the cushy softness of grass cradle her, and the air smelled clean and crisp. In the distance, she heard a cow moo and a dog bark.

Kit smiled and shifted slightly, testing her body function control. Logging into a game was a slightly discombobulating experience for the brain, so it was better to take the first few minutes easy.

She relaxed and gave herself a moment to adapt. It was then that she faintly heard a steady, metallic beat. The perfectly timed tempo sounded suspiciously like a blacksmith hammering a horseshoe. But that was wrong. It had to be wrong. Kit had used her game card to purchase the *Sky's End* experience—a sci-fi game. Blacksmiths and swords did not belong in it.

Kit snapped her eyes open and shot upright. She blinked in the abrupt sunlight, but from her position on the grassy hillside, she could see perfectly into the medieval-esque village—complete with thatched roof cottages—and the pastureland that stretched around it. Far off on the horizon, snowcapped mountains pierced the air, and Kit thought she could make out the form of a dragon flying in the sky. "No. No!"

As if brought on by her disbelief, huge golden letters the size of elephants appeared in the sky, spelling out, *"Welcome to Retha. Your adventure awaits!"*

"Dang it!" Frustrated, Kit plucked a wad of grass and threw it at the letters before they dissipated. "What possessed that game architect to ignore my request? I was very clear I wanted —" she cut herself off as she ran a hand through her hair and her wrist brushed the tapered tips of her ear. "Oh, no."

With new dread, Kit scrambled to her feet. "Show character screen," she ordered the interface.

A transparent screen marked off with glowing lines appeared in front of her, swirling for a moment before displaying an image of her character: a long-legged female elf that sported Kit's natural dark brown eye color and hair a decidedly unnatural shade of champagne pink. Granted, it was a light, rosy gold color, but it was undisputedly *pink*. Kit narrowed her eyes until they were little more than slits. "Bryce," she growled as she flicked the screen away.

Kit's cousin, Bryce, had to be the culprit behind this prank. Bryce worked for Eternal Chase—the parent company of both *Sky's End* and *Chronicles of Retha*—as one of several community managers for Retha. As an employee, he would easily be able to create a new character under her login information.

But how did he get me dumped in here? Did he put some kind of note in my user profile?

Kit sighed. "It makes no difference. I'll twist it out of him when I get out of here. But where—" She froze as she brushed grass off herself and her palms touched silk. She peered down at her clothes and opened and closed her mouth several times.

Her character was dressed in a flimsy golden skirt that had

strings of coins layered around the waist, gold sandals, and a closely tailored shirt made of gold silk that cut off at her ribcage and boasted short sleeves made of the same flimsy cloth as her skirt.

"Show character panel." Kit bit her lip in worry and tapped one sandaled foot on the ground as the display popped up. She peered at her character information and felt the blood drain from her face.

"I'm going to stalk you at night and shave off all your hair, Bryce!" Kit howled at the blue sky when she could finally spit out the words.

It wasn't bad enough that she was an *elf*. She was also one of the most useless character classes to ever grace Retha's soil: a dancer.

———

Shortly before waking up in a fantasy game as a joke of a character, Kittredge—or Kit as most called her—adjusted her earpiece as she strode across the mall, listening to her cousin chatter.

"And then Chalupa ate the cord to my submersion headset! I had to call the rental company and see if animal damage was covered on the renters' insurance," Bryce said.

"And was it?"

"Yes, though I had to argue for half an hour that even though he is a rat, Chalupa is my daughter's pet and not a pest," Bryce said.

"This is why you should have just bought her a pony when she was little." Kit glanced at the giant clock that hung on the mall wall as her cousin scoffed. "In any case," she continued, "I have to go."

"Oh, are you at the arcade?"

"Just about."

"You're going to an EC arcade, right?"

Kit struggled momentarily to adjust her backpack—which contained her work laptop—and didn't answer.

"Kit, you're not *betraying* me, are you?"

"Sorry. Of course not," Kit said. (Since Bryce had become an Eternal Chase employee years prior, he had turned into a zealot for EC games.) "I'm going to the West Towne Mall EC arcade."

"Nice choice—they just remodeled their full submersion units."

"It won't make much difference to me, as long as I don't get a crick in my neck while I'm out of it."

"You won't," Bryce promised. "Be sure to have a pleasant time!"

Slightly weirded out by his overly friendly tone, Kit paused. "Thanks..."

"Mmhmm! I'm sure you'll be *dancing* with glee."

She frowned. "That would be a little weird, honestly."

"Oh?"

"I'm planning on playing *Sky's End*—the alien invasion game. I can't really see myself doing much of anything gleefully in there besides shooting aliens." She peered up and down the main drag of the mall, then found the correct side hallway and trotted down it, doing her best to avoid making eye contact with the rather pushy kiosk employees situated in the center of the hallway. (The last time she had mistakenly glanced at them, she had walked away with three bottles of lotion, a huge box of chocolate truffles, and a foot massager.)

"Why don't you play one of the fantasy games? Like *Dragon Rider* or *Chronicles of Retha*?" Bryce asked.

Kit almost collided with a kid that came pelting out of a shoe store. "I've only occasionally played *Dragon Rider* with you, and I haven't logged into Retha in years."

"True," Bryce said. "But maybe it would be worth a laugh to check it out again."

"Yeah, some other time," Kit said.

"We'll see."

"What was that?"

"Nothing! I should let you go—have fun!"

"Thanks." Her earpiece beeped, signaling Bryce had ended the call before she could say anything more. Kit swerved around a couple holding hands, then paused outside the darkened doors of the EC arcade. She glanced up at the glowing neon sign that read *Eternal Chase—we're waiting for you*, slipped her earpiece off, shoved it into one of her backpack pockets, and then entered the arcade.

The arcade itself was dimly lit, but the area flashed with lights from the screens that advertised its game lineup. Whatever floor tile she set foot on glowed like the night sky and emitted a rush of orchestra music. Cold air blasted down on her, and the screens on the wall flickered when she drew closer to them, rearranging so they displayed 3D advertisements of the games she had played the last few times she visited an EC arcade. An image of a dragon leaped off one of the displays as a warrior from the next screen over shot an arrow at it.

Kit ignored the advertisements and trotted up to the ticket counters, which blocked off the way to the submersion rooms.

Most of the game architects were already serving other players, but Kit spotted an empty slot and approached, smiling cheerfully at the architect—a guy who wore the blue and silver EC uniform and was probably a university student.

"Welcome to the Eternal Chase Arcade—where your adventure is our story," he said, breaking off to cough into his elbow. "How can I help you today?"

"Hi, I'd like to purchase a two-hour submersion game," Kit said.

"Okay." The game architect rubbed his nose and sniffed. "Do you have your login information?"

Kit held out her cellphone and bumped it against the architect's tablet, loading up her gamer ID on the countertop screens.

"Welcome back, Kit. Do you know what game you would like to experience today?" His fingers flew across his keyboard as he paged through Kit's profile.

"Yeah, *Sky's End*."

The architect paused. "Really? You don't want to try a multiplayer game—an MMORPG, perhaps?"

Kit wrinkled her forehead in confusion. She hadn't played a MMORPG—or massively multiplayer online role playing game —in a long time. For at least five years now she had almost exclusively played single-player games. "No. I'm not interested in multiplayer games."

"But you've played some recently...for instance, *Chronicles of Retha*."

Kit blinked, getting a sense of déjà vu from her conversation with her cousin. "I haven't played Retha recently."

The architect tucked his head into his neck. "Yeah, um, but your profile shows you used to be an avid Retha adventurer," the architect said.

"*Used* to be," Kit stressed.

"Did *Chronicles of Retha* fail to meet your expectations?"

"No, it just doesn't interest me anymore," Kit said. In truth Retha had been the last multiplayer game she seriously played, and she hadn't returned to it since Bryce had been hired by EC, and the guild they had been a part of left the game. "So, yeah. *Sky's End*, please."

"Retha has better reviews, and a new expansion just launched: Sword of Deceit," he said.

"I don't care. I want to play Sky's End." Kit held up her phone again, waiting to pay.

The game architect tapped his fingers on the desk for a moment, then reluctantly bumped his tablet against her phone, completing the transaction. "Your account has been billed," he said. "Here is your EC gauntlet, which contains all the information about your experience today." He passed over a metal cuff that had stylized edges, several plug ins for the submersion units, and snapped around the player's wrist.

It looked more like a piece of jewelry than an ID bracelet, but that was one of the many touches EC used. It was an expensive gaming company to go with, but they were stubborn in their desire to give users a high quality experience in all areas of their business.

"Your submersion unit is in the Atlantis wing, room number three." The game architect pointed out one of the hallways that broke off from the main room with the tired expression of someone who had done so hundreds of times before. "I'll send your information ahead; they'll be waiting for you."

The little gate next to his counter swung open, letting Kit through.

"Thanks," she said.

The game architect nodded, but his focus was on his computer as he finished up her order.

Kit made her way to the directed room. The floor picked up on the signal from her EC gauntlet and began displaying blue arrows to steer her in the right direction. She hitched her backpack higher up her shoulders and smiled.

It had been at least a month since she had been to an arcade, and her apartment wasn't configured for a submersion hookup, so she hadn't been able to play a game since.

With the launch of full-submersion games, video game companies had begun building their own arcades for a truly immersive experience in which the game would feel, to the player, like reality. A secondary market had opened up for home submersion units. The units were too expensive to buy outright, so gaming companies brought in most of their revenue by renting out submersion units tailored for their games. The rented units weren't quite as good as an arcade experience— they were smaller and didn't have as much processing power— so while the game felt realistic, players wouldn't experience as wide of a variety of smells, tastes, and textures.

Unfortunately, after graduating college and acquiring her first job approximately five years ago, Kit had taken up residence in an older apartment complex that hadn't been outfitted with the necessary cables and life-support systems that the submersion units required, so visiting arcades were her only option if she wanted to play a submersion game.

Still following the floor arrows, Kit approached a submersion room.

She held her gauntlet to a panel next to the door, and a light blinked above it. A woman who was perhaps in her mid-forties popped out of the room. Her short, messy red hair was pushed back from her face, and a pair of EC-blue glasses were propped up on the top of her head. She had a stylus clamped between her teeth like a cigar, and she squinted at her tablet screen until she flicked her glasses down over her nose. "Kittredge?"

"Kit, yes."

"Come on in. Changing rooms are located at the back of the room—follow the blue lights." The woman marched off to an empty submersion tank without bothering to check that Kit followed her instructions.

Kit took a moment to let her eyes adjust to the darkened room—illuminated only by floor lights, monitors, and soothing blue lights that pulsed on and off in the submersion units— which were basically glass bathtubs that held sleeping players and the tubes and plugs used for the submersion experience.

She slid her backpack off her shoulders and made her way

to the changing rooms, exchanging her clothes for a wetsuit and locking her things in a foot locker located under a bench.

Once ready, she slipped out of the changing room, and the older woman waved her over to a submersion unit that churned as it filled with water.

"Hop in," the woman said. "Unless you want a new image scan of your body? The scan will be used so your in-game character closely resembles you—should you desire it."

Kit dipped her toe in, then eased herself into the sponge-like chair sculpted into the tank as the water—bath-water-warm—sloshed over her. "I'm good, thanks. I had a rescan the last time I came here."

The woman shrugged and used her stylus to make a mark on her tablet, then clamped it between her teeth again. "Your gaming experience will last two hours, although it will feel much longer," she said around the stylus as she began suctioning nodes to Kit's skin. "If you are killed while in-game, your character will be reset to the last spawn point or save point you passed. Eternal Chase is not responsible for the actions of other players you meet while submerged in the game."

Kit frowned. *Sky's End* was a single-player/first-person shooter game. *I shouldn't meet anyone while submerged....* Before she had the chance to ask, the woman rolled on without stopping to take a breath.

"If you have not finished the game by the end of your purchased time, your progress in the game (as well as your character) will be saved. The average play time of a virtual game is four to eight hours, or approximately two to five visits," She thumbed through the screens of her tablet. "Please take the prescribed sleep drops now. It is a quick-acting sedative that will make your transition into the game easier." She held out a small bottle that was capped with an eye dropper.

"Thanks," Kit said, reaching out to take the bottle. She

unscrewed it and squeezed a drop of the liquid into both her eyes before handing it back.

The woman took the drops, then shut the lid of Kit's capsule. "Please stand by while I set your adventure." She affectionately slapped the unit, then swaggered away.

The computer attached to Kit's capsule was flipped on. Kit listened to the lady type away before slipping off into sleep...and waking up with pink hair.

2

_____

AN ENEMY APPROACHES

KIT STALKED down a dusty dirt road. Every step she took was marked by the bells hanging from her many anklets, making her anger with Bryce build.

"I hope his cellphone gets infected with a virus," she announced. "This was a mean-spirited joke—and *wasteful*! How much of my time is going to be eaten by this? Does he think money grows on trees?"

It *had* to be Bryce. A prank of this caliber had his thumbprint all over it.

As one of the community managers for EC, he would be one of the only people who had access to her profile. Most likely he made a note that convinced that scruffy game architect into signing her up for a Retha experience *even though* she had made it clear she wanted *Sky's End*! Bryce was also the only person she knew who could have gotten one of his company buddies to register such an embarrassing character—because that's what the elf dancer was, embarrassing.

As Kit stomped along, the walk gave her time to glance over a little more of her character information. The pink hair was bad enough—although Bryce had at least made it an attractive, dusty-golden-pink, like champagne—but he had gone the extra mile to make her look as newb-like as possible, and had given her elf a black swirly tattoo—a trait that was meant to be limited to several tribes of magic-using humans—on her left cheekbone. He must have used her body scan as the base for the rest of the image, though, as her character sported her same dark eyes and eyebrows that arched a little too sarcastically for fashion, and a heart-shaped face. The extra height he had added, though, kept throwing her off.

She scrunched her nose and checked her map again, taking a moment to glance back at the tiny village she had left behind. She had spawned just outside one of the starter villages, where EC corralled all players for their character's first five levels.

The villages had only the bare bones, as they were meant to be constantly repopulated by new players, not returning ones. So if Kit wanted to get out of this special torture Bryce had arranged for her, she needed to get to the nearest legal town. If she had been playing in a rented unit from the comfort of her apartment, she could have just logged off, but as she was in full submersion, she had to manually log off by visiting a village and talking to the right NPC—or non-player-character.

"Killing Bryce would be too kind," Kit decided as the breeze played with her gauzy skirt. "I'm going to systematically break his spirit."

She heaved a sigh of relief when she spotted her goal—Vippa, a small trading post town. "Almost free!"

Her elf ears twitched, picking up rustling bushes. Kit slowed her ruthless march and peered suspiciously at a couple of leafy hedges that edged the road. As she slipped past them, they shook, and out popped a glob of something that looked like a soccer ball-sized gob of grape jelly—a monster called gelata.

Kit jumped to the side, but the gelatinous creature rammed

into her with a surprising amount of force given that it was basically a land jellyfish.

Kit yipped and almost fell flat on her face, but she was able to correct her step at the last moment. It did nothing to save her health bar—the green bar indicating her health level that hovered near the top of her field of vision.

The single hit from the gelata sliced a third of the green bar off. Kit's jaw dropped. "You've got to be kidding me." Grumbling, she turned a spiteful eye at the gelata, which rolled toward her again. This time she was better prepared and jumped to the side to avoid it.

Her evade bought her some time, and she quickly opened up her character panel, fumbling through her skills. "What starter skills do I have...*nothing?*" Kit stared in horror at the blank space that was her skill list. There were a few race skills and starter skills—like basic cooking—but no attack skills.

The gelata made a suctioning noise as it adjusted itself for another pass.

"But I at least must have a weapon...right?" Kit fumblingly exited out of her skill list, opened up her inventory, and flicked over to her weapons slot. "*Nothing?!* Not even a club?"

Kit would have sworn with great vigor, but as *Chronicles of Retha* was marketed to all ages, swear words were immediately bleeped out. (Players who persisted in using them were eventually muted—unable to make a sound.)

So instead, Kit had to get creative to sneak around the language-rule. "Crabcakes and quinoa—this is rubbish!"

The gelata rolled toward Kit, who was grateful for the chance to vent some of her frustration as she stomped on the thing.

It bulged like a water balloon, but ruthlessly advanced, grazing her leg with another stinging blow.

Kit scrambled a few feet, retreating as her health bar

dropped by another third. "This is pathetic. It's so embarrassing I want to cry." She crouched briefly, then jumped directly on top of the glob. She had to jump up and down several times to deliver enough damage for it to pop, then fade away.

Kit brought up her character panel, screwing up her mouth into an ugly frown. She had gotten a few measly experience points from the gelata, but her low health was more concerning. "I don't believe this. I'm level five; I have no weapons, no skills, and I can barely kill a Jell-o jiggler."

Kit had never been a big fan of elves—they stuck out too much and were always harping on about the stink of shadows— but she knew there were some serious advantages to the race. The same could not be said of the dancer class—at least not these days, evidently.

EC offered a wide variety of character classes to choose from, but strictly speaking, they were divided up into five basic types: healers, melee fighters, tanks (who could soak up damage but dole little of it in return), magic fighters, and support classes.

Dancers fell into the support class. They could increase their friends' stats, trip up enemies, and more. Back when Kit had played the game, they were prized for conducting large-scale raids and completing dungeons, and she had loved the few dancers that were a part of her guild. But now most submersion games catered to small-group content rather than large-group content, making the dancer with its lack of damage or healing traits less useful when there were only a few slots to fill. (The change in content was one of the many reasons why Kit no longer played MMORPGs.) Moreover, dancers had an extremely low number of attack skills as their specialty was support. For a damage junkie like Kit, that was the worst.

Kit twitched her skirt in irritation.

The bushes rustled some more, and to Kit's horror, five more rainbow-colored gelata rolled into the road. Kit stared at them. An air bubble popped on the surface of one of the gelata.

"Nope!" Gripping her skirt, Kit sprinted toward the town of Vippa, the five gelata bouncing after her. *If one gelata almost killed me, five will take me down in a second!* She heard a sucking noise behind her, and groaned as a wad of jelly struck the back of her head, making her health drop a few points. "That's not fair! How come they can throw things when I don't even have a basic bludgeon skill?" One of the gelata almost caught up, and Kit forced herself to run faster.

The colorful gelata lost interest in Kit when she was a stone's throw from Vippa. Kit was tempted to throw a rock after the globs as they rolled off, but the last thing she wanted was to bring them back. She took a moment to collect herself and noticed that at least she wasn't panting heavily like she usually did when playing Retha. *Must be the elf stamina—it is a nice trait,* she admitted grudgingly as she glided the last few feet into town.

Vippa was a circular-shaped town corralled in by a rough wooden wall, but it burst with a wide variety of shops and colorful flags. The air was liberally spiced with the scent of hay, horses, and fried food. It was mostly filled with NPCs—shopkeepers, guards, and the like—but Vippa was a popular starting point for quests and raids as it was a short distance away from Luminos, the capital of Retha, so a fair number of players gathered in the streets as well.

Kit had to walk the circle twice before she could remember where the Fibbit stall was.

To "further the experience," EC had created Fibbit Services, an in-game company that served all players' more technical problems: from logging off full submersion players, to filing the necessary forms and paperwork to create guilds, and even providing teleportation gates to other cities.

Vippa was small, so its Fibbit station was little more than a stall, and it had only two NPCs stationed behind it.

Kit headed for it, weaving her way between a huge crusader and a slender illusionist. She was close enough to the Fibbit stall to touch the counter when someone cleared their throat behind her.

"Kitten Lovemuch?"

Another wave of fury with Bryce—who had given her character the ridiculous name—washed over Kit as she spun around. "Yeah?"

Two town guards narrowed their eyes as they studied her. One—an older guard with a thick mustache nodded. "It's her. Take her out."

Kit scratched her head. "Um...what?"

Mustache's companion—a young man—unsheathed a short sword and stabbed Kit in the shoulder.

Kit grit her teeth—it was quite painful until the attack dropped the last remaining bit of her health bar and made her collapse. "You as—" She didn't have time to finish the curse word before her sight went fuzzy, then black, and she died.

———

Kit snapped upright, respawning on the very hill she had first woken up on when logging in. "What the heck was that?" She furrowed her brow in concentration as she reviewed her memory. There was no way around it. Two NPC guards had killed her in broad daylight. "But guards only kill anyone affiliated with the Court of the Rogue..." she trailed off, deep in thought. "Display character panel."

Her character panel popped up. This time Kit flicked past the image of her character and instead activated the social panel. A list popped up, displaying Kit's reputation and kinship levels with the various races of Retha, as well as the different factions.

Her eyebrow twitched as she took in the stats. "*BRYCE!*"

She was going to murder her cousin.

It hadn't been bad enough that he made her a stereotypical elf with the horrible class of *dancer*; instead, he had manipulated her character's reputation level as well.

Reputation was usually about gaining favor with specific races—although there were certain races that did not get along, like elves and dwarves—but it also involved social balance. For instance, it was incredibly difficult for a player to be allied with the Imperials—the good NPCs, like city guards—as well as the Court of the Rogue—assassins, smugglers and the like. (In fact, back when Kit had played Retha frequently, only a handful of players had ever managed the feat.)

But Bryce hadn't *positively* manipulated her reputation level, oh no.

He had made her into a social outcast, so she was hated by both the Imperials *and* the Court of Rogue. And they weren't all! Dwarves *and* elves disapproved of her as well!

She sighed. *He must have gotten away with the obvious manipulation through the excuse that he's trying to break the algorithms that run the game.*

As an EC employee, Bryce was given a lot of sweet bonuses, but all EC employees were forbidden by contract to create characters that were positively manipulated. (So, he couldn't create a level 110 monk with the best equipment in the game.) The company didn't have the same rules, however, in creating terrible characters. In fact, EC encouraged employees to create characters with awful stats, just to see how the game reacted. (Kit had learned this when—one of the few times she agreed to play a multiplayer game after leaving Retha instead of a single-person game—she played *Dragon Rider* with Bryce. He had logged into the game with a pyro dragon that could only fly over water and a rider that was afraid of heights.)

Kit tapped the little question mark located next to her elf kinship bar. "How can my own people dislike me?"

Another transparent screen popped up.

Elf Reputation is low due to selected character class.

Kit groaned. "Of course! I forgot, elves think the dancer class is below them. Not that I blame them."

The tranquil and reserved nature of Retha's elves meant they thought dancers—with their flashy spells and horrid armor —were an embarrassment to one of their kind. Instead, if you wanted to be an elf and a support character, you could take up the class of bard, songstress, engineer, or many others.

Kit rolled her shoulders back. "No matter, I shouldn't ever see many elves anyway—and even if they disapprove, I don't think they'll shoot me on sight. But if both the Imperials *and* the Court of the Rogue hate me, how on earth am I going to get into a town that has a Fibbit Services location and log off?"

She rubbed her shoulder—although physically she was fully healed, her brain still screamed at the memory of being stabbed —and stared at the starter village. It didn't have a full service Fibbit desk, but it did have a teleportation gate. "I could buy a ride through a teleportation gate and pop out in the middle of a city. But can I get to the desk and ask to log off before the guards see me?"

Once again, Kit stood and brushed off the gauzy material of her skirt. She heaved a sigh as she set off down the grassy hill, making her way to the thatched roof cottages.

The starting area was little more than a handful of cottages arranged in a ring. There was a blacksmith (so players could buy weapons and armor) a food vender who was busy dipping apples in a vat of candy coating, and a few villagers. Chickens and children alike ran through the dirt streets, and at the far end there was a Fibbit stall—where tickets were sold to use the teleportation gate—and a post box where players could retrieve mailed packages.

The area swarmed with new players—many of them wore nondescript clothes as they hadn't yet reached level five, which was when they were allowed to choose their character class.

Kit in her orange dancer outfit and pink hair stuck out like a flame as she edged her way through the crowd, finally popping out by the desk.

"Greetings, customer!" the Fibbit stall attendant chirped. "How can I help you?"

Kit fanned her face with a hand and adjusted a shoulder strap of her belly shirt. "I'd like to purchase a ticket for the teleportation gate, please."

The stall attendant smiled and tipped her head. "I'm afraid I can't do that, valued customer."

Kit's stomach dropped to her toes in dread. Had Bryce gotten her banned from Fibbit Services as well? "Why not?"

The attendant raised a finger and pointed to the sky. "Heroes must reach level ten before they are allowed access to Retha's teleportation gates."

Kit ran a hand through her hair and was tempted to pull it, because it seriously couldn't cause her more pain than Bryce had already plunked her in. "But I thought it was allowed at level five?"

"It was level five a number of years ago," the NPC acknowledged. "But the minimum was changed last year." The attendant continued, ignoring the shriveled look Kit was giving her. "We at Fibbit Services apologize for any inconvenience this might cause you."

Kit stopped assaulting her head and turned around, propping her elbows up on the counter as she stared at the chaotic swirl of her fellow players. "Well that bites. What am I supposed to do now?"

The question was meant to be rhetorical, but the attendant answered her anyway. "You may enter the Aridus Plains and begin fighting monsters, if you choose, or you can check with the Heroes' Representative. He's hanging about the blacksmith's shop and likely has a few errands you can run for experience and loot. Or—"

The NPC stopped mid-word, her voice dragged out in a tinny sound. Kit tried to move, but found she couldn't, and she noticed all the players were frozen in the middle of an action.

Lag. Kit reasoned. *A lot of players must be online.*

Whenever EC experienced an influx of players, the game sometimes worked slower as the servers adjusted.

Sure enough, after a few more moments, the world exploded into action again. The attendant talked on, and the other NPCs continued with their business, but, Kit was surprised to see, many of the players had suddenly disappeared.

Kit frowned and brought up her character panel, her eyes settling on the dimmed community tab.

In order to foster comradeship, EC had created a cohesive community where players and staff members alike posted and interacted. Players could post recorded footage from their gameplay, create guides and walkthroughs, and access the many databases EC provided. It could be accessed both in and out of game, but while most used it like a social network offline, ingame it was an invaluable resource that players could refer to when searching for information on certain quests, skills, and more.

The dim color of the tab signaled it was offline and unavailable—which was not shocking. It usually went down when the servers lagged.

"Yep, must have been the lag," Kit decided. She turned around and nodded to the attendant. "Thanks for your help."

The attendant waved farewell as Kit wandered through the now significantly less populated village. If she had to guess, the lag and subsequent surge had knocked at least 80% of the players out of the game.

"Maybe it affected everyone using rental units at home," Kit muttered. "It's a shame it didn't affect me—I could be off this character, then."

Kit brought up the world map and was trying to estimate how long it would take her to walk to Luminos—the capital of Retha—when a computerized voice rang through the village circle.

"*Attention, Heroes. Retha is currently experiencing server difficulties. Log off capabilities are temporarily unavailable. Thank you for your patience.*"

"Oh that's just *fabulous*," Kit grumbled—but even she knew this was one thing she couldn't blame on Bryce.

One of the few remaining players—a woodland elf—cheered. "This means we get more game time," she said.

"As long as we don't have to pay extra for it," a guy still in the beginner armor (cotton clothes) grumbled.

Kit suspected the logout function wouldn't be down for more than a few minutes, so she ignored the impromptu assembly and continued with her exit strategy.

She instead approached the food vendor—a grandmotherly woman who had a sweet smile and a critical eye for bartering—and spent a few minutes haggling for what few food rations she could afford. (She was *not* going to walk all the way to Luminos just to die by a gelata once within sight of the massive city.)

Kit popped her purchases—a loaf of bread, two baked apples, and a waterskin of cider—into her inventory and was making her way toward the edge of town when a bell rang and an envelope shook in front of her—the in-game notification that she had received a letter.

Briefly, she considered ignoring it. No one from her guild still played *Chronicles of Retha*, and even if they did, they wouldn't know about this asinine character Bryce had created for her. Most likely, it was a welcome message from EC or a letter that would direct her to a quest.

In the end, she decided she may as well read the message. If she didn't, the white envelope would pop up every hour of in-game time, which was sure to get irritating quickly. *Plus, it might have more information about what's going on*, Kit thought as she squinted around the village, though she knew it was unlikely as no other players were rushing to the post box to collect mail messages.

Kit meandered back to the Fibbit stall, where the mailbox— a blue box the size of a large bird feeder nailed to a post—was situated. As she opened the mailbox and retrieved her message —a heavy parchment envelope—it struck her that none of the players who had been disconnected with the wave of lag had come back on.

It made sense given the ability to log off was temporarily offline. EC was probably scrambling to fix it...but if the situation was that dire, why hadn't they forced a logout of *everyone*?

Still mulling over the idea, Kit opened her letter. She glanced at the sender's name and almost ripped it up in her anger. There, at the bottom of the rather lengthy letter and under an EC company letterhead, was Bryce's name.

"He's probably gloating," Kit grumbled. "Yeah, laugh it up while you can. As soon as I get out of here, I am going to..." she didn't finish delivering the threat as she started to read the letter, and worry clogged her throat.

Kit, you are in danger.

The Fable-Stay server, the one you're currently on, experienced a power surge and shut down. All rental units were automatically disconnected, but the full submersion units were shuffled to the emergency backup server. That's where the problem is.

The backup server, which was designed to take over in hosting and running the game should the main servers fail, is corrupted. All players who were transferred to the backup server are locked inside. No one, not even EC employees, can log on, and you can't log off. You won't be able to leave until they successfully transfer you back to the main server—which is unlikely as they need to fix whatever corrupted the backup server first.

The obvious option would be to turn the servers off and shut down the game. It may come to that, but management wants to avoid it if at all possible. The game has filters built into it for logging on and off to help players make the switch from game life to reality. As the login features are down, so are those filters. Without them, management estimates that approximately 26% of players would experience light to serious brain damage. Most likely it would be about as serious as a concussion, but probability says a number of players would experience significant damage.

Kit's fingers shook. For a split second she hoped wildly this was all part of the trumped-up joke Bryce was playing on her. But while Bryce would happily drag her pride through the mud and frustrate the heck out of her by giving her an elf dancer, he would never make a twisted prank that involved such steep stakes.

She took a deep breath and tried to calm her irregularly beating heart, then continued reading.

EC will not rest until they have you guys safely out of the game,
but there is a chance for you to free yourself.
Several of the biggest quests/events in the game automatically
boot players off once completed. This was done so EC employees
could check over the data and verify that the quest/event was
completed without any sort of manipulation or cheating. That
function should still work—though there is no way to verify it at
this time.

A bubble of dread popped in Kit's stomach. "Oh, no..."

The easiest quest for you to complete that does this is to kill
Malignus.

"You've *got* to be kidding." Kit's legs gave out, and she sat
down hard on the ground. The Fibbit Services attendant gave
her an odd look, but Kit ignored it and stared unseeingly at her
letter.

Malignus was the final boss of the game. He was part of the
lore of the world. No one had beaten him. It had long been
suspected that he was impossible to defeat *because* he was a
cornerstone of Retha.

I know what you're thinking, but it can be done. A full raid of
EC employees completed it during beta testing before the game
was commercially released.
You can do this, Kit. Get as big of a group gathered as you can,
and kill him. If EC can repair the server before you manage this,
great. Otherwise, it's your only chance.

Kit set the letter down and rubbed her face, trying to organize her racing thoughts. Her ears rang, and her chest felt like
someone had her lungs clenched tightly in their fist.

Eventually she finished reading the letter—which did nothing to make her feel better.

Tell everyone about this way out. No one else knows of it—
knowledge of the EC employee raid is part of the confidentiality
clause we have to sign.
After this message, I don't think it's likely I'll be able to contact
you again. Getting in contact with the server is hard enough, but
with this crap-show, EC is locking down tight on us employees.

Reading between the lines, Kit could see that Bryce was almost certainly going to lose his job over this—first of all for reaching out and personally contacting her and telling her what was going on, and secondly for revealing that slaying Malignus was possible.

Remember to check our guild zone in Luminos. We probably
have leftover equipment and materials you can use. Good luck,
cousin. If anyone can bust out of Retha, it's you.
Senior Community Manager
Bryce N.

Kit snorted at his closing line. Out of *everyone* who had been a part of their guild, she was probably the least qualified to do this. She had never led a raid or even a quest. She had always been the damage-dealer of the party...and now she was a dancer.

She tilted her head back and stared at the sky. "I am so screwed." Her hands flopped to her lap, crinkling the letter.

3

PARTY FORMATION

IT WAS TOO MUCH—THE threat of mental injury, the inability to log off, the pressure of slaying Malignus and completing a quest that was thought impossible... An unhappy future was staring her down, and Kit didn't think she could survive it.

The ringing in her ears grew louder, and her vision grew fuzzy.

What am I going to do? What CAN I do? I can't beat these odds.

Kit shook her head so hard she felt her neck crack. "Enough!" she whispered fiercely. "I can't just sit here freaking out—I have to at least *try* to fix this! I'm not going down without a fight!" She stood, impatiently straightening her skirt as it twisted around her legs.

Bryce was right. The best first step would be to go to Luminos. She could rummage around her house and the guild zone for anything helpful—maybe she could even get in contact with some of the major guilds that were still on.

Kit and her friends had left the game five years ago, but there were bound to be players who would remember them.

She opened her inventory panel and pushed the note into the screen, popping it into her character's inventory, already feeling better.

She had a plan, which was a good start. The situation might be tense, but falling apart wouldn't help her. Kit planted her hands on her hips. "Besides. As real as Retha feels, it's still a video game. Everything here is about balance. I just have to figure out how to tip the scale my way."

Kit eyed the two dozen or so players who still wandered around the village. *One thing is for certain: even though Bryce said to tell people about this, I don't want to start mass hysteria—particularly among the newbies—when there is still a chance EC will fix this. I'm better off sharing what I found in Luminos with the more veteran players. But I don't want to leave everyone here hanging...*

Nodding, Kit cleared her throat, then shouted through the village. "Has anyone been able to log off yet?" She asked, knowing perfectly well they could not.

A dwarf lingering by the blacksmith shop shook his shaggy head. "No, I expect they'll make an announcement once everything is back online."

A couple of new players who still wore the nondescript cotton clothes nodded.

"I hope they get it fixed soon," a girl said.

"Why? We're getting free playtime," one of her companions said.

"Yeah, but I don't want to pick a class until I can access the community tab and figure out which of the magic user classes is the best!" The girl said.

"It's been down for a while now," Kit carefully said. "Isn't that a little odd?"

"It's nothing to worry about," the dwarf said.

"I'm not so sure," said a girl—some kind of thief class based on the daggers holstered at her hips. "Bits of lag and services being temporarily unavailable happen in any game every once in a while...but usually it's fixed in a matter of minutes. It's been a while since they made the initial announcement."

Kit eagerly capitalized on the girl's point. "I agree. I'm going to head to Luminos. Someone there might know what's going on."

The group of players who still hadn't chosen their character class shuffled. One of the guys shrugged. "Go if you want, but by the time you get there, everything will probably be fixed. You'll just be wasting your playtime."

The dwarf nodded his agreement. "It shouldn't be much longer," he said.

"I'm not so sure," Kit said.

Her half-baked warning fell on deaf ears. Several of the new players rolled their eyes and turned their back to her. A guy who had a sword nearly as big as himself strapped to his back snorted as he made his way to the Fibbit desk. The dwarf raised his shoulders, as if saying he had tried, then waved to her before he approached the blacksmith.

"Well." Kit scratched an itch on her hip. "That wasn't exactly a fruitful endeavor."

"Pardon me young lady, but you said you were going to Luminos to investigate this game breakdown?"

Kit spun around, her best sales smile on her lips. "Yes. Luminos is the biggest city in Retha. If anyone knows what's going on, they'll be there."

The speaker, a human man who looked about middle-aged with slightly weathered features and dark circles under his eyes, smiled, revealing the good-natured twinkle in his dark eyes. "If you are not opposed, I should like to join you. Retha is the first full submersion game I've ever played, but this situation seems...odd. I, too, would like to gather more information."

"Wonderful! I'd be glad to have you come with me...." Kit glanced at the crown of his head, making his character name, health bar, and basic information appear. "Old Man Bluff?"

He laughed. "Yes, it's a little odd, but I'm ashamed to say the character name creation screen stumped me. Every name I came up with was taken. But please, call me Gil—short for Gilbert...Miss Kitten Lovemuch," he said, referencing her nameplate.

Kit made her smile bigger in hopes that he wouldn't recognize her shiver of revolt at her own name. "Just Kit will do great, thanks." She glanced at his information again. "So you're a level eight crusader?"

Gil nodded and flicked his shaggy hair out of his slightly narrowed eyes. "Yes—a tank class, I believe."

"Mhmm," Kit said, refraining from saying anything else. She never would've guessed Gil was a crusader if not for his nameplate; he still wore the cotton clothes of a newbie player.

"Excellent! All we need is a healer. Then we will be a true-blue party." The female thief who had spoken up earlier folded her arms behind her head and sauntered in their direction. "That is, I assume you don't mind if we come as well?"

Kit blinked. "We?"

The thief waggled her thumb back and forth between herself and a female wizard who reluctantly trailed in her wake. "Me and Vic, that is. We think it is probably best to head to Luminos, as well, so we'd love to join you."

The wizard scowled and flipped a lock of her silky black hair over her shoulder. She would've been quite pretty, particularly for a human, if not for the fact that her dark eyes were barely more than narrowed slits. "There is no we in this situation. I'm still furious with you for dragging me into this!"

The thief laughed sheepishly. "This is Vic's first full

submersion game experience. After this, I am honestly not sure how I will get her back into one."

Kit eagerly clasped her hands together. "Then you've played *Chronicles of Retha* before?"

The thief shook her head. "This is my first session in-game. I played a lot of other submersion games, but I was saving this one to play with Vic. I love your character design, by the way!"

Kit smiled—though she internally questioned the thief's sense of aesthetics. "Thank you...." She glanced at the thief's head. "Nevarro Kuro."

"You may as well call me Cookie. I haven't been able to get Vic to call me by my character name at all anyway. I'm a night stalker, by the way." The thief grinned, her big eyes combined with the bow that marked the end of her blonde hair braid made her look cute rather than deadly. "I'm level six. Vic is a level five wizard."

The wizard studied her nails as Kit glanced at her name, which was *Ihatethis*. "So, what would you like us to call you?"

The wizard shoved her hands into the sleeves of her voluminous cloak. "Vic or Victoria will do. Thank you for including me in your party."

"We're glad to have you with us. I'm Kit, a dancer, and Gil over there is a crusader."

Cookie used one of her wicked-looking daggers to scratch her cheek. "We really are a pretty well-rounded group, then. Too bad we couldn't recruit a healer."

As a member of the thief class, Cookie fell in the class of fighter. (Most thief classes—like night stalker, rogue, or assassin —used speed and stealth to their advantage and inflicted great damage.) Vic, on the other hand, was a magic user—which meant she was far easier to kill but also packed massive amounts of damage. (Mage classes also had the most Area of Effect skills —AoE skills—which impacts a set area as opposed to a specific target, allowing the player to kill more than one baddie at a time.)

"It can't be helped. The perfect small group party wouldn't include a dancer anyway." Kit looked back and forth between Cookie and Gil. "Do either of you want to lead this party?"

"Party?" Gil asked.

Cookie shook her head. "I barely figured out the combat system. I assume you've played *Chronicles of Retha* before?"

Kit nodded.

"Then you're the natural choice to be the leader. We will be in your care, thank you!"

Kit laughed sheepishly and scratched the back of her neck. "I hope you don't have your hopes set too high. I haven't played Retha in years, and I'm not an experienced leader. But with luck, we'll find someone more up to date on the game in Luminos." Resigned to her role, Kit pulled up the necessary screens and made the party, creating a name (*Travelers to Luminos*) and selecting one of the standard banners—a periwinkle blue one— to represent their group. "Does anybody need to get anything before we go? Or maybe put on their armor?"

Cookie slung her arm across Vic's shoulders, unbothered when the pretty girl shrugged her off. "We're great! We were about to go level grinding when the announcement was made."

"I believe I'm adequately prepared as well," Gil said.

Vic's frown deepened, if that were possible. "Aren't you a crusader? Don't you have special armor to put on?"

Kit wanted to bless the prickly-tempered wizard. "She's right, Gil. The crusader armor they give you when you signed up will have much better stats than the stuff you're wearing now."

"It won't wear out?"

"No," Kit said. "Your armor won't degenerate, but your weapons will. Even so, it's easy enough to get them fixed. Just visit the blacksmith whenever you stroll through a town, and you'll be set."

"I see." Gil flipped through his inventory panel and began highlighting his armor— switching out the newbie gear for the heavy yet durable suit of crusader armor.

Kit brought up the world map, then consulted the mini-map screen to get herself correctly positioned. "It shouldn't take us too long to get to Luminos. They put the starter points near it so once players reach about level ten, they can walk there or use a teleportation gate."

"Then let's get going," Vic said. "I don't want to stay in this game any longer than I have to."

Cookie sighed and placed a hand over her heart. "It grieves me every time you say that."

Kit flicked the big map away and began marching out of the village.

"Then shall I say it again?" Vic asked as she, Cookie, and Gil followed behind.

"Please don't," Cookie pleaded.

Vic gave a derisive snort, and Gil released a rumble of laughter as they cleared the small circle of buildings.

"Hey! You four!"

A guy—the one who had snorted at Kit earlier and sported a sword nearly as big as himself—jogged after them. Presumably he was some sort of fighter class based on the sword and his armor, as both were of a significantly lighter build than Gil's. "Yes?" Kit asked.

"I want to come with you to Luminos." The guy had bright red hair that was pulled back in a man-bun so tight Kit wondered if it pulled on his eyebrows.

"You also wish to seek out more information?" Gil asked.

"Heck no!" Man-Bun lifted his chin up and hooked his thumbs in his sword belt. "I think you're all worrying over nothing. But I gotta go to Luminos anyways for a quest, and you all look like you'll croak if a monster even glances at you."

Vic stabbed a finger at Gil. "I don't think he would."

"You probably wouldn't either, Vic." Cookie said.

"Of course," Vic sniffed.

"Yeah," Kit said. "You'd kill it before it could reach you."

"That's not the reason at all," Vic said. "I would survive because I would throw Cookie in the fiend's path and run."

Gil eyed Cookie and Vic. "Are you certain you two really are friends?"

"Totally!" Cookie chirped. "We're besties! Vic just doesn't know how to express affection without using sarcasm."

"That was not sarcasm," Vic said.

Kit combed her fingers through the low ponytail of her champagne pink hair. A glance at the fighter revealed his name, Axellent; class, fighter; and level, nine. While the guy was not winning any personality prizes, a warrior would be able to take more damage than a night stalker or wizard. And as they lacked the healer, extra damage and resilience was their best hope. *And who knows, by the time we reach Luminos, maybe he'll understand how weird all this is.*

She gave him a friendly smile. "You can come with us if you want," she said as she sent him a party invitation.

Axellent accepted. "I'll hold the front lines," he promised.

"Welcome to the group, Axellent." Gil smiled at the warrior and shook his hand. Though Gil was thick through the shoulders and Axellent had more of a lithe build, both players were similar heights and stood eye to eye. (Kit wryly noticed she was as tall as them—perhaps even a bit taller—which would explain why the extra height her elf character boasted had thrown her when she first started.)

"You will be called Axel," Vic declared.

"What? No way! My name is Axellent! It's a legitimately cool name!"

"Do you really think so? Then I pity you. And it doesn't matter. I would be absolutely embarrassed to call you Axellent in public. Moreover, it is unnecessarily long," Vic said as they started walking again.

"Choosing a name that isn't already taken can be pretty difficult—that's why so many players now have last names as well," Kit said. She purposely curved their path a little, aiming for the road that ran between Luminos and Vippa—the outpost town she had visited earlier.

"You mentioned previously that you've played Retha before," Gil said. "I assume Kitten Lovemuch is your second character?"

"You could say that," Kit said wryly.

Axel adjusted his sword on his back. "Why would you ever choose a *dancer* as your character class?"

"Let's just say it wasn't my choice."

————

Kit switched her attention back and forth from glancing at the party members' health bars to watching Cookie and Axel fight with a small group of gelatas.

The warrior and night stalker were making quick work of them, but both Cookie and Axel's health were dipping down past half way, and their teamwork was a little rough.

"You're a kill stealer, night stalker," Axel growled when Cookie sliced cleanly through a gelata he had been attacking and slayed it.

"Sorry. I thought we were trying to kill these monsters as fast as possible." Cookie said.

Kit noticed a gelata rolling towards Vic and automatically

made a few of the gestures she used on her old main character to jump-start a spell. When nothing happened, she shook her head. *I'm a different class, now. No damage skills for me—as maddening as it is!* She cleared her throat and announced, "A gelata is going for Vic." She meant to tell Gil who would taunt the monster and draw its attention, but Cookie pounced on the glob before it reached the wizard, leaving Axel surrounded by four gelata that immediately convened on him.

"Hey!" he growled.

Cookie was back in an instant. "Sorry."

Axel stabbed two gelata with one strike. "I'm never trusting *you* with my back."

"Miss Kit, look out!"

Kit turned around and yelped when she saw the emberling —a wisp-like creature of flames that had a jack-o'-lantern smile— bearing down on her. She started running when the creature spat a fireball at her, setting her gauzy skirt on fire.

She almost collided with Gil but managed to sidestep him at the last moment. The crusader tried to punch the emberling, but the creature bobbed over his fist and continued pursuing Kit.

Kit could feel it gaining on her, the sparks it shed hitting the bare skin on her lower back. "Can I get a little help?" She shouted.

Cookie jumped a gelata and ran at her, but Vic beat her to it. "Bubble Barrage!" The wizard traced her finger through the air, creating a glowing symbol, then thrust her pointer finger at the emberling. A river of bubbles slammed into the creature, putting it out with a puff of smoke. "That was a surprisingly effective skill, despite its pathetic name," Vic said.

Kit gratefully stopped running and finished slapping out the last tiny bits of flames that ate at the singed hem of her skirt. "Thanks, Vic," she said as Axel finished off the last gelata.

Vic nodded queenly, though she jumped when a thunder-cloud formed directly over her head and lightning rained down around her. Similarly, black shadows swirled around Cookie, and rainbow-colored lights and white musical notes poured down on Kit like a waterfall. Simultaneously, big, beveled, golden letters formed over the three girls' heads, reading: "LEVEL UP."

Kit smoothed her bangs as her character panel automatically popped up.

Congratulations! You have learned the dancer skill: Battlefield March
Your beauty and poise in battle heartens those around you.
Skill Effect: Increases party members' physical attack and defense power. Can be interrupted.

Kit felt as weary as an old woman as she gazed off listlessly into the horizon. "Ahh, yes, a buff, as expected of a support charac-ter. An attack skill was too much to hope for, I see." She flicked the screen away. "Did you get any new skills, Cookie, Vic?"

Cookie shook her head and holstered her daggers. "Nothing for me."

"I finally have a useful skill: Fireball," Vic said.

"But Bubble Barrage was quite powerful," Cookie said.

"It's most effective against flame-based monsters," Vic said. "Otherwise, I would've tried smothering you with it hours ago."

"Aw, I love you too, bestie!"

"I apologize, Miss Kit, for my failure in keeping the ember-ling's attention on me," Gil said. He furrowed his eyebrows, making his weathered features appear even harder than usual.

"It's not your fault," Kit said.

"But it is," Gil insisted. "My entire role is to keep monsters from attacking other members of the party."

"Yeah, but you're only level eight, and we're still a pretty inexperienced party. Of course, someone's going to pull aggro off you," Kit said. Tanks were designed to hold the attention of monsters—it's why they were immovable walls of health. However, monsters could still drift away if another party member put out too much damage, taking on that monster's aggression—or aggro. Monsters would attack players besides the tank, though, for other reasons as well.

"The dancer is right," Axel said, as if he could hear her thoughts. "Monsters are always drawn to the weakest member of the party. In Kit's case, it's even worse than usual because she can't fight back or even heal. Basically, she is a bleeding, wounded seal frolicking through a swarm of sharks."

"Thank you, Axel, for that complimentary review of my character," Kit said wryly.

"What? Everyone knows support characters are a royal pain to keep alive."

"You seem to know quite a bit about game mechanics," Gil said.

Axel shrugged and sheathed his sword. "I played *Beast Master* a lot. But it's gotten so abandoned, they're shutting it down in a couple months, so I thought I'd give Retha a try."

"*Beast Master?*" Vic said, her voice acidic with disdain.

"It's a good game!"

"Uh-huh. I bet."

Kit used her superior elf eyesight to peer off into the distance. She'd been able to see Luminos for a while—it was impossible to overlook as it was a brilliant white spot in the middle of the rolling plains. "Hey Cookie, can you see Luminos yet?"

The night stalker joined her. "That blob on the horizon? Yep, I see it finally."

"Good. We're almost there. I'm pretty confident we'll reach it before nightfall." Kit marched toward the city, her new friends following behind her.

"I'm glad to hear it; particularly given that neither the community tab nor our log off capabilities have returned," Gil said.

Kit bit her lip, internally agreeing with the crusader. Despite Bryce's letter, she had hoped the EC geniuses would be able to get them transferred back to the main server. *It's probably been half an hour outside of the game. We still have time.* The reassurance seemed paper thin, but Kit wasn't very eager to organize a raid to throw themselves at Malignus.

Axel grunted. "I still say you're all just worriers."

"What will we do when we reach Luminos?" Vic asked.

"The marketplace is a good spot to hear local gossip," Kit said. "But the Guildhall will be where all the big players are. If we really want to figure out what's going on, the Guildhall is our best bet."

Cookie adjusted her black armguards. "Then we'll go straight to the Guildhall?"

Kit squinted, able to make out the nearest entrance to Luminos, a giant drawbridge that was lined with guards. "Not exactly."

Vic frowned. "What do you mean?"

"I can't enter Luminos through the main gates; I'll have to get in a different way. But all of you can walk right in. So we'll split up. You four head on in, and I'll meet you at the marketplace—which is in the center of the city. It will give you a chance to repair your weapons and restock up on any supplies you need. The Guildhall is north of it, so it won't take us out of our way."

Gil tilted his head. "Why can't you go through the main gates?"

"The Imperials don't really like me."

"Then you're allied with the Court of the Rogue? How did you pull that off at such a low level?" Cookie asked. "Before logging on the game, I read that it took a while before you gathered enough reputation with them to make the Imperials dislike you."

"I'm not allied with the Court of the Rogue, either," Kit said. "They hate me, too."

Axel whistled. "What did you do to tick off both of them at the same time?"

Kit's shoulders slumped. "It's complicated."

"If you can't get in through the gates, how do you expect to enter Luminos?" Vic asked.

"There are a few backdoor methods," Kit said. "None of them are really appealing, but I don't have a choice."

The furrow of Gil's brow deepened. "I don't think you should go alone."

Kit patted the crusader on his pauldrons. "Don't worry about it. It can't be helped. I'll be fine; the method I'm considering isn't really dangerous—just super annoying. And smelly."

"Still..."

Cookie unsheathed one of her daggers and tossed it in the air. "Not to worry, Gil! I'll go with Kit."

"It's really not necessary," Kit said as the city grew larger on the horizon.

"Maybe not, but you should still have someone there to help if things get rough—especially since you're a support character," Cookie said.

"She's got a point, shark-bait," Axel said.

"Maybe you should wait to officially offer help until you hear how I'm getting in," Kit said.

"Nonsense. Together, I'm sure we will be able to handle it." Cookie gave her a thumbs up and a brilliant smile.

"Then it's settled," Gil said. "Vic, Axel, and I will meet you two at the marketplace."

"How about at the mermaid statue in the marketplace? It's a pretty sprawling area, so it would take a while for us to meet up even though all party members are marked on our mini-maps," Kit said.

"The mermaid fountain in the marketplace. Understood," Gil said.

"This is going to be great fun," Cookie said. "And it will be good practice for avoiding guards."

Kit was not convinced. "We'll see."

After all, she knew there were several secret ways to get into Luminos. But the only one she thought she could pull off as a dancer...was going up a garbage chute.

4

LUMINOS

KIT PUT her hand on a rancid piece of meat, and tried not to gag when a maggot wiggled against her thumb.

"You okay back there?" Cookie was farther up the garbage chute, having crawled through the horizontal chute with the slipperiness of an eel and popped into a vertical shaft.

The walls of the chute narrowed as Kit climbed forward on her hands and knees. "I'm managing."

"The intersection where you go from a horizontal to vertical position might be tough for you," Cookie said.

Kit breathed shallowly through her mouth so she wouldn't gag from the rotten, overwhelming stench of garbage that filled the chute. "Why? I'm pretty nimble as an elf."

"But you're also tall," Cookie said. "And it's your height that might make it difficult."

A gelatinous glop landed on Kit's shoulder. She flicked it off, but it left an algae-ish slime behind. "I don't think I get what you...oh." Kit reached the end of the horizontal chute and poked her head into the vertical shaft. The horizontal chute made a T intersection with the vertical shaft, which fell at least ten or fifteen feet deep. Because of the sharp angles of the intersection and the tight width of the shaft, Kit could see she was going to have a difficult time maneuvering her body out without falling.

Cookie was comfortably situated about four feet above Kit's head. She was braced with her back pushed against one side of the shaft, and her feet on the other side. "Here!" She slid down a bit and offered her arms. "I'll pull you up."

"Won't I be too heavy for you?"

"Nah. You're an elf. Elves are always light as feathers. Come on!"

Kit took the night stalker's hands to steady herself, then inched to the end of the horizontal chute. With a surprisingly strong pull, Cookie yanked on her arms and popped her out of the chute like a cork coming out of a potion bottle. Kit dangled in mid-air for one terrifying moment, then scrambled to brace herself similarly to Cookie, heaving a sigh of relief when she was secured. She wiped off her forehead, grimacing at the sticky residue some of the trash remnants had left on her hands. "There has got to be an easier way to get inside Luminos without being discovered," she said.

"Maybe you can disguise yourself?" Cookie wriggled further up the shaft with enviable ease.

"Maybe," Kit agreed as she tried to follow her friend. Unfortunately, her sandals didn't exactly make the greatest footwear for scaling walls, and she slipped. She threw her arms out to catch herself, banging her elbow in the process. Kit hissed out a breath of air, then squealed when she slipped down another few inches, this time smacking her head on the wall.

With both her head and her funny bone smarting, she groaned. "Son of a biscuit! I hope the EC designer who came up with the pain scale is plagued by papercuts!"

A cute little trumpet chord sounded, and sparks of red, purple, and blue light fizzed around her.

Congratulations! You have learned the life skill: Swear
Proficiently!
Your salty tongue is creative enough to make a nun wallop you.
Effect: Unknown
PASSIVE SKILL

Kit stared at the announcement, half stuck between being stunned and furious.

In *Chronicles of Retha*, players were able to learn four different types of skills: class skills, which they received for leveling up their character's class; crafting skills, which were awarded once players chose the two kinds of crafting they would like to take and leveled up their crafting level; race skills, all of which were granted upon character creation and were different based on the race of the character; and life skills, which were learned naturally throughout the game and varied greatly from player to player.

Life skills were meant to balance out characters to create a fair gameplay system. For instance, fighting and mage classes were normally given more passive skills that would do very little to help in battle. Things like "Bow gracefully," "charismatic speaker," or even "fast reader." Healer and tank classes were often given more useful skills, like "quick learner," "excellent observer," or "fast walker."

The pool of possible life skills ranged in the hundreds of thousands, and the skills you were given depended heavily on the way you used your character, as well as your general character build. Players who shared the same character race and class would still receive different life skills. That was why typically the more fragile or non-combative classes received some of the most useful skills. As a dancer, Kit should have been a prime candidate for some amazing life skills. So to have her first life skill be "swear proficiently"?

"Did I ever really find this game enjoyable? Or was I just being unknowingly traumatized?" Kit wondered.

"Did you say something?" Cookie asked.

"No. I was just musing over the curse of this character."

"Oh. Well if it makes you feel any better, I reached the end of the shaft."

"Really?" With renewed vigor, Kit tried crab-waddling her way up the shaft.

"Yep! I'm going to pop out and make sure there aren't any soldiers around."

"Great. I'll see you soon." Kit said.

"Roger that, good buddy!"

Kit shook her head, impressed with Cookie's upbeat attitude even though they were squirming around in trash. She took in a shallow breath, then resumed inching her way up the shaft. With the promise of release just ahead, Kit didn't even shudder when she touched the slime-coated wall and narrowly missed crushing a yellow-toothed rat who sat upon a brick that jutted out of the wall.

Soon, she reached the square opening of the shaft. Blinking in the sunshine, she wormed her way out, falling out of the shaft and landing in garbage piled in front of it with a wet splat. She leaped from the pile and sucked in great gulps of air.

"Cold-hearted-designers. There's no possible way that chute could be legitimately used to get rid of garbage."

Cookie popped out of the shadows. "Good job getting out all by yourself! And there aren't any guards around, at least not right now anyway."

Kit tottered away from the garbage, shaking refuse from her clothes and limbs. Her hair, ironically enough, had not even a speck of dirt in it, nor a lock out of place. "The guards are on rotating patrols; but I'm not too worried about that. Back when I played, they were mostly posted outside important buildings."

"That's good to hear. So, should we head to the marketplace?"

"No. I don't want to walk around smelling like a sewer rat—I'll get kicked out of any stores we try to enter. Let's take a quick detour. There's a city well nearby we can use to clean up."

"I'm game if you are," Cookie said.

Kit, her clothes smeared with grime and smelling powerfully enough to make her eyes water, took a quick look around. The garbage shaft had popped them out in one of the residential areas of the city. It took her a few moments to rummage through her memories and recall the layout of Luminos—with which she had once been so familiar, she could probably have drawn it out by hand. "This way." She started up the cobblestone street, ignoring the horrified looks an NPC innkeeper gave her when she passed his doorstep.

They didn't see any other players until they reached the edge of the residential area, popping out in a small circle that held a well and a stable.

Situated in front of the stable was a gallant-looking female knight who was entertaining a small, mostly female audience. When the knight glanced from her companions to Kit and Cookie, she grimaced in sympathy. "The lost ring in the garbage quest?"

Kit shook her head and wiped crusted dirt off her wrist. "We used the garbage chute to enter the city."

The knight shook her head, making the high positioned ponytail of her blue-black hair flare behind her. "That's never a fun experience."

"Tell me about it," Kit grumbled.

"Alistair." One of the knight's friends tugged on the knight's armor. "Are you going to finish your story?"

The knight smiled—the combination of her white teeth and sincere light in her eyes making the gesture charming. "Of course, milady." She nodded to Kit and Cookie, then returned her attention to her friends.

Two of her crowd—a male who had goggles pushed up into his hair and wore a crazy amount of buckles, and a girl with tawny-colored skin who wore druid robes—watched Kit curiously for a moment before they too returned their gazes to their companions.

Kit ignored the extra attention and waddled over to the well, freezing momentarily when she realized too late that a pair of soldiers were entering the street circle. She was paralyzed with fear—and dearly tempted to break in her new "Swear Proficiently" skill as they walked the circle.

Oddly, the soldiers didn't even glance at her—though they poked their heads in the stable—and continued with their patrol.

Cookie rubbed her chin and joined the still-paralyzed Kit. "Huh, I wonder if they didn't notice you because of the garbage."

"Could be." With the threat of insta-death out of the way, Kit darted to the well and, using a crank mechanism, drew up a wooden bucket filled with water. Without hesitating, she dumped it on herself, washing away some of the slime.

It took several more buckets of water before Kit felt she could breathe through her nose again. She closed her eyes, sucked in a gulp of air. "At long last...I don't smell sour enough to make myself sick."

"I didn't think it was quite that bad, but in addition to superior sight as an elf, maybe you have a superior sense of smell, as well?" Cookie splashed water on herself and cleared away some of the sewage grime, but she wasn't even half as dirty as Kit.

Ahhh, the athleticism of a night stalker. Kit brushed her

damp bangs out of her eyes. "Maybe. The important thing is that now we won't drive everyone away with our stench."

"Yes, Vic would kick me in the face if I tried to hug her while smelling like garbage." Cookie tossed the empty bucket back in the well. "Are you ready to go meet up with the rest of the group now?"

"Yep. Follow me. It's this way." Kit trotted off, leaving the quiet city circle for a busy street that was filled with NPC shops and players meandering from store to store.

As a city, Luminos was practically an ode to straight lines and tall buildings. Almost every city structure had multiple floors, and the buildings were always pristinely straight up and down and built out of the same gray rock as the city's walls. In spite of the uniformity, or perhaps because of it, each section—and in some cases each street—brimmed with its own brand of character, achieved with beautifully colored banners, stained glass windows, unique lamp posts, and eye-catching signs.

Strolling through Luminos was comforting for Kit. Though it had been years, the city was still much the same. There were a number of new stores, but many of the same NPCs strolled down the street as they had back in Kit's day.

The familiar sight of a little girl NPC who was always accompanied by her pet pig made Kit smile as they meandered past. *I still can't believe we're in danger—it's like coming home again.... But maybe that makes it worse. I find it hard to fathom being in danger when I spent years playing this game.*

When unease tugged on her stomach, Kit opened her character panel and grimaced. The community tab was still darkened. *I've got to keep my priorities straight. Until EC starts making some announcements and transfers us back to the main servers, killing Malignus needs to be my focus.* She shook her head to clear her thoughts, then picked up her pace to a brisk walk.

Cookie gazed wide-eyed at a pet store that sold beautifully colored cats. "I'm glad I saved *Chronicles of Retha* to play with Vic. If any game can make a gamer out of her, it'll be Retha."

"They put a lot of effort into making every part of the game be a true experience." Kit rounded the corner, which opened into the city marketplace—the most popular place for players to try and hawk their wares to fellow players.

"+10 agility sword, only a hundred silver marks!"

"Poison antidotes, mana potions, and health potions—get 'em all here at Snooty Moody's store."

"Rare buccaneer saber—private message me with best offer."

Cookie staggered back under the onslaught of shouts. "What a thriving economy."

Kit peered at the marketplace, which was a checkerboard of player stores and potential customers. "This is actually pretty empty—probably because of the technical difficulties." She scowled when two male players standing nearby hid no attempt to take a screenshot of her.

Cookie gaped. "Are you serious?"

"Yep. Usually if you walk near the marketplace, you get a wave of lag because there are so many people packed in it." Kit plunged into the stands, shouldering her way through the crowds. Once, she had to save Cookie from a particularly aggressive merchant, but in no time at all the pair popped out of the thickest of the crowds and staggered their way to the gigantic mermaid fountain.

The fountain was huge—easily the size of a small cottage—and made completely of marble. Three carved mermaid maidens sat on rocks, which gushed with drinkable water.

Cookie squinted up at the giant display. "It's so beautiful!"

Kit studied the monstrosity. "It's certainly eye-catching. Look, our group is over there."

Kit and Cookie trotted around the fountain, waving to catch the attention of the rest of the party.

When Gil saw them, he smiled and nodded—giving him a fatherly aura. "I'm glad to see you made it safely into the city," he said when they drew close enough to hear him.

"It was certainly an experience." Kit flapped the gauzy material of her skirt, trying to dry it faster. "One I hope not to repeat."

"Vic!" Cookie squealed and sidled up next to her friend. "Did you enjoy yourself?"

"Of course not," Vic scoffed. "I'm stuck in this rustic-aged game; how can I enjoy myself? Here!" Vic shoved a fist-sized, cinnamon-covered, cat-shaped cake at her friend.

"You bought this for me? Aw, Vic! You're too sweet!" Cookie beamed as she took the cake.

"You're making a big deal over nothing. I only got it because I thought you wouldn't have eaten yet." Vic lifted her nose and refused to look at her friend.

Though players didn't strictly *have* to eat and drink in-game, usually the mind and stomach eventually sensed the time spent between pseudo meals and revolted, and players grew hungry— although mostly food was consumed to heal after a battle. The same went for sleeping. Players could stay awake for days in game time—though if you were on long enough, exhaustion usually won out and even the best of gamers crashed to get a few hours of rest.

Kit turned her attention from the two younger girls, and studied Axel. She was a little perplexed that he was still with them. *Is he starting to realize the severity of the situation?*

The warrior scratched at an itch under his armor. "What?" he asked when he caught her staring at him.

"I was wondering why you're still tagging along when you said you only wanted to come to Luminos for a quest."

"I thought I'd stick with you guys for now to make sure no one mugs you. You're going to the Guildhall, aren't you?"

Kit nodded.

"And where is the Guildhall located?" Gil's armor clanked as he shifted.

"Not too far from here. It's pretty close to the Fibbit Services' headquarters." Kit pointed north, toward the top of the city.

"Then let's go," Vic said. "The community tab still isn't up, and I want some answers."

"Right." Kit paused to re-orientate herself, then circled around the mermaid fountain and headed north.

Rather than traveling on the broad main roads that were wide enough to ride mounts on and housed the more important buildings, Kit wove through smaller streets—doing her best to avoid soldiers. It took longer, but eventually they strolled into the North Ward of the city.

Luminos' most important buildings were all located in the North Ward, on a hill that pitched them higher than the rest the city. The Guildhall and the Fibbit Services' corporate headquarters were only two of a handful of the spectacularly beautiful hillside buildings.

The Guildhall was in the center. The main part of the building was cylinder in shape, with smaller hallways that branched off into towers so it almost resembled a snowflake. A massive garden sprawled in front of the Guildhall, though a wooden walkway peppered with guards split the grounds in half.

Kit sighed. "I'll have to meet you all inside."

"How will you get in this time?" Vic asked.

"Certainly not another garbage chute, I hope?" Cookie asked.

Kit rubbed one of her tapered elf ears. "Nope. I can avoid

the guards if I circle around through the gardens. It will just take a little extra time."

Gil relaxed his grip on his massive spear. "That doesn't sound so bad."

"It shouldn't be. I'll meet you guys just inside the front doors. It's a really pretty building, so feel free to look around while you wait for me. There's a bunch of beautifully themed meeting rooms you can check out." Kit waved as she started to walk away, but she was still able to hear their conversation for a few more moments.

"I wonder what sort of meeting rooms a fantasy game can create," Vic said.

Axel shifted the sheath of his sword strapped to his back. "Can't say I'm interested in interior design."

Kit approached the large, green hedge that walled in the gardens in front of the Guildhall. Cringing, she squirmed her way through it. It was nearly as wide as she was tall, and she popped out the other side as she spat out a green leaf. "Far easier than garbage-chute spelunking." She took her merry time, darting behind white birch trees, flowering lilac bushes, and even a birdbath fountain.

Once in the Guildhall, I'll have to try to tell everyone what Bryce told me...hopefully they won't think I'm a lunatic.

When she was flush against the Guildhall wall, she trotted toward the entrance and was again forced to fight her way through the thick hedge. She made it almost all the way through when her skirt snagged on a hedge branch.

She gritted her teeth and tugged on her skirt. "I wonder if Bryce had his little designer friend mess with my character's gameplay balance. Because this is enough to make a saint swear." She leaned back, and her skirt abruptly gave. She crashed out of the bush, almost falling on her rear before righting herself at the last moment.

She shook her clothes out, shedding a few leaves and grateful her skirt was still in one piece. She was combing her fingers through her hair to make sure she didn't have any greenery stuck in her thick locks when a deep voice interrupted her.

"Could you move, please."

Startled, Kit belatedly realized she'd been blocking one of the doorways to the Guildhall. "Oh, I'm sorry." She backed up to let a large man exit the building.

He wore a dark-colored cloak with a hood that shadowed most of his body so Kit couldn't see more than the faint gleam of his armor. His face, however, was visible. He had a square chin, piercing gray eyes, and dark eyebrows that had a strong slant to them.

As he looked at her, he raised his eyebrows in open disdain and made a noise in the back of his throat.

Kit blushed. She was aware that between her class and character design, she looked like the sort of person most serious gamers would look down on...but he didn't have to openly remind her! She narrowed her eyes at him, purposely flicked a leaf in his direction, then flounced around him and slipped into the Guildhall.

"Kit!" Cookie called.

Kit swiveled around, searching for the night stalker.

"Over here," Vic added.

Kit spotted her party just a little in, gathered around the base of a marble statue of a knight. "Hey."

"Did he say anything to you?" Cookie eagerly asked.

Kit blinked. "Who are we talking about?"

"Solus Miles." Gil folded his arms and stared thoughtfully at the door Kit had entered through. "He was just confronted by two players. He shot them down as coolly as you please."

Still lost, Kit tilted her head. "...So?"

"He's apparently the top player in the game," Vic said wryly.

"How did *you* know that?" Kit asked.

Vic shivered in horror. "I didn't. A bunch of inane girls squealed loudly about it when they saw him."

"He was the amazing knight that almost ran into you at the door," Cookie chimed in.

Axel adjusted his sword. "He isn't *that* amazing."

Vic rolled her eyes. "Your eyes were practically filled with stars when you watched him shut down those other two players."

Axel frowned sharply and shifted his weight from one foot to the other. "Yeah? Well, his name sounds like some kind of emo punk band."

"Like *you* should be the one to criticize," Vic snorted.

So the top player is a bit of an elitist, is he? That's it, from now on I shall think of him as Intimidating Eyebrows, Kit thought rather ungraciously.

"What part of the Guildhall do you think will offer us the most information, Kit?" Gil asked.

"If we follow this hall, it opens up into a circular chamber. That's usually where big news items are posted, and the bigger guilds meet to discuss game business."

Vic began marching down the hallway. "Then what are we waiting for?"

Cookie trotted to catch up with her, and Kit, Gil, and Axel trailed in their wake.

Even before they reached the chamber, the murmur of muted conversations crawled down the hallway. The volume increased when the passageway opened up. The area was designed for discussion. Giant chalkboards were bolted to several walls, displaying some of the more important records held by various players. Higher up, all the banners of the most esteemed and powerful guilds were hung. Although they were brilliant spots of color, they couldn't compete with the complex stained-glass window that made up the ceiling.

A wave of nostalgia hit Kit as she gazed at the banners that hung from the stone walls. She only recognized a handful of them—the rest were all new since she and her guild had left Retha.

The room was ringed with chairs and cushions to sit on, and although the game was far emptier than usual, a fair number of the seats were occupied. Players were listening to a discussion held between several representatives from guilds who had their banners on the walls.

"I still say there's nothing to worry about! There haven't been any more announcements. If we were in danger, EC would say something," a werewolf roared. He folded his arms across his massive chest and stood in a small crowd of players— mostly males—who ranged from muscled humans to more werewolves.

"EC is a brilliant organization," a male elf said. "They may not be telling us because they are trying to cover their butt legally speaking, or because they are afraid bad news could create chaos among us players." His nameplate marked him as being a member of the Silver Army Guild, which greatly encouraged Kit, as the Silver Army had been around when she played.

The werewolf scowled. "Players should be strong enough to face dire situations," he growled.

"Your guild may be able to do so," a gruff dwarf—who Kit thought *might* be a girl based on the slightly higher voice pitch, but couldn't tell because the player's helm completely obscured his/her face—pointed out. "But what about all the new players who joined the game just before this? How do you think they would respond?"

The werewolf curled his upper lip, revealing pearly white teeth, but said no more.

"Does it really matter if something bad is happening or not?" A gnome asked. "We're mere players. There is nothing we can do to change the situation."

Sensing her opening, Kit scooted farther into the room. "But what if there was something we could do?" She gulped, fighting a blush when she felt the attention of the room swing to her, no doubt taking in her champagne pink hair, elf ears, human face tattoo, and obviously low-leveled armor. She never liked speaking up in a big group, but sticking her neck out while dressed as she was made it even worse.

The werewolf snorted, but the dwarf thumped the arm of her chair. "Let her speak," she said.

"She's clearly a newbie," the werewolf argued.

"Everyone gets a chance to speak," the elf from the Silver Army said. "Now, young lady. What are you saying?"

"There're several quests in Retha that are so massive, players are automatically logged off if they complete them," Kit started. "If we finish one of them, we'll automatically log off due to pre-existing code in the game."

"And we're supposed to believe that you, a level six dancer, are the only person to know about it?" The werewolf asked.

Without missing a beat, the dwarf threw her warhammer at the snarky canine, nailing him in the head.

"And what quest do you believe we should attempt?" the Silver Army elf asked.

Kit licked her lips. "The quest for Malignus's destruction."

The room erupted with laughter and scathing remarks.

"Killing Malignus is impossible!" a hunter shouted. "Everybody knows this. It's a throwaway quest!"

"Dozens of guilds have banded together to try and defeat him, but no one has managed it," a priestess added.

The dwarf heaved a great sigh. "I'm afraid they're right. The quest is only included so you learn more about Retha's world lore."

"But it *is* possible. I know an EC employee. He told me this," Kit shouted.

"Perhaps he meant it as a joke," the Silver Army elf gently suggested.

"It's not a joke!"

The werewolf stabbed a clawed finger in Kit's direction. "Then why hasn't EC come forward and told us this?"

"I don't know, but all employees are under a confidentiality contract so they *can't* tell anyone," Kit said.

A sage pushed her eyeglasses further up her nose. "And you just happened to be such great pals with your EC contact that they broke their employee contract and told you?"

"I smell a liar," the werewolf announced.

"Don't be too harsh," the Silver Army elf warned.

"Harsh? She's a newbie who waltzed in here without any kind of in-game credentials to back her up. Not only is she low level, but she doesn't even have a guild!" The werewolf said.

"I know my character looks stupid, but she's a secondary character that was made as part of a joke," Kit said.

"Oh?" The werewolf snarled at her. "And who's your main character?"

"Azarel."

"Never heard of her," the gnome said.

"I used to be part of Milk Crown," Kit added, desperately naming her old guild.

"You're still not convincing anyone," the werewolf said.

The Silver Army elf leaned back in his chair. "I'm not so certain," he said.

"You know of Milk Crown?" Werewolf asked. "Are they some small-time RP Guild?"

"No, I don't know of them...but the name sounds oddly familiar." The elf trailed off as he rubbed his forehead.

"We used to play here over five years ago," Kit said.

Someone in the crowd snorted. "That's convenient."

Kit ignored the comment and kept her eyes on the elf.

He shook his head. "I'm sorry, I can't rightly recall if I really have heard of Milk Crown. I can ask my guild mistress..."

"You Silver Army freaks are too kind-hearted. The bottom line is ain't nobody buying your lies, dancer," the werewolf snapped.

Kit, her face still hot with embarrassment, was unable to take it any longer. She turned on her heels and stormed from the room, grinding her teeth when she heard the bellows of laughter behind her.

I can't really blame them. I know it sounds ridiculous, and if the roles had been reversed, I probably wouldn't have believed it either. But still!

In her anger, Kit allowed her feet to automatically choose the path, and she wound up outside a huge, gold-gilded door. A crown was emblazoned on it, as were the words "Milk Crown," in a fanciful script.

Kit lovingly caressed the door, making a screen pop up in her face.

Speak the Password to Enter.

Kit stared at the screen, and she startled when Cookie spoke.

"So Milk Crown must've been a pretty powerful guild."

"How can you tell?" Gil asked.

Cookie nodded at the door. "Most of the doors we passed by have been pretty plain or only have an ornate frame. To be able to have a fancy door like this must mean that its members had some serious money. I'm assuming all these doors are guild zones?"

"Yeah," Kit said.

Vic shoved her hands in the wide sleeves of her robe. "What are guild zones?"

"Guilds can buy spaces for themselves in this Guildhall," Kit said. "There're a couple of other Guildhalls, but space here is especially desired given that Luminos is the capital of Retha. The kind of space you get depends heavily on how much money your guild is willing to spend and how many upgrades they can afford."

Axel rubbed the back of his neck as he stared at the door with furrowed brows. "You guys must have been a huge guild. You did raids, I'm guessing?"

"We did a bit of everything: raid, PVP, and a lot of questing." Kit unthinkingly rubbed at her tattoo.

"PVP?" Vic asked.

"Player vs player—it's when players fight each other, usually in sessions organized by Fibbit Services, but there're also duels and stuff like that," Cookie said.

Kit nodded. "Milk Crown's leaders were pretty choosy in who they allowed in, so we weren't a huge guild. But we never had a shortage of players, and everyone was incredibly competent with their character."

"So you weren't trying to show off back there." Axel hooked his thumbs on his sword belt. "You really know an EC employee, don't you?"

"He's my cousin. He used to play in Milk Crown as well." Kit leaned against the hallway wall, and let the tale spill from her lips. She told them everything about the situation and of her dislike of Kitten Lovemuch. She even showed them the letter Bryce had sent to her.

Cookie twirled one of her daggers and bit her lip. "This is worse than I thought."

Vic tugged on the sleeves of her robe, smoothing them into place. "We'll be okay, won't we?"

Gil smiled and patted her shoulder. "Yes. I'm certain EC will spare no expense in freeing us. In the meantime, we can follow Kit's direction and start this quest chain to kill Malignus." Besides Vic, Gil had the least experience as a gamer, but with his soothing baritone voice, even Kit felt highly encouraged by his words.

"So that's our next step?" Axel asked. "We find whatever quest it is that will take us to this Malignus guy, and kill him?"

"We can and should start the quest," Kit said. "But there's no way we can defeat Malignus with just us."

"If EC still hasn't reached out by then, more players might be willing to hear what you have to say," Cookie said.

Kit shrugged. "We can hope, I guess."

"What are we standing around here for then?" Axel grinned wickedly. "Let's get going! I assume you've got tons of loot left in your guild zone. You can take us in there?"

Kit glanced over her shoulder at the golden door. "No."

Axel's jaw dropped. "No? Why the heck not?!"

"Because I've forgotten the password to get in," Kit finally admitted.

Axel groaned and swung around so he could lean against a wall. Vic frowned at Kit in open disappointment.

"It's not entirely my fault!" Kit said. "We only had to enter the password once a year, then it automatically allowed your character entrance. Plus, it's been ages since I've been in there."

"Then I guess we're truly starting from scratch." Cookie sighed and slid her dagger into a hidden sheath on her wrist.

"Not necessarily," Kit said. "There's one place we can check out and get a bunch of starting gear and goodies."

"Where's that?" Gil asked.

Kit fixed a string of twisted coins from her skirt that were digging into her hips. "My original character's home."

Cookie brightened considerably. "That's wonderful!"

"Yeah..." Kit tilted her head back and stared at the ceiling with an uncomfortable frown creasing her lips.

"What's wrong?" Gil asked, as astute as ever.

"It's where my place is located," Kit said.

"Where is it?" Vic asked. "In a different city?"

Kit shook her head. "No, it's in Luminos. It's just off the main city square."

"Sounds like a nice location," Cookie said.

"It is; that's why I got it. Except the main city square is heavily patrolled by NPC guards."

Axel shrugged. "So? Oh..."

"And how do you propose you reach it if you are so wanted by NPC guards that you are to be shot on-sight?" Vic asked.

"I'm still thinking about that," Kit said. "But our best opportunity will be at dusk."

"Great," Vic crouched. "I don't even play video games, and even I know that dusk activities are never a good sign."

Cookie hugged her. "See? I knew we'd make a gamer out of you yet!"

Vic elbowed her away. "I am not a gamer!"

"So where exactly is your house?" Gil asked.

"It's not really a house per se," Kit said. "Pull up your maps —there should be a city map on display in addition to the world map. I can point it out on your screens."

5

THE LOFT

"I'D LIKE to take this moment to remind you that you described your place as a small loft just off the city square, and to say that I think you're absolutely delusional," Vic grumbled as she stabilized Kit.

Kit pinwheeled her arms, briefly losing her balance as she stood on Gil's shoulders in spite of her supposedly superior elf athleticism. "It might be a bit bigger than I remembered."

"A bit?" Vic scoffed. "It's the entire upper floor of an outfitter and directly overlooks the city square! Furthermore, your front door is next to a guard station! Didn't it ever occur to you that perhaps you shouldn't buy something so flashy?"

Gil inched closer to the wall so Kit could grab the wooden crossbeams and white plaster walls. "This is less flashy! One of my guild mates bought an apartment that's on the top of the Cathedral here in Luminos, and another bought a palace in one of the human cities. By comparison, my apartment is quite humble."

"Do you have a solid grip, Miss Kit?" Gil asked.

Kit clung to the wall like a gecko. "I think so."

Gil ducked out from under her and backed up in the alley so he could watch with Vic as Kit tried to scale the building's wall.

It took Kit a few minutes of waffling back and forth between logic—because she *knew* she had the athleticism of a water buffalo—and the innate knowledge and abilities her character possessed. She clung to her knowledge of reality for too long, making her progress up the wall slow. As she tried to edge around a protruding window seat on the second floor of the building, her grip failed, and she slid down a foot or two.

"Aren't you elves supposed to have superior athletic skills?" Gil asked.

"Can it!" Kit ordered as she scrambled up the asymmetrical side of the building.

Vic snorted, but the pair fell silent as Kit continued climbing upwards.

By the time Kit reached the crest of the vaulted roof, she was starting to hate her apartment almost as much as Vic did. She splayed herself across the wooden shingles, gulping in the cool night air. She shot upright when Cookie leaped from the next-door building and landed neatly at her feet.

"Axel gave the signal," the night stalker cheerfully said. "He's drawing the soldiers away—I think he's asking them where the Guildhall is located so they're pointing him down the correct street. It's time to move."

Kit carefully inched herself to her feet and began climbing down the other side of the building. The plan was to drop directly in front of her front door, and get inside before the guards noticed her.

It sounded like a grand idea when Cookie first proposed it, but Kit was coming to regret the extreme climbing component of the plan.

Cookie jumped from ledge to ledge, clearing the building in a matter of moments. Kit took a little longer, stretching her long limbs to their limit as she climbed down. Naturally, as she was reaching for a ledge her grip gave out, and she tumbled and fell into a prickly rosebush planted next to her door.

"I love elves so much," Kit declared dryly.

Cookie laughed and helped pull her out of the bush. "Honestly, I'm a little jealous. I love elves, and I think your hair is adorable!"

Kit grunted and brushed her palm against the door, making the password screen popped up.

"Excuse me, this isn't your house."

The blood in Kit's veins froze in fear before she and Cookie swiveled to face the speaker. The tension in her shoulders eased, and she could breathe once again when she realized that two players, a druid and a guy decked out in buckles, were addressing them, and not guards.

Cookie tilted her head. "Is something wrong?" She asked the pair.

"Yes," the druid tucked a strand of her brown hair behind her ear. "Please allow me to assure you that no matter what your stealth level is, you cannot break into another player's house."

Worried, Kit looked from them to the house number posted over the door. "No, it's fine. This is the place we want."

The buckle-covered guy narrowed his eyes and chewed a mint leaf. "There's no way that's your place."

"Please move on, or we'll be forced to signal the guards," the druid said with a cheerful smile.

Kit's eyes bugged. She had not monkey-crawled her way up the house to avoid the guards just to have another player call them out. "No, seriously. Everything's fine. I have permission to get in here."

Buckle boy folded his arms across his chest. "That's impossible," he said. "The owner of that apartment hasn't been on this game in at least five years."

Oh? Are they someone I know? But I thought everyone from Milk Crown left! ...Or did they come back and not tell me? Kit squinted at the pair, but didn't recognize their faces. Whoever they were, she hadn't met them. (She didn't know if that was comforting or upsetting.)

Vic and Gil finally turned the corner, popping out of darkened alleyway and into the moonlit city square. "Is there a problem here?" Gil rumbled.

"No," Kit started.

"Yes," the druid and buckle boy said.

"What should we do?" Cookie whispered. "The druid is level forty, and the saboteur is level thirty-five. There's no way we can take them."

Kit groaned. "Crap on a cracker, this is not what I need."

A trumpet sounded.

Congratulations! Your life skill, "swear proficiently," has risen to level two!

Kit waved the notification away and turned to the door. She heard the druid and saboteur shift from their spot on the street as Kit blurted out into the password screen, "Honey, I'm home!"

The lock on the door clicked, then the door itself swung open as braziers fastened to the wall burst into flames.

Kit sighed in relief and sagged against the door frame. She looked up when the druid spoke in wonder.

"Who are you?"

Kit offered her a wane smile. "Azarel."

The saboteur took a step closer. "From Milk Crown?"

Kit nodded.

"Then you must be the dancer everyone in the Guildhall

was talking about—the one who claimed she knew an EC employee," the druid said excitedly. "You know how to get out of here!"

"You mean you believe me?"

"We were playing back when Milk Crown was at its most influential." The druid pointed back and forth between herself and the saboteur. "I even attended Milk Crown's farewell party. I know your guild. None of you would lie about something like this."

Kit stared at the pair, wondering if she could trust them.

Vic peered over her shoulder. "Axel is on his way back, and he's got some company."

Her mind made up, Kit darted into her home. "Everybody inside."

"Us, too?" the saboteur asked.

"Yeah, just get in," Kit said as she hurried up the steps that led into her apartment. "Gil, could you make sure that Axel gets inside as well?"

"Yes, Miss Kit."

"Thanks!" When Kit reached the landing at the top of the stairs, there was another door—this one as golden and elaborate as the Milk Crown guild door. Kit pushed it in, and for a moment stared into the darkness of her apartment. When she crossed the threshold of the doorframe, all the lights—magically fueled—twinkled to life.

On the side of the building that overlooked the city square, there were giant floor-to-ceiling windows. The apartment—like the building—was asymmetrical, with several bulging window seats that popped out of the side of the house, as well as one small turret.

The ceilings were vaulted and painted with the sun motif, and a giant chandelier hung from the largest sun painted in the center of the room. The floor and furniture were all a golden maple color, accessorized with jewel-colored cushions and plush carpets.

The sprawling main room was part study, part sitting room, and part kitchen. Bookshelves were pushed against whatever solid bit of wall there was, and in the dead center of the room was a circle of chairs and low-back benches.

The side of the building that overlooked the alleyway held a small kitchen with shelves stacked tight with vials, sacks, and wooden dishes.

Two rooms connected off the main chamber—a modest bedroom, and a ridiculously lavish bathroom.

Though she had been gone for years, there was not a speck of dust in the place, and the air was still heavy with the fragrance of dried oranges.

For the first time since logging into Retha, Kit felt like she was back.

"I have quite a bit of extra gear here—though it might not be class-specific. At least I have a lot of potions, weapons, and other useful stuff. I think I may even have a pet cat for you, Vic." Kit marched into her apartment, opening cabinets and peering at her bookshelves. "You'll mostly find things in the storeroom off my bedroom. You can take whatever you want, as everything of serious worth is locked to my main character already."

Vic and Axel wasted no time in trundling into the bedroom after Kit pointed it out.

"So many clothes!" The warrior complained as he waded through the bedroom.

"This way, Axellent," Vic sneered.

"Watch it, wizard, or I'll let you die on the field."

Gil inched toward the bedroom, but almost took out a suit of armor with one of his pauldrons. "You have a rather impressive array of material items," he noted.

Kit flipped open a tiny jewelry box and frowned at the

contents. "When you've played as many videogames as I have, you learn that sooner or later you need just about every drop or armor item you come across and become a hoarder." She offered the tall crusader a quick smile. "I'm almost positive I have several spears with better stats than the one you're carrying. If they're not in the back room, let me know. They might be with one of the suits of armor in the bathroom."

Gil bowed to Kit, then maneuvered his way around Cookie, the druid, and the saboteur—whom the night stalker was filling in.

As Cookie explained to them about Bryce, and that killing Malignus was the one way out of the game, Kit continued to search the main chamber of her apartment. She eventually found what she was looking for: mount medallions, tossed carelessly in a gold bowl that was situated on an end table.

There were lots of ways to get around Retha, but when one was not traveling by a teleportation gate, the fastest way was to ride a mount. There were all kinds of mounts—from regular horses, to flying dragons and pegasus, to giant elk. The most common, and perhaps the most dependable, were everyday horses.

While mounts of any kind were usually quite expensive to purchase, thankfully, players were often given mounts as gifts from NPCs or as rewards for completing quests.

Kit had an abundance of them, as she had been obsessed with collecting as many of the horse mounts as possible, and she hadn't even bothered to bind all of them to her character. She fished a handful of the mount medallions—the tiny metal trinket that would allow a player to summon a mount and bind it to their character—out of the bowl and considered calling the rest of the party.

"I'm sorry, we swooped down on you and never bothered to introduce ourselves."

Kit swiveled her attention to the druid and saboteur, nodding to Cookie as the night stalker—having finished her explanation—slipped into Kit's bedroom to join the rest of the party. "Don't worry about it. Everything is a little crazy and upside down right now. I'm Kit—though as I mentioned before, this character is a secondary character and my main is—was —Azarel."

"Cookie explained to us that Kitten Lovemuch was your cousin's idea of a joke," the druid said.

"An elf dancer *is* a joke," the saboteur stressed as he adjusted the goggles that were nestled into his hair. "But Azarel...You were Milk Crown's echo of arcane, right?" he asked, naming her original character class.

Kit nodded.

The saboteur raised his eyebrows. "How the mighty have fallen. Uck!" He gurgled when the druid elbowed him directly in the face.

"I'm Riko, and this is Prowl. We're both from the guild La-Lune," the druid said.

Kit shook Riko's hand when she offered it, though she winced at her seemingly poor memory skills. "Nice to meet you. I'm sorry to say I don't really remember hearing about La-Lune."

"I should think not," Riko laughed. "It wasn't established until after Milk Crown disbanded. We're only a medium-sized raid guild, but our guildmaster is Tough Beard."

Kit brightened considerably after hearing the dwarf's name. "I've played with Tough Beard!"

"Yeah, the old man got around," Prowl said as he scratched his side. "La-Lune has a pretty decent ally list and contact list because he's old as dirt."

"Is he online?"

Riko shook her head. "I'm afraid not. He and everyone else

from the guild who were playing when the server crashed all had rental units. Prowl and I are the only two who were in full submersion. That's why we would be particularly thankful if you would let us join you."

Kit discreetly glanced at their nameplates to confirm they were members of La-Lune. Pulling up their public profile, she could see that La-Lune was indeed run by Tough Beard. It gave her some comfort to know players she had been acquainted with were still around.

Confident she wasn't inviting less-savory players into the party—like a player killer—she extended a party invitation to them. "We'd be happy to have you. Though I'm sorry to say we aren't as well organized as you're giving us credit for. I know we need to kill Malignus, and I also know there is a quest line that pits you against him in the final stretch, but I don't know where it begins."

"You never played it as Azarel?" Prowl asked.

"Nope. It seemed like a waste of time, as I thought Malignus was unbeatable," Kit said.

Prowl grunted. "I don't blame you."

"It's a big problem, though, as we can't exactly look up a guide on the community tab," Kit said.

Riko beamed. "Have no fear! These are our secondary characters. Prowl has actually gone through this quest on his original character and was violently killed by Malignus multiple times!"

"Careful, your glee is showing," Prowl said wryly.

Riko's smile grew. "I wasn't there, but I was told it was such a beautiful sight, watching Malignus take him out with a single stab."

"Yeah, which is how I know it's not possible for us to do it with this dinky little group," Prowl said.

"Even with you guys joining us, we would never attempt it with this small group," Kit said. A druid and a saboteur would be welcome additions—the druid was a mage class that used mostly nature-based spells, whereas saboteurs belonged to the thief class and used lots of traps and tricks to stop monsters and then strike when they were weakest. "My hope is that by the time we finish the quest line, EC will have either fixed every-thing, or players will be more open to the idea given the amount of time that will have passed."

"So we're gonna leave soon, then?"

Kit, Riko, and Prowl turned to face Axellent, who was leaning against the bedroom door frame.

Prowl raised an eyebrow—a gesture he seemed quite fond of. "Are you trying to get gossiper or busy-body as a life skill?"

"No." Axel held up a fur cape. "The old guy wanted me to double check with you that I can take this as it's got quite a bit of attack boost."

"Go for it, as long as you can actually wear it," Kit said.

"Jackpot!" Axel slung the cape over his shoulders, fastening it to his dented metal breastplate.

"The gossiper does bring up a point," Prowl said. "I assume you want to set out on this thing as quickly as possible?"

"No," Kit said. "We don't want to go out ill-prepared, or we'll just have to come right back. Besides, at bare minimum, all of us lower-level characters should choose our crafting jobs."

In addition to their character class, players were given the opportunity to select two crafting jobs for their characters. Players could learn anything from armorsmithing, to cooking, or even toy-making. Usually players chose useful crafting classes for their main characters. Azarel, for instance, was a jeweler—giving her the ability to make enchanted jewelry—and an excavator—so she could mine ore in search of jewels for her work.

Leveling a crafting job could be frustrating and boring as all get out, but even having basic skills for some of the crafting classes—like potion making—would be extremely useful as they set out on the quest.

"That's reasonable enough," Riko said. "I can take the four greenhorns around and advise them about the best crafting classes."

"Are you sure?" Kit asked. "I need to choose crafting classes too, so I have to go anyway."

"Perhaps, but it will take you quite a bit longer to escort them around as you'll be busy dodging guards and members of the Court of the Rogue," Riko said.

"I wonder if they'll be shot on sight as well if they're seen wandering around with you," Prowl said.

"While I'm handling the crafting thing, Prowl can send out private messages to some of our contacts who are still online," Riko said.

Prowl frowned at his fellow guild member. "When did you get administrative privileges, old lady?"

Riko's smile was flawless as she grabbed Prowl by the cheek and yanked his head up and down. "You're so cute, for a potty-mouthed juvenile delinquent."

Prowl freed himself and frowned, then wisely scooted out of Riko's reach.

"It's settled, then," Riko said firmly. "My, this might be fun! It's been quite a while since I've hung out with young folk—they are so refreshing."

"And you wonder why I call you old lady," Prowl muttered.

"I don't know that Gil is as young as the others," Kit said.

"Perfect! He'll add a touch of the distinguished to the party. It will be such fun!" Riko held her hand to her cheek and smiled happily.

Prowl eyed Kit. "Are you going to be okay?"

"I'll just keep to the heavily populated areas where I can creep around in the shadows. I think it's harder to spot me in a crowd of people. I'll go shopping while I'm at it. I have a lot of stuff here in my house, but there are a few extra status cures and potions I think we should have on hand, just in case."

Riko nodded. "Sounds like a plan. Good luck!"

"Thanks. You, too." Kit could barely keep from gleefully rubbing her hands together. Besides survival, she had a more selfish desire to get a crafting class—specifically that of armor-smith. If she could make her own armor, she wouldn't have to waltz around baring her belly to every monster as a convenient target.

Soon! She promised herself. *Soon Kitten Lovemuch will be just a bit more respectable.*

She should have known better.

6

SELECT CRAFTING CLASS

WHEN KIT HEARD the synchronized stomp of a squad of soldiers marching down the street, she stopped rummaging through her inventory long enough to adjust the gauzy scarf she had wrapped around her head. Nonchalantly, she scooted closer into the shadows cast by a stall cabana, and smiled at the NPC merchant with whom she was bartering.

The woman placed her folded hands in front of her and smiled. "Do you have anything else you wish to share, customer?"

"Possibly..." When she could no longer hear the soldiers, she returned to considering her inventory again. Before leaving the loft, she had ransacked her home for any spare items she could sell. Though her main character was flush with money, Kitten Lovemuch had no way to access it. Just as it was in the real world, money and economics played a key role in Retha, so Kit was highly motivated to gather as many funds as she could before leaving.

She pulled a few more items out of her inventory screen, making them manifest in her hands. "How about this gold ingot, these three sharpened daggers, and one hundred and fifty-two pieces of fluff?"

"Hmm..." The merchant poked over the goods with a critical eye before renewing their barter session.

Kit haggled heavily, securing a number of humility potions —which, when drunken, significantly lowered the amount of aggro a player pulled. (She had a feeling those would come in handy, particularly given that they still didn't have a dedicated healer.)

"Thank you for your business!" The woman called when they finished the transaction. "Please come again!"

Kit smiled and waved, then joined the stream of players that trickled up and down Retailer Row—the street where most NPC run shops were located in Luminos.

"Let's see...I bought the extra health and mana potions; we have plenty of antidotes and cures; I got about as many aggro potions as we can afford, and enough sugar and cocoa powder to choke a giant. All that's left is to get weapons and become an apprentice armorsmith."

There was an extra spring in Kit's step, making the bells of her anklets jingle extra annoyingly. She was in high spirits as no soldiers had caught sight of her yet, and joining the candy maker's crafting guild had been a great deal more fun than she'd expected.

Kit had settled on candy making as her second crafting class, mostly because she knew the second class would be almost completely ignored as her greatest interest was in crafting armor. She also picked it as a futile attempt to buy her way back into the goodwill of Retha's general population.

Managing a character's reputation was always a confusing exercise as various groups would like and dislike you based on the opinions of other groups, and your reputation changed marginally based on anything from the NPCs you spoke with to the kind of game you hunted in certain areas. It was constantly changing, and each race had its own requirements in order to gradually accept you. There were big things, of course, like completing large quests. Players could often give specific items to NPCs in order to strengthen those relationships, as well. Each race or organization had a customized list of things they liked, so no one liked the same things, making collecting those items a real pain. The only exception was candy. Everyone, from dwarves, to elves, to even the Empress of the remaining bits of the Solis Empire loved candy.

Candy crafting's only point was to give treats away to NPCs and improve the character's reputation. As such, most people never bothered with such a crafting class—unless perhaps it was on their second or third character. Kit had always been curious about the crafting class, and she suspected it perhaps was the only way she could actually win her way back into anyone's good graces.

Kit dodged a chicken, ignored a guy who cat-called her, and wove around a huddle of players who were loudly bargaining with a merchant over a keg of apple cider. *It probably would've made more sense to take up a more useful secondary crafting class, but after I get out of here, I'm never going to use Kitten again. Besides, if it really works, giving out candy might be the only way to reverse the effects of Bryce's meddling.*

She paused outside the open door of a clean and carefully arranged store—Griffin Hill Armory. Inside it smelled of leather and wood varnish, and it was just as impressive as she remembered. Racks of weapons lined the whitewashed walls, and barrels of carefully fletched arrows were sorted according to their elements—with light arrows on one end and ice arrows on the other.

Kit had never bought a weapon from Griffin Hill Armory before. Her main character had been a magic user—which meant her weapons mostly consisted of ancient tomes or extravagantly carved wands and staffs. But she had visited the store hundreds of times with her fellow guild members, and it held many memories for her.

The same two NPCs that used to run Griffin Hill Armory back when Kit played Retha were still there: a tall, slender man who wore an archer's armguard, and a squat woman with thick muscles who could have passed for a dwarf if she had more hair.

The woman briefly smiled at Kit. "Welcome!" She barked. She went back to polishing a broadsword, until her slender companion nudged her when Kit lingered nearby. "Do you need help finding something?"

"Can you tell me if you have any weapons for dancers?" Kit asked.

The woman nodded and waddled around the wooden counter. "Back here." She led the way to the rear of the store, pausing next to a roaring fireplace. "We got the basics—your leather whips and dancers' mallets." She pointed to the oversized wooden hammers that were as tall as Kit and designed to use more as an anchor for dances than for actual damage. "We can order something special if you know what you want—and if you've got the money for it."

Kit let her scarf slide from her head. "Is there anything you'd particularly recommend?"

The woman shrewdly eyed Kit's tapered ears that poked out of her silky hair. "You're an elf?"

"Yes." Kit tried to respond without sounding like death, but she was not convinced she actually pulled it off.

"You must be on an...interesting journey," the woman said.

"And you're probably the least judgmental person I've met yet," Kit sighed. "I would choose a different...path...if I could, but unfortunately I'm stuck. I badly need a weapon—I've encountered too many monsters to waltz around without one."

The woman scratched her chin. "Most dancer weapons aren't made with damage in mind."

"That's just great," Kit said dryly. She glanced out the window and noticed two soldiers patrolling the street. She tried to discreetly edge out of eyesight, but it seemed nothing got past the weapon dealer.

"You're an elf dancer who is also wanted by the Imperials?" The woman asked.

Kit tried to keep her face blank. "I don't know what you're talking about."

The woman shrugged. "Makes no difference to me. We get customers on both sides of the law here. But if you're wishing to avoid the Imperials, I suggest you take the back door out after you've made up your mind."

"Thank you, but you still haven't made a weapon recommendation."

"I don't think there's anything we have in stock that will suit your needs. The mallet does the most damage, I reckon, but it breaks real easy. If you're traveling with a weaponsmith, they may be able to mend it, but each time it's mended, it will get more fragile. If you're not in a rush, I'd say your best bet is to order something—or perhaps to check the market. Someone might be selling something rare."

The woman was right—the market where other players peddled their goods more than likely had dancer weapons. The problem was that players didn't theme their stalls like the NPCs did. Kit would have to check every single stall herself, and even then it wasn't guaranteed she'd find something in her price range that her character would still be able to use with such a low level.

She sighed. "Unfortunately, I'm in a bit of a rush. I will keep your words in mind if we happen to pass through here again. Thank you for your advice, though."

The NPC nodded, then began shuffling back to her counter. "Holler if you need anything."

Kit nodded absently as she stared at the array of dancer weapons. She brushed the mallet with a fingertip, calling its stats up on a pop-up screen. "It has a luck bonus? What good will that do? Dancer spells can't receive critical upgrades, and they really shouldn't be physically attacking monsters."

She shook her head and looked over the leather whip with a grimace. She was pretty sure she'd rather have Prowl and Cookie mug a bobokin—a blue-skinned goblin—and use its wooden club than a leather whip, but she was desperate to have *anything* that would protect her in the meantime.

The bell attached to the door jingled, and Kit glanced over her shoulder long enough to see two guys—a pirate and a beast tamer—enter the shop.

The NPCs greeted them cheerfully. The beast tamer returned the greeting as they perused the two-handed swords.

Kit furrowed her eyebrows and went back to staring at possible dancer weapons. She was considering a stick covered in bells when she felt a hand on her shoulder. Kit, being a tall elf, looked down at the pirate who smirked as he squeezed her.

"Hey there. Did it hurt when you fell from heaven?"

Kit's brain flatlined for a moment as she was struck dumb. *People actually use lame pickup lines like that?* She'd received more unwanted male attention in the past game day (assumedly because of her class's awful armor) than she had in her entire existence as her main character, and she was feeling particularly unsympathetic. So she pasted a wooden look on her face and said,

"Welcome to Luminos!"

The pirate blinked. "Um, what?"

Kit jerkily clasped her hands in front of her. "Retha needs your help, hero!"

Wrinkles spread across the pirate's forehead. "You're...an NPC?"

"The shadow of darkness stands over the land," Kit parroted.

"One of the anniversary NPCs," the pirate muttered.

In homage to the old RPGs, Retha had released a number of anniversary NPCs during the second year Retha had launched. These rare NPCs parroted dozens of old lines from even older games.

The pirate stared above Kit's head—looking at her name-plate probably—when his friend nudged him. "Hey, I think I found a saber for you. It's not as good as the one you were telling me about, but it's way cheaper. Hello." The beast tamer finished by nodding at Kit.

"Welcome to Luminos!" Kit repeated.

The beast tamer shifted his gaze from Kit to his friend. "And you are staring at an anniversary NPC."

"I thought she was a player."

"Let me correct that, you were apparently hitting on an anniversary NPC."

The pirate scratched his ear. "I think she really is a player, she's just pulling our legs."

The beast tamer rolled his eyes. "If she is, then you've obviously made her super uncomfortable. Come on." He yanked his friend along by his arm, pulling him away.

Kit relaxed as they approached the counter, and returned her attention to the dancer weapons. She had nearly gone over all of them when a pair of blue silk fans covered with painted petals caught her eye. It had both an intelligence bonus and a vitality bonus, two important stats for dancers. Intelligence determined the amount of mana Kit had, and vitality would help keep her alive longer and increase her health—a particularly important thing as dancers were given a pathetic amount of health points.

The fans didn't do much damage, but then again neither did any of the other dancer weapons.

Her mind made up, Kit selected the fans and waited until the pirate and beast tamer had left before carrying them up to the front counter.

The slender male NPC wordlessly took her money (the fans had cost her nearly a third of the remaining gold she had left) then bowed low.

"Come see us again," the female NPC said in a singsong voice.

"Thanks!" Kit slipped out of the shop and into the street, accidentally stepping directly into the path of an Imperial guard.

The guard narrowed his gaze as he studied her. "Are you...?"

"No! Definitely not me!" Kit zipped back into Griffin Hill Armory so fast she almost shut the door on her skirt.

The female shopkeeper didn't look up from polishing the sword. "Told you," she said.

Kit scurried to the back of the store, passing the dancer weapons once again before she reached an unassuming door in the back corner. It opened directly into the back alleyway that was surprisingly cool. It smelled faintly of over-ripe fruit, but was shaded by the buildings and riddled with shadows.

Kit shut the door behind her and leaned against it. "Whew." *That was more stress than I would've liked to encounter.* When her heart stopped frantically beating, she took a moment to equip her new fans, both of which hung from her wrists on pink silk cords.

She admired them and tried snapping them open and closed a couple times with a flick of her wrists.

Gravel crunched under a boot, and Kit whirled around to see a woman dressed in all black ghosting down the alleyway. A moment of scrutiny revealed she was NPC—probably thief based on her elegant gait.

Satisfied, Kit returned her attention to her fans and flicked them open again. Just as she shut the fans with a click, she realized an NPC thief would undoubtedly be allied with the Court of the Rogue. Kit glanced back at her as she drew closer, and this time saw the glittering dirk in her hands.

Kit sprinted down the alley faster than she'd ever run before. "Fudge. Fudge! I mean it, fudge!" She shot out of the alleyway, skidding into the main street and raising a small cloud of dust.

"There she is!"

Kit turned around, and this time was treated to the sight of several Imperial guards marching after her.

"Halt!" the leader called.

"Nope!" Kit darted between the crowds, heading west to the armorsmith guild. *If anything, this afternoon has taught me it will take more sugar and cocoa than Retha has to make enough candy to worm my way out of this. Maybe I should have just chosen furniture maker. At least then I would have a hammer I could throw at them!*

Kit reached the armorsmithy much faster than expected, likely due to her elf athleticism that seemed to inconsistently kick in. She leaned up against the smithy and peered up and down the road, looking to see if the soldiers or thief had successfully followed her.

Good. I'm in the clear!

Kit stepped into the smithy, her eyes stinging from the heat of the forge, where a dwarf worked on a giant warhammer.

"What do you want?" A snot-nosed kid asked. He was

perched on a precariously leaning stool and had a huge book sitting on a wooden bench in front of him.

"I'm here to apply for an armorsmith apprenticeship."

The kid rubbed his nose and tore a page out of the book. "Are you aware of the guild rules, which clearly state once you are accepted as armorsmith you cannot leave the guild. 'N you can only be a part of two crafting guilds. After you are accepted as an apprentice, you are expected to abide by guild rules— which includes not pestering the senior smiths to make stuff for you because you're a wussy beginner and haven't got enough strength to your blows. You got it?" He looked at her as if he doubted she understood much of anything as he dipped a white feather quill into an inkwell.

Kit took the paper and quill from him. "I know how it works. I just sign at the bottom?"

"Yep."

From sheer habit, Kit skimmed over the apprenticeship paper. She paused when she heard a little bell ring and a transparent screen popped up in front of her.

You have a private message from: Riko.
Accept message?

Kit flicked the yes button.

"*Hey, Kit. The group is all set. Everyone has their crafting classes and is geared up about as best as we can do at this local level.*"

"Great! Thanks, Riko."

"*It was my pleasure. So where are you? Prowl and I will come pick you up. We'll bring you to the quest starting point, then we can all get started at the same time.*"

Kit brushed her cheek tattoo with the feather quill. "I'm at the armor smithy."

"We'll be there shortly."

"Okay."

Kit finished reading the paper—which was the same basic rules all crafting guilds presented their apprentices—then signed her character name with a grimace. "Here." Kit handed the paperwork back to the skinny boy.

He glanced at it, then carried it over to a crate and filed it. On his way back to his stool, he grabbed six scrolls and a grease-covered tool belt.

"These are yours now. It's the basic starter set all apprentices are given, and the six basic armorsmith recipes. As you get better, you'll be able to understand more recipes and forge more armor, but it will take a lot of practice."

"Thanks," Kit said. She picked up the scrolls and opened them, making them disappear as they were added to her skill inventory.

Congratulations! You can now forge: Bronze Armor.
Congratulations! You can now forge: Bronze Boots.

It continued in the same vein as she opened up the last of them, then added the toolbelt to her inventory.

"If you want help getting started, talk to Bailbrock over there." The kid pointed to a jolly-looking man who stood next to a cool forge.

"Maybe some other time," Kit said. "Thanks for accepting me!"

She waved to the kid, then stepped outside after cautiously poking her head out and peering up and down the street.

"Kit!" Riko waved to her from farther up the street, with Prowl at her side. "You decided to become an armorsmith?"

Kit trotted up to the pair with a smile. "Yeah. I want to be able to forge something that covers up more of my body so it doesn't look like I'm walking into battle asking to be run through the belly with a spear. Plus, I really don't like walking around like this, feeling only half dressed."

Prowl frowned at her. "Didn't you pick the wrong crafting class then?"

Kit blinked. "What do you mean?"

Prowl adjusted his goggles. "Dancers don't wear metal armor like plate metal and chainmail. Their clothes are always made of silks and linen, which you need to be a tailor to make."

Kit stared unseeingly at a building and curled her hands into tight fists. She was so angry that not even so much as a single thought was able to surface in the churning pits of her mind.

"Did you not know that?" Riko gently asked.

"No."

"How could you not?" Prowl snorted. "Your main character is an echo of arcane. They also only wear cloth armor."

"I never really paid attention to my armor class," Kit said.

Prowl snapped his goggles off his head. "You were in one of the top raid and PVP guilds. How could you not be aware of armor classes? You had to have purchased gear for your character!"

"One of my guildmasters gave me all the battle gear I ever owned," Kit said.

Prowl opened and closed his hands like a cat flexing its claws. "You sound like a MMORPG equivalent of a clueless trust-fund kid when you say something like that."

"Prowl," Riko scolded.

Kit pressed her palms into her eyeballs. "This is awful! It

isn't bad enough Bryce saddles me with this terrible character, but I sabotage myself, too!"

Riko tilted her head. "Are you really that angry?"

"I'm *FURIOUS!*"

Riko smiled and patted Kit on the back. "Perhaps it isn't so bad. Do you have your other crafting job open?"

Kit shook her head.

"No? What did you decide on?" Riko asked.

"Candymaker."

Kit, Riko, and Prowl were all silent as they marveled over Kit's poor choice in crafting jobs.

"Considering you're Azarel, you're a lot less intelligent than I thought you'd be," Prowl said bluntly.

Riko frowned sharply. "Prowl!"

"I killed your guild leader whenever I faced him in a PVP match," Kit said darkly. "You should ask him how intelligent I am."

The threat seemed to appease Prowl, for he nodded. "That's better. Well, you're screwed. But standing around isn't going to change anything. Let's go to the quest starting point." Prowl folded his arms behind his head and began to stroll away.

"It isn't that bad, Kit," Riko said as they trailed behind him. "It's not like you'll have time to level your crafting class anyway. If I remember correctly, this quest takes you all across Retha. And you can always buy more...protective clothing. Prowl can lend you the money if you need it."

"Stop volunteering me to bankroll everything!" Prowl barked.

Kit sighed. "Thanks, Riko. I'm sorry...I know I've been gone five years, but I've still been playing other games. I didn't think I'd be so...*out of it.*"

Riko laughed. "I'm fairly certain that anyone who has to

deal with the class, race, and reputation you've been given would be 'out of it' as well. Try not to let it get to you."

"Yeah."

"*Attention, Heroes. Retha is still experiencing server difficulties. Log off capabilities remain unavailable, but we are investigating the issue. Thank you for your patience.*"

The announcement was made in a computerized voice, making it pleasant sounding but flat.

Prowl shook his head. "I still think it's stupid to attempt this quest line with such a small party...but I'm glad we're doing *something* to try and get out."

"Yes," Kit agreed. "Did you notice the sneaky wording? They said they're 'investigating' the issue, but they didn't mention a patch installation or a fix that will solve it."

"They probably don't want to make it public that the issue is more urgent than it seems," Riko said. "Either way, I agree with Prowl. We need to make this quest our priority. Our lives might depend on it."

Kit grimaced. "I really hope it doesn't come to that."

The druid smiled sadly. "Me, too."

7

A NEW QUEST RECEIVED

KIT WAS UNSURPRISED that the NPC responsible for handing out the mission was an ancient geezer who reeked of alcohol and was so old his skin was papery and mottled. He was splayed out in a back alleyway behind one of the many Luminos taverns, clutching an empty pint mug the way a baby holds a bottle.

The rest of the party stood near him. Cookie and Axel looked around with interest while Vic pinched her nose closed and Gil waved to them.

"Are you ready to begin?" Gil asked.

Kit fussed with the silver bells that were attached to the leather cord that tied her hair back. "As ready as we'll ever be. Let's talk to him."

"Before we begin, if he asks you anything about having approached Malignus's stronghold, just say you have," Prowl said.

"Yes, sir." Cookie saluted him.

Axel ignored him and poked the drunk with the toe of his boot. "Hey. Wake up!"

"What? What do you want? I ain't hurting nobody!" The old man scowled at Axel and cradled his mug.

Prowl crouched in front of him. "I've heard rumors you can tell us how to get into Malignus's stronghold. Are the whispers right?"

The old man peered at Prowl with bloodshot eyes. "Maybe they are, maybe they ain't. What's it to you?"

"We're looking to remove the wall," Riko said.

"Wall?" Axel parroted.

Prowl slapped his hand over the young warrior's mouth, but he was too late.

"Ah, the wall." The old man stared unseeingly at an empty crate. "The wall that seals in the ancient evil. Once our world was on the brink of ruin. All the free peoples were under siege by Lord Valdis Moarte, who filled the land with blood and death."

"Now you've done it," Prowl growled.

"What has he done?" Gil asked.

Kit flipped a broken crate upside down so she could sit on it. "He asked what the wall was, so now the old guy has to fill us in on Retha's lore. You may as well make yourself comfortable; we're in for a wait."

"An alliance of elves, fae, dwarves, and men fought together and locked up the Lord Valdis, sealing his spirit and locking it away.... But the success came at great cost," the old man rattled on. "Man, once powerful and united under the Solis Empire, lost so many armies that the empire crumbled, and now only a small remnant remains. Elves found their forests polluted—"

"And let me tell you they never shut up about it ever since they found that out," Kit complained.

"Dwarves were forced to mine some of their most precious quarries into desolation, and more. But with Valdis Moarte sealed in what once was his castle, peace returned. Centuries passed, and the great sacrifice of our ancestors was forgotten until a new evil stirred, Malignus. Twisted and dark, he is a necromancer who forced his way into the lands that once belonged to Lord Valdis. His sole goal is to revive Lord Valdis Moarte and cast Retha back into ruin."

"I had forgotten some of this backstory," Riko said.

"I don't see how," Prowl said. "They shove it down your throat from the moment you first step foot on Retha."

"There was a pretty lengthy cut-scene when we first logged in that covered a bit of this," Cookie added.

The old man droned on, oblivious to their conversation. "Unfortunately, even during the peaceful times after the war that nearly tore Retha apart, we were unable to return to the strength and power we once had. Many feared Malignus would succeed in his mission with no one to stop him. That was when the first hero appeared," the old man huffed the last line so reverently, Kit wouldn't have been surprised if a halo suddenly ringed his head.

"Hero?" Vic asked.

"That's what NPCs call us players in-game," Cookie said.

"That's not narcissistic or anything," Vic said dryly.

"The heroes have pushed back Malignus's forces, but the people of Retha still fear that Lord Valdis may return..." The old man trailed off and hummed in the back of his throat.

"Yeah, yeah," Prowl said. "That's why we're here. We want to defeat Malignus, but we can't get past the sealed wall our...er...ancestors placed to keep Valdis Moarte locked up."

"Of course," the old man coughed so deeply it rattled his chest. "Only with the four seals may one remove the wall and cross into the lands of the dead—into the lands of Moarte."

Gil stroked his chin, scratching at his five o'clock shadow. "So the quest to defeat Malignus is really the quest to open up his lands."

"Exactly," Prowl said. "It is most widely believed they did this to keep idiot newbies from wandering into endgame material—which is really what we're about to do."

"It's also been acknowledged that the quest exists only to teach players about Retha's lore, and to forcibly introduce them to other races," Riko added.

"How so?" Cookie asked.

"Let me guess." Kit leaned back on her crate and her head rested against the alleyway wall. "We're sent to each of the races to retrieve those seals the old guy was talking about, which all happen to be scattered in four opposite directions."

Prowl nodded as the old man gasped. "How did you know?" He asked in his quivering voice. "But then again, you are an elf. It can only be your great wisdom and vast years of life. Were you perhaps alive in the ancient days when Lord Valdis roamed Retha?"

Kit frowned. "He just called me ancient, didn't he?"

"Thank you for sharing your wisdom with us, Sir," Riko said with a smile. (Kit had no idea how she was able to keep it in place as the old guy puffed his stale beer breath in her face when he cackled.) "Can you tell us exactly where the four seals are?"

"One lies with the elves, who hide away in their secret forests," the old man said.

Cookie counted off the four seals on long and slender fingers. "The dwarves probably have another; I'm guessing the descendants of the Solis Empire have the one for the humans; and the fae have the last one."

The old man banged his mug on the dirt ground. "If you already know everything, what use is there in coming to me?"

"But we don't know everything," Riko said soothingly. "We need more than a general idea of where the seals are. We need specific locations. Like cities."

The old man smiled slyly, revealing black holes where he had lost many of his teeth. "Oh, I can give you cities. For a price."

"You want us to pay you after we were forced to listen to you ramble on for so long?" Axel demanded.

The NPC folded his bony arms across his equally bony chest. "Where else are you going to go for such prime information?"

Kit scratched her forehead. "Is this really part of the quest, or is he just being a pain?"

Prowl yawned. "Yep, this is the quest alright. He is the only way to officially receive the quest and allow you to move past this."

Riko scowled. "I'm with the kid on this one. I'm not forking over cash to this lush."

Vic frowned at the old man. "Are we really sure we should give him the money, though? He looks like he may die before he finishes telling us everything."

"It does not seem like we have a choice," Gil said.

"Hey, Mister," Cookie said. "What's your price?"

The old man held up five fingers.

"Five gold pieces?" Kit asked hopefully.

"Five thousand," he said with an evil smile.

Kit wanted to shriek. Five thousand gold pieces would've been a drop in the bucket for her main character, but as Kitten, she had limited funds and had less than a thousand remaining after her epic shopping spree.

"Five thousand?" Riko looked murderous as she clutched her staff and eyed the old man.

"I don't even have a hundred gold pieces," Vic said.

The NPC rubbed his red nose. "That's five thousand total, for all of you to find out."

"Five thousand?" Riko repeated in shock.

"Riko and I can cover most of that. Just toss in a bit each, and we'll call it even." Prowl initiated a group trade session. "Riko, cough it up."

"But five thousand!" Riko said. "That's far too pricy. Why, back when I first started playing—"

"We're not interested in learning about the economy's inflation. I know you have to have at least a million on this character, so pass it over," Prowl said.

Riko stared at him with narrowed eyes. "You're getting cocky, you juvenile delinquent."

Prowl and Riko passed over the majority of the funds to Kit, with the game system automatically moving the funds and making the transfer.

Vic and Cookie each threw in twenty gold pieces; Gil added fifty; and Axel surprisingly topped all the newbies with one hundred pieces.

"My money," Riko moaned.

"Is that enough?" Prowl asked.

"Yeah. But why am I the one giving it to him?" Kit asked.

"You're the party leader," Prowl reminded her.

"We should change that." Kit reluctantly drew closer to the old man. When she gracefully crouched at his side, he smiled widely at her.

"Pleasure doing business with you," he said as she passed the funds over. Kit had to cough into her elbow to keep from gagging at his foul-smelling breath.

"Yes, it has been charming. But you have your money now, so where are the seals?" she asked.

"The human seal last resided in Elba, the last remaining city of the vestigial Empire. No one knows for certain where it is now, but if you wish to track it, you will have to begin there. Your path to the fae seal will begin with the gnomes. The fae are a secretive bunch and never openly shared where they kept their seal, but as the gnomes are the scholars of the fae, they will know where it is. As for the elf seal, it resides in Lèas, the central city of the forest elves." The old man's head rolled to the side, as if keeping it upright on his neck was too much work.

"What about the dwarves?" Vic asked. "You didn't mention them."

"Yes, them dwarves. Their seal is enshrined in their oldest city, Brunascar, in the White Needles mountain range." The man groaned, then all the muscles in his body went slack as he fell to the side.

Immediately, a new transparent screen popped up in front of Kit.

You have received the quest: The Lost Seals of Retha.
For quest information and goals, view your quest log in your
character panel.

Kit flicked the screen away as Axel prodded the old man with the scabbard of his sword.

"Vic called it," Axel said. "He just kicked the bucket."

Kit peered down at the old man and watched his chest rise and fall. "No, he just passed out. I suspect he's drunk out of his mind. Well, at least we got what we needed." She stood and brushed off her skirt. "I vote we start with the dwarves."

"They're the farthest away," Prowl said.

Kit almost smacked herself in the face with one of her fans when she brushed her bangs out of her eyes. "Yes, but the White Needles mountain range is also the lowest-leveled area of the four options. I prefer to work our way up the levels as we go —especially given that this is pretty much a suicide run."

"I'm game," Riko said. "Prowl and I will be above the level of most the monsters in that area. We'll just have to watch out for the few bosses who spawn there—and the dragons of course."

Vic made a strangled noise. "Dragons? The dwarves live near *dragons?*"

"Dwarves almost always end up near dragons—or at least large lizards. It must be a mountain thing," Axel said.

Gil adjusted his chest piece. "I recall seeing dragons in the promotional material for the Chronicles of Retha. While I hope we do not face a dragon, I do hope we get to see one."

"I don't," Kit said. "They're a bugger to kill, and if you're close enough to see one, it can most assuredly see you. Is everyone ready? Since we've received the quest, we may as well set out."

Cookie caressed the hilt of one of her daggers. "We have our crafting classes, and all the new gear you gave us, so I think we're good."

"We have to travel to Brunascar by foot, yeah? We can't use the teleportation gates?" Riko asked.

"Since none of us have been there yet, yes," Kit said.

When players first started out in Retha, there were a handful of places available to travel to via teleportation gates. All other areas—like the dwarven city of Brunascar or Solis Empire's Elba—had to be reached by foot. Once players arrived in previously unvisited cities and checked in with a Fibbit Services Stall, they were officially registered and available for use the next time they chose to use a teleportation gate. (This unusual method forced players to explore and stick to places that matched their level as opposed to zipping around without a care.)

Prowl brought up his city map. "We're near the southern exit, which is technically the wrong direction, but we may as well take it, or we'll have to waste time trying to avoid Imperials and members of the Court of the Rogue for Kit."

"It will also be faster because we can't use our mount medallions for the first time inside the city limits," Kit said. "We have to be outside to call our mounts to us so we can bind them to our characters."

"So the southern gate it shall be," Gil said as the party started down the alleyway.

"Beware!" The old man called after them. "Beware the power of the seals, and the darkness that will seek to destroy you. The ancient evil stirs again!" He trailed off, and for a moment Kit thought he really might be dead. Then his snores filled the alleyway.

"I do have to commend EC," Cookie glanced back down the alleyway even as the rest the party darted out into the main street, eager to return to fresh air. "They're very good about including atmospheric details within their games."

Kit paused at the alleyway entrance and waited for the night stalker. She also glanced back at the old man—who was still passed out on the ground. For a moment, Kit thought she saw black shadows ripple behind the NPC, and a flash of white bone. She blinked, and whatever it was had left.

"Is something wrong, Kit?" Riko called back to her.

Kit studied the alleyway for a moment more, but even though the hair on her neck stood on end, there was nothing there. "No. Sorry. Anyway, I agree with you, Cookie. But sometimes I wish they weren't quite so good at it." She grimaced, as she stepped around a pile of oxen droppings.

"That reminds me, Kit. If you want to exit the city via the garbage chute, I'd be glad to go with you again!" Cookie made her offer with a brilliant smile.

Kit waited until Prowl turned a corner and had signaled that it was clear of Imperial guards. "No, I'm afraid I don't think my gag reflex could take another trip there. But thank you for your extremely generous offer."

"How will you get out then, if not through the garbage chute?" Gil asked.

"Guts and courage," Kit said.

Vic adjusted the collar of her wizard robes. "You're going to make a break for it?"

"Yep."

"You're nuts," Prowl said.

"Maybe a little, but I need to test my abilities against the NPCs anyway, or I'll never know what my limits are," Kit said.

Axel gave her a thumbs up. "Spoken like a true warrior. You're wasted as a dancer. And an elf."

Kit's smile turned brittle as they joined the main road and the city gates—a set of giant double doors that were taller than her apartment—loomed above them. She did her best to stand behind Gil as they drew closer.

"Maybe we could crowd around you and screen you from view," Gil suggested.

"That method works for some players, but Kitten Lovemuch is a bit..." Riko paused and searched for the right word.

Kit flicked her champagne pink ponytail over her shoulder. "Obnoxious?"

"I was going to say eye-catching."

"Close enough. Alright, I'm going to wait for an opening here and then book it. I'll see you all on the other side," Kit said.

"Are you *sure* you don't want to do the garbage chute again?" Cookie asked.

Kit shivered. "Positive. Don't worry about me."

"She's right," Prowl said. "If she's killed, we'll hear her screams and know what happened. Let's go. URK—" He choked when Riko nailed him in the windpipe with the flat of her hand.

Kit laughed and waved to Gil, who kept looking over his shoulder at her while the party trooped down the cobblestone road and out the giant doors.

She adjusted her skirt and shirt to make certain they wouldn't slip when she ran, fussed over her sandal straps, and then clutched her fans.

There were only four guards standing watch at the entrance, but Kit still gulped nervously. She waited longer than necessary until she knew she couldn't stall much more, or Riko or Prowl would PM her.

"Here I go!" She shouted and then barreled her way through the crowd.

She passed the first guards, who snapped to attention as she sprinted past them.

"Stop her!" the guards shouted to their companions on the other side of the doors.

One of the guards poked his head around the wall. "Stop who?"

Kit zipped past him before the other guard could answer, but she heard him fall into pursuit after her as she cleared the gate.

"Halt, you!" the guard shouted as he chased her into the flower-spattered field that surrounded Luminos.

She risked a glance over her shoulder and yelped when she realized he was closing in on her fast. "Roll the dice—he's quick!" She tried to run faster and barely evaded the soldier when he leaped at her.

He landed off balance and had to adjust, giving Kit a few moments to add to her lead. "Why won't you give up?" She shouted when he doggedly followed her.

"You're an enemy of Luminos," the guard grunted.

"The only thing I am is a twit of an elf with no self-respect! You people have poor priorities!"

"Surrender yourself, and you'll only be arrested."

"Never!"

The soldier pursued her all the way to a tiny stream before he finally stopped and turned back to Luminos.

Kit paused to catch her breath, but noticed she wasn't as winded as she had been during her previous games of cat-and-mouse. *Hmm. I wonder why...*

"Kit!" Cookie shouted as she trotted in her direction.

Kit and the guard must have passed everyone even though she had dragged her feet about it, for the rest of the party lagged behind Cookie and were closer to Luminos than Kit.

"That was impressive," Cookie said. "I don't think I've seen any player sprint for so long!"

Kit winced. "It's an achievement I'd like to avoid committing again."

"I understand, but maybe you'll get a good life skill out of it," Cookie suggested.

Kit sighed. "I don't think my luck is good enough to pull that off. But never mind that. Are you ready to summon your first mount?"

"Yeah!"

"Great. Just fling the medallion I gave you into the air and whistle on the count of three. One, two, three!"

Solus Miles checked the community tab of his character panel. It was still dimmed and unavailable.

They haven't fixed whatever the issue is yet? That is...troubling.

He rested his hand on the hilt of one of his swords and pulled his cloak over his shoulder, hiding the glint of his armor in the twilight that settled over Luminos.

I don't know why I bothered to come. No one knows a thing here, and it's been nothing but obnoxious.

As *the* top player on the American Retha servers, Solus Miles was constantly dogged and followed. Even now, inconspicuously wrapped in his cloak, he felt the eyes of two girls—an illusionist and a priestess—bore into his back as they whispered to each other. How they had spotted him when he was skulking in the shadows of an alleyway was beyond his comprehension.

He was tired of the whispers. He was tired of the flattery. It was time to move on—even if it meant continuing to play in ignorance.

It was a foolish hope. How could anyone figure out what is the cause for our inability to log off without being in contact with EC management?

Miles crouched, then—tapping one of his character's passive skills—made an impressive leap and landed on the roof of a small outbuilding. Another jump, and he reached the second floor of an inn. He sauntered across the rooftop, enjoying the breeze and the quiet.

Luminos was a city that crawled with players and NPCs, but few ventured across the rooftops as Solus Miles did, making it something of a haven even though he could still hear the swirl of voices below.

He made his way across town, intending to exit Luminos via the east gate. He was gliding across the rooftop of a residential area when he heard several players chorus, "Guildmistress!"

"Yes, you said you wished to speak to me?" A woman with a melodic voice asked.

Curious, Miles peered over the side of the roof.

White Lady—the guildmistress of The Silver Army, the largest raid guild on the American servers—stood in the street. She wore her usual kind smile and silken summoner robes. White flowers were plaited into her dark hair, and they glowed in the rising moonlight as her fellow guild members fidgeted before her.

"Yes," a male elf said. "There was a player who claimed to have knowledge about the state of the game in the Guildhall. She said she had been in contact with an EC employee."

White Lady tucked her ink black hair behind her tapered elf ears. "When did this happen?"

"A day ago in game time."

"I assume you must not have believed her claim, or you would have brought the matter before me sooner?"

"Indeed. She was a lower-level character—not even to level ten yet—and no one knew her well enough to vouch for her."

Miles' interest dwindled, and he climbed the apex of the roof once more. Half the city was filled with players who claimed they knew what was really going on. He was not interested in the ramblings of another greenhorn player who had nothing to back up her word.

"But?" White Lady asked.

Her minion continued, "She claimed she had a different main character and had once been a member of a guild called Milk Crown."

Miles froze. *Milk Crown.* No one had spoken of that guild in years, even though its name had been synonymous with greatness before Miles had begun playing Chronicles of Retha.

He drifted back to the edge of the roof, his attention hinged on White Lady and her guild members.

White Lady's posture straightened. "Milk Crown? Did she say her character name?"

"She did, but I'm afraid I do not remember it." The elf hung his head.

White Lady placed a gentle hand on his shoulder. "It's fine. I can speak to her myself. Where is she now?"

"She left the Guildhall rather quickly, for several other players were quite brusque with her."

"What is her name? I will send her a PM."

"I can look through my logs and see if I still have it. I'm sorry, Guildmistress. I have failed you."

"You couldn't have known. Milk Crown has been gone so long, not many remember it. Come. Let us go inside, and you may tell me more."

Miles stood on the roof many minutes after the Silver Army guildmistress and guildmember retreated indoors.

A member of Milk Crown had returned to Retha.

I have to find her.

8

COMBAT TRAINING REQUIRED

KIT FLICKED both of her fans open and twirled. Though she performed her dance flawlessly, she kept her gaze on the swirling battle that surrounded her.

"I gotta give it to you." Axel grunted and struck out at a nether wolf—a fiendish, large wolf that was the size of a pony and had red eyes and bigger teeth than a regular wolf. "Your character might be wussy as all get out, but I can tell that your little dance does actually add to my attack and defense power."

"Indeed," Gil echoed as he stepped between one of the wolves and Vic, drawing its attention away from the wizard. "I know you are quite frustrated with your character, Miss Kit, but I must say even I can tell that you've been leveling up as your dance has grown in potency."

"Thanks," Kit said. "But I feel like an idiot for prancing through the battlefield while everyone else actually does something to contribute to the fight." Out of the corner of her eye, she saw Axel attack a nether wolf, unheedful of the wolf cub that bit at his legs as he fought its parents.

He bleeds health points like its mana.

"Kit, could you come a little closer? I'm out of your range, and I want that physical defense buff," Riko called.

Kit grimaced at her mistake and, against her instinct, plunged deeper into the battle. Azarel, her previous character, was a damage dealer who always stood at the back of the party for safety reasons. It had given her a propensity to lurk at the outskirts of any fight, and she hadn't managed to break that habit yet.

She glanced around and saw Cookie lingering in Vic's shadow, attacking any beast that drew near to her. "Cookie, could you help Axel?"

"Okay!"

"Don't worry about your skills, Kit. Your dances will be more helpful as you grow higher leveled," Riko said. She pointed at a nether wolf and shouted, "Nature's Bindings!" Vines shot out of the ground and wrapped around the animal, pulling it to the dirt.

"They may grow more helpful," Prowl corrected as he moved to help Gil—who had used his taunt skill and attracted too many wolves for him to handle. "It depends how the game reacts to the way she plays. If they give her the party build, she'll be worth something, but if they give her the soloing build…"

"Fireball!" Vic chucked a soccer ball-sized glob of flames at a wolf. When the creature started chasing her, she fled. She scrambled through the battlefield, stopping only when Prowl threw a dagger at the wolf, killing it. "What do you mean by a soloing build?" she asked.

"All classes have various builds available to them." Kit said with another flourish of her fans. "The style they get depends on the way they play, as Retha itself will react to your playing style and give you skills that match it. For example, you can have speed-based knights or strength-based knights. The speed knights move much faster, but the strength knights hit harder—though they take much longer to cast their skills." She spun, then leaped into the air. After landing, she glanced at her party display—which showed everyone's health bars and statuses, to confirm that her dance was affecting everyone. *We have to be careful. Even with Prowl and Riko adding greatly to our attack power, with an entire pack of nether wolves attacking us, things could go downhill fast.* Not to mention Vic was still understandably prone to newbie mistakes—like running when a creature started chasing her—and their party's teamwork was pretty shotty.

"Support character builds, however, tend to be extremely different," she continued. "The most favored dancer build is meant for party playing. That dancer does an excellent job of buffing her party and of adding status ailments and de-buffs to enemies. However, there is another dancer build that is meant to be a solo runner—which means they are supposedly capable of fighting alone. However, dancers are, at their hearts, a support class; so, though the soloing build has several damage-based attacks, they're pretty awful compared to melee and mage classes, and due to those damage attacks, their support skills aren't leveled as high, so they're not very good for support roles either."

"I think I'm starting to understand." Vic nonchalantly finished off a wolf with her Bubble Barrage skill. Another almost jumped her from behind, but Gil smashed its head with his shield, and it fell like a rock. "What it basically means is that EC can be downright cruel and force your character to be something you don't want it to be."

"Absolutely," Kit said.

Riko laughed. "Not really. Kit is a little jaded right now—not that I blame her—but EC uses advanced algorithms to determine how it can best improve your playing experience. As the game changes and people change the way they play, the builds change with it. For instance, back in the beginning of the game, there was a dancer build that was made specifically for giant raid parties. The build isn't around because players don't often play in huge raid groups anymore and now tend to play in smaller party groups of six to twelve players. Oop." Riko, who could one- or two-shot the wolves thanks to her far higher level, used her vine attack and grabbed a wolf that had been stalking Kit.

"With the amount I use Battle March, I'm fairly confident Retha will give me the stereotypical party build." Kit snapped her fans and elegantly twirled them as she kept on dancing.

"It doesn't *just* depend on the skills you use," Prowl grunted as he jumped a wolf. "The game also takes into account the armor point bonuses you prefer and divvies your points into appropriate stats."

Vic started tracing the sign for her Bubble Barrage skill, then paused. "Stats?"

Riko, using Nature's Bindings, dragged a wolf across the ground like a child dragging a toy behind them. "Agility, intelligence, dexterity, vitality—that sort of thing. Almost all armor has stat bonuses. If you usually go for armor with agility points, the next time you level the game will put points into agility. As a wizard, you should be doing everything you can to pump up your intelligence."

"So the game decides what sort of build you should have based on what you *wear*?" Vic snorted.

"It's only one part of the algorithm." Kit snaked her way behind Gil—who was tangling with a half-dead nether wolf. "You can also visit training grounds to specifically target a stat—that helps the game recalibrate to what you want if your stats aren't going the way you like. Also, each class build has a secret skill you can forcibly learn—either through questing or visiting class trainers and being told how—which will help the algo-rithms re-target your build."

She frowned when she noticed Axel had drifted out of range of her dance while chasing a wolf. She moved towards him, hoping he wouldn't go much farther or he would cut himself off from the rest of the group, then continued. "And if the game has really screwed up there is also a potion you can take to reset your points—though it's super expensive, can only be used once per account, and costs real life money." Kit twirled on one foot and popped the other up behind her for balance. She roared when a nether wolf grabbed her by her extended leg and sank its fangs deep into her muscles. The attack dropped her health bar by twenty percent of its points, but it also inter-rupted her dance—canceling out the attack and defense buffs the skill gave.

"Son of a motherless goat!" Kit swore as she hopped next to the wolf. Its spit was caustic and started to burn her skin—further eating away at her health.

"That is physically impossible," Vic said.

Cookie slung a dagger at the wolf that still held Kit by her leg, nailing the creature in the flank. It didn't even turn to look at her. "See, Kit? Your dance does make a difference! When you had it up a minute ago, I was doing much more damage," the night stalker said.

"That's great," Kit said through gritted teeth. "I'm super glad to hear that. But can we do something about the wolf attached to my leg?"

"Cry of Challenge!" Gil shoved his shield in front of him in a taunt skill. The wolf ignored him.

Kit glared angrily at her paper fans. Everyone, besides Prowl and Riko, had leveled as they continued to make their way through the Aridus Plains and journeyed to the White Needles mountain range. Unfortunately, unlike everyone else who had leveled, Kit hadn't received any new class skills—though Battlefield March improved with each level she got. "What idiot decided I couldn't even have a basic attack, like stomp?"

Her health bar continued to inch down, so Kit grabbed Axel's scabbard, which he had flung aside as soon as the fight had started, and smashed it down on the nether wolf's head. She hit it with enough force that it let go of her and staggered a bit.

A trumpet chord blew around Kit, and a few sparks crackled near her head.

Congratulations! You have learned the life skill: Violent Outburst Your overly-aggressive temperament can be funneled into a physical attack.

Kit was torn between irritation and glee. After all, she finally had an attack skill! But she could have done without the criticism of her personality.

The wolf she had attacked growled, snapping Kit out of her thoughts. A glance at its health bar confirmed that her new skill hadn't done much damage to it. Kit backed up slowly, but the wolf pressed closer to her, flashing its fangs that were red with her blood.

"Kit, fallback to me," Prowl shouted. Kit needed no further encouragement and turned on her heels and ran back to the saboteur. She wove around Gil and Vic—the wizard was once again fleeing a nether wolf, and Gil was chasing after them while trying to simultaneously cast a taunt—then skid several feet so she could stop directly next to Prowl, who was crouching on the ground.

The wolf wasn't far behind her. It launched itself into the air and snarled, but when it landed, a steel trap clamped around its leg. The wolf howled, and Prowl threw a fistful of red colored grit at the creature.

"Pepper grit," he said when Kit glanced curiously at him.

The pepper grit and the steel trap ate away at the wolf's health, but Prowl finished him off with a dagger to the throat.

"I forgot how slick traps work in this game," Kit said.

Prowl dusted his palms off. "Traps are easier to use on some enemies than others."

Kit eyed the party screen again. "I'll keep that in mind."

Prowl pointed at the chaotic fight. "You should tell them what to do."

"Why?"

"Because you're the party leader?"

Kit winced. She still hadn't managed to pawn off the role—which was a shame as she was not skilled at it and it was likely the group would suffer as a result. She cleared her throat and shouted loud enough for everyone to hear. "Everyone pull back and gather close. We need to hit them with one strong strike to run them off—or they're going to bleed us dry of mana shortly. I want us to funnel them to Riko, who can hit them with her Earthen Pit skill."

"Got it," Cookie said. She and Axel finished their targets, then joined Gil and Vic. "Vic, bestie! Have you missed me?"

"Like a gangrene-infested wound," Vic said

Kit stuck next to Prowl as they slowly rejoined the group. The saboteur planted traps behind them, catching the wolves that attempted to stalk them.

"Ready, Riko?" Kit called.

The druid waved from across the fight. "I've got the spell loaded!"

"Great. I'll start my dance. Once the buffs settle, I'll give a signal, then everyone strike the wolves with any attack that pushes the target backwards."

Gil was shoved back several inches when a wolf rammed headfirst into his shield, and Prowl tossed out traps and poison-coated needles. "Hurry up, would you?" the saboteur asked.

Kit was already starting to twirl, flicking her fans and artfully slicing them through the air. As soon as the buffs symbols popped up by everyone's names, she shouted, "Now!"

"Gut Buster!" Axel shouted.

"Bubble Barrage!"

"Hammer Strike!"

Cookie and Prowl were the only two fighters who hit the wolves without skills and instead attacked with daggers— Cookie because most of her skills involved shadows and striking from behind, and Prowl because he didn't have any physical attacks that would push the wolves back.

A number of the nether wolves were sent sprawling backwards. Standing alone, Riko shouted, "Earthen Pit!"

The ground beneath the wolves cracked, and the dark canines fell into an open chasm.

Several of the wolves managed to avoid the attack. Prowl drop-kicked one in the face, sending it sprawling backwards and straight into the pit, but at least four other wolves fled, loping away with snarls.

Vic immediately sat down—which helped replenish her mana points faster. "I thought fighting would grow less stressful as I got used to it. So far I've been wrong."

"It's extra stressful because we're fighting stuff so much higher than us," Cookie said. "Those wolves were level thirteen —they were on level for Axel and Gil, and they're only one level above me which isn't so bad, but you and Kit are still only level eleven."

"Fighting a monster above your level really makes it that much harder?" Vic asked.

"Yep," Kit affirmed. She was only half listening as she was stuck sifting through the list of drops the party had received as the defunct party leader.

"I know you're not a gamer," Axel said. "But wouldn't it logically make sense that a higher-level monster is harder to kill?"

"I don't want to hear that coming from you, Mr. Man-Bun."

"Leave my hair out of this!"

"It's only going to get worse, I'm afraid," Riko said. "Most of the monsters in the White Needles Mountains are between levels fifteen and twenty-eight."

"We'll have to be more careful and try to avoid as many fights as possible," Prowl said.

"Thankfully, that's something I happen to be extremely skilled in," Kit said.

"True. You have been forced to evade just about everyone," Gil said.

"No, I wasn't talking about being a dancer—although you're right and this has only added to my experience. It's because my previous character class was about as fragile as a glass Christmas ornament. Even if she was ten levels higher than an opponent, she could be slaughtered easily, so I always had to place myself as far away from the battle as possible."

"What's the point of playing with such a fragile character?" Vic asked.

"The trade-off was her incredible magical attack power. But I could never wander in an area alone or solo things unless I was ridiculously over-leveled." Kit frowned slightly as she reviewed their drops. They hadn't received anything particularly useful, but everything could be sold for money—which they continued to badly need.

"Echoes were—and still are—over-powered," Prowl said.

"Maybe, but they're so hard to use, no one bothers much with them anymore," Riko added.

Axel reclaimed his scabbard and sheathed his ridiculously giant sword. "Magic classes always bail out when the road gets rough."

Riko ignored the insult and adjusted the hood of her druid robes. "That's another class that was abandoned when small parties began to be more popular."

Axel looked speculatively at Kit. "It seems you're into unpopular classes."

"They weren't unpopular five years ago, but I guess things have changed since then." Kit shoved aside the flicker of sadness that tugged on her heart, finished sorting the drops, and flicked the screen away. "Is everyone good? Are we ready to move on?"

"Just about," Vic said. She was still sitting on the ground, recovering her mana.

Prowl meandered through the singed and blood-spattered battlefield, reclaiming a few of his unused traps. Axel, Cookie, and Gil joined Vic on the ground as Riko approached Kit.

The druid held her hand out in front of her. "Nature's Blessing."

A leafy green light enveloped Kit, and the fragrant scent of flowers tickled her nose as the skill gradually restored her health points at a slow crawl and gave her a light blessing that upped her stats.

"Thank you," Kit said.

"My pleasure. I only wish I had more healing skills."

"Druid is a mage class, isn't it? I was always under the impression that they only had a few self-healing skills."

Riko shifted her elaborately carved wooden staff from one hand to the other. "That used to be so, but with the smaller parties now, most druids end up using healing skills more, which gives them more of a combination build. There's been a real lack of support characters in-game for a while now, so most everyone ends up going hybrid."

Kit shook her head and looked from the rolling plains to the mountains that bloomed directly in front of her. "The landscapes may be the same, but in many ways, *Chronicles of Retha* is not the game I played."

"Sure it is," Riko said confidently. "You forget, this is my secondary character. My main character is a buccaneer—and she is damage all the way, sweetheart!"

Kit grinned as the spell surged again, bringing another trickle of health back into her bar. "Sounds fun." She hesitated, then added, "Are you certain you and Prowl don't want to lead the party?"

Riko scratched her nose. "Yeah, totally. Why do you keep asking?"

"Because I'm out of my depth here," Kit said.

"I think you're doing great. You just have to get used to bossing us around more. That's the point of being the party leader, you know; you have to be the responsible one who tells everybody what to do. Didn't you have to do that a lot with Milk Crown?"

Kit shook her head. "Never. An echo of arcane is not a class that is conducive to leading people. Neither is a dancer, come to think of it. Anyway, I think I was party leader only a dozen times or so with Milk Crown, and usually it was when we were killing creatures in search of specific items—not leveling, raiding, or entering a PVP battle."

"It doesn't matter," Riko said confidently. "You're still the most senior, and you do know what to do even if you are a little skittish about telling us. You just need practice at giving orders."

"You have far too much confidence in me."

"I'm ready," Vic called as she stood up.

Kit glanced at her own health bar and was pleased to see the last surge of Riko's heal had completely restored her. "Excellent. Let's go find the horses." As the wolves had attacked them rather suddenly, the horses had shied and ran off.

"Can't we just call them?" Vic asked.

"I'm afraid not," Riko said.

"But Prowl just did that," Vic said, pointing to the gray mare Prowl had summoned with the whistle and was already mounting.

"That's because he and I both have maxed affection levels with our horses." Riko whistled, summoning her horse. "It's pretty much a given that by our level you would have max affection, but with Prowl's scary mug it was quite the uphill battle to get his horse not to shy away from him."

Prowl scowled down at Riko from the back of his horse. "Excuse me?"

Vic blinked. "What."

"You have to build a relationship with your pets and mounts," Cookie said. "Once they trust you more, they'll come whenever they're called, right?"

"Yes," Kit said. "Once your horse or pet trusts you enough, they'll be willing to do a lot more for you—including returning after running away. Until then, I'm afraid we're stuck going after them on foot. Or we'll have to wait a few hours until they're reset, and then we can automatically summon them again, but I don't feel like waiting that long. So...did anyone see what direction they all ran off in?"

Gil rested the edge of his shield on the ground. "I believe I saw them run for the mountains."

"Alrighty then. Let's head out." Kit started trudging in the direction of the mountains, and, using her superior elf eyesight, started scanning the land, searching for the wayward mounts.

"I swear, everything in this game is all about leveling." Vic rolled up the sleeves of her robe and started trudging after Kit. "You have to level your main class, your crafting skill class, your reputation with all the various factions, your stinking pets! Whoever designed this game is absolutely obsessed."

"That's the point—to improve and become stronger." Axel grinned savagely. "Or is that too difficult for a pristine magic user like yourself?"

Vic did not rise to the bait. "Isn't that exactly like real life though?"

"Perhaps," Gil said. "However, a videogame is more enjoyable, probably because it is so much easier to level, and if you face any difficulties, it can usually be solved by leveling a bit more. In life, there are some obstacles you cannot overcome no matter how you improve."

"Congratulations." Prowl leaned back in the saddle. "You have managed to simultaneously cause discouragement for real life and psychologically ruin games."

"At least the horses are going in the direction we wanted to head in," Cookie said.

"They may have even run into the White Needles zone." Riko shielded her eyes as her horse—a pretty palomino with gold fur and white mane and tail—tossed its head. "It's probably about a five-minute walk from here."

For days, the mountains had loomed on the horizon, but now they were so close, Kit had to lean back and look up to see their peaks.

"Does anyone happen to have a tracking skill?" Kit asked. "I don't see them up ahead, which means Riko is right, and they moved into the mountains. Once in the White Needles Mountains, I won't be able to see as far ahead, so tracking is our best bet."

"Yeah, I can do it," Prowl said. "We just need to find a clear hoof print."

Unfortunately, they didn't find a hoof print until they reached the very fringe of the plains where the wide road they had been traveling on shrunk to a well-maintained—but much smaller—path.

Kit warily turned in a circle, gazing up at the impressive mountains.

"Are you worried about the monsters?" Gil asked. "Riko said they will be higher leveled now."

"I don't think they'll be too much of a problem," Kit said. "What bothers me is that we're heading into dwarf territory."

"So?" Vic asked.

"Have you ever even cracked a fantasy book open? Elves and dwarves don't get along," Axel said. "And based on the way the Imperials were willing to shoot her on sight, I'd reckon it's pretty safe to say the dwarves won't have much fuzzier feelings for her."

"Thank you, Axel, for that encouraging moment," Kit said.

Prowl, who crouched over a track as he activated his skill, stood and brushed his hands off. "It looks like the horses continued down the main road."

"All of them?" Cookie asked.

Prowl nodded.

"Great," Kit said. "They can't be too far. When horses shy, they flee enemies, but they don't altogether abandon you."

"Better than I can say for most of my ex-boyfriends," Riko laughed.

"It's because of your personality that they do that," Prowl said.

Riko looked murderous and held her staff aloft. When her hands started to glow mint green, Cookie shouted, "Please don't hurt him, Riko! If you kill him, we won't be able to find our horses."

Riko paused, considering Cookie's plea.

Prowl mounted again and nudged his horse. He had the good judgment to zip out of the way lest Riko change her mind. "This way."

The path started as barely more than a slight incline, but it meandered a lot—zigzagging around the mountains so only pieces of the road were visible at a time.

The horses—or most of them—were milling around the first bend in the road. When the party approached, the mounts nickered and sidled up to their owners.

Vic's horse affectionately nuzzled her and chewed on a lock of her black hair. (Although the wizard complained about all the leveling mechanics in the game, Kit had not missed the fact that Vic poured out affection on her horse more than any other person in the party.) Gil's, Axel's, and Cookie's horses stood patiently, letting their owners mount up.

The only animal missing was Kit's mount.

"Where's Chester?" Vic asked after she settled onto her horse's back.

Kit propped her hands on her hips and looked up and down the road. "I don't see him."

"Give me a second." Prowl slid off his horse's back and poked around the road until he found a smaller hoof print. "Looks like he kept moving. That way." The saboteur pointed to a flattened bit of ground that wiggled between two cliff-like ledges.

Herbs grew on the cliff sides, and a few bushes dotted the ground. "Yeah, this would appeal to Chester." Kit sighed, then left the path and started blazing her own trail. The rest of the party—still mounted on their horses—followed behind her.

Kit had to go deeper than expected, but it wasn't long before she saw Chester's plump pony butt.

Cookie, Vic, Axel, and Gil had all received normal horses from the mount medallions Kit had given them. But, because

Kit seemed to have the worst luck ever, she happened to have gotten a pony mount medallion so, instead of a normal-sized horse, Kit's pony—Chester—was far smaller, rounder, and sprouted hair as if he was concerned an ice age would soon strike Retha. He was cute, with black socks, a white mane and tail, and black spots dotting his white hide. But as a pony, he was incredibly food motivated—which occasionally made him resort to naughtiness.

"Chester," Kit called.

The pony looked up, still chewing on a patch of grass he had ripped out of the ground so ruthlessly its roots and clods of dirt hung from it. He swished his white tail, then returned to eating.

Vic gave an uncharacteristic sigh. "He's so adorable."

Kit pushed her way between two bushes. "He's so fat. I don't understand why he acts like I starve him."

Chester started eating faster, and Kit was almost concerned he would choke himself when she reclaimed his reins and pulled his head up. When he finished chewing his grass, he nickered cutely and nudged her with his dimpled nose.

Even Kit was unable to resist his sweet brown eyes, so she patted his neck before she swung up on his back. As a tall elf, she looked absolutely ridiculous riding the short-legged pony. But while Vic would have happily traded for the pony, there was no swapping as the horses were bound the moment they were summoned.

"We should be able to start making better time now," Kit said as she turned Chester around. "Although everything will be higher leveled here, if we stick to the path, there will naturally be fewer monsters."

"That would be yer mistake." Two parties of dwarves were crouched on either cliff side. Many of them hefted warhammers and axes, but the majority of them had bows with arrows nocked in place. Their eyes glittered like the gems they mined, and their posture was stiff as they glared down at Kit and the party.

"It ain't monsters you need to fret over," one of the dwarves sneered.

Kit groaned. "Great googly moogly, we just don't have any luck."

A trumpet sounded.

Congratulations! Your life skill, "swear proficiently," has risen to level three!

9

BRUNASCAR: A DWARVEN STRONGHOLD

ONLY A SHORT TIME LATER, Kit had completely changed her tune. In fact, as two guards frog-marched her down a dank hallway, she hummed.

The dwarf who had slapped manacles over her wrists when she first arrived at the dwarven city of Brunascar eyed her suspiciously. "Why do you make a joyful noise, you loyal-less elf? Don't you know you are about to be imprisoned?"

"I'm totally aware of it," Kit reassured him.

He exchanged glances with his companion, who walked on her other side. Together, they shook their heads, making the silver beads woven into their beards click.

One of the dwarves sharply prodded her with the butt of his axe. "Move along!" He ordered.

Kit willingly let them herd her along, as being captured by the dwarves had actually turned into the first bit of luck she had encountered since starting the game again.

With the dwarves as their escort, they hadn't been attacked by monsters even once, and the dwarves had taken a back way into their city, cutting their travel time down to minutes as opposed to hours.

Moreover, Kit was the only one the dwarves seem to behold with real suspicion. Everyone else had been allowed to stay in the city.

The dwarves tugged on giant metal doors that groaned as they muscled them open. Beyond the door were a number of jail cells, all divided with iron bars. Kit didn't see a jailer; that was probably because all of the cells were vacant, with the exception of one, which held two blonde-haired elves.

The elves, dressed in green and brown suede, shifted when Kit and her escort marched into the dungeon. But they settled down again and scowled when they saw it was Kit the dwarves had taken captive.

The dwarves opened the door to one of the empty cells. "You are to stay in here, until our king sorts out what to do with you," one dwarf said.

"What will happen to my friends?" Kit asked.

"Don't know," the dwarf said.

The dwarf that was unlocking the manacles on Kit's wrists and ankles glanced curiously at his companion. "I thought you said the King personally knew two of them?"

His companion glared at him and jerked his head in a gesture for him to back out of the cell. "They'll be well taken care of, for we dwarves care for our visitors. Unlike you elves." He added to the scorn in his voice by slamming the cell door shut and locking it with a thick metal key.

The two dwarves turned on their heels and stomped out of the dungeon, leaving Kit alone with the elves.

Kit looked around her cell—which, by all standards, was actually quite nice. There was a little cot mounded with furs, a cushion to sit on, and even a little fire with a stack of wood to feed into it.

Kit felt a breeze brush the back of her neck, as the party chat —a channel that would allow party members to speak privately to one another even when they weren't in a close geographic location—activated.

"Are you all right, Miss Kit?" Gil asked.

"Yeah, I'm fine. How are you guys faring?"

"Quite well. We've been given rather luxurious rooms and told we may stay as long as we like."

"Any news about the seal?"

"Nope," Axel piped in. "Though I don't reckon Riko and Prowl have been asking anybody much about it."

"Their primary concern seems to be to free you," Gil said. "Unfortunately, even though they are allies with the White Needles Mountain dwarves, the king is entirely unwilling to listen to them vouch on your behalf."

"I can't say I'm terribly surprised by that. If the roles were reversed, and we were trying to smuggle a dwarf into elf territory, they'd react just as poorly." Kit sat on her cot and wrapped one of the furs around herself. "It looks like we're going to have some down time. You should try exploring the city. Once we get the seal, I don't think we'll hang around very long, and this place is one of my favorite dwarvish cities in the game."

"Wouldn't that be rude as you are locked up and Miss Riko and Prowl are working to release you?" Gil asked.

"Nah. You guys can't help with this anyway, so you may as well enjoy yourselves. Although, can someone tell me what happened to Chester?"

"He's stabled with our mounts," Vic said. "I will see to it that he is fed and watered."

"Thanks, Vic. You guys enjoy yourselves, and stock up on anything if you need it."

"I'm going to train," Axel announced.

"Ay-aye, leader," Cookie said.

The party channel fell silent, and Kit was left to muse over her situation. She thoughtfully considered the elves, who sat with their backs to her. "Excuse me," she called out.

Neither of them turned to look at her.

"Hello? I know you can hear me!"

"Do you hear something, Faladia?" One elf—a male whose hair was as silky-looking as Kit's—asked.

"I only hear the insipid buzz of an insect trapped deep in the ground," said his companion—a female whose eyelashes were dusted with gold.

Kit rolled her eyes. "So much for elvish camaraderie," she grumbled. She wasn't surprised they looked down on her, though their disdain was a bit much. She was still an elf, after all. She twisted the large fur for a few minutes—idly wondering what creature could possibly provide such a huge fur—before boredom finally got the best of her, and she approached the campfire. She opened her inventory and scanned the screen. She had been hoping she could use her armorsmithing skills and build something in her cell to use to her advantage, but the little information box that popped up when she selected her forge hammer informed her she had to use a forge with it. Kit thoughtfully rubbed her chin, and her gaze fell on the tool set she had been given when she became an apprentice candy maker.

Reluctantly, she unearthed the apprentice recipe for caramels and dug the necessary ingredients out of her inventory. "It's not like I've got anything more important to do."

An hour passed, and in that time Kit made three different batches of caramels. (The first two were health hazards as she had terribly burnt them, and they were about as hard as rocks, but the third batch had come out reasonably well and had also garnered her a level.)

Kit was rustling through the basic candy recipes she had been given—trying to figure out if there were something she could make besides caramels as her stomach was starting to roll from the scent of burnt sugar—when the dungeon door opened.

Kit slipped her recipes back in her inventory, and watched a dwarf carrying a tray of food traipse down the walkway, making a beeline for her cell. He unlocked the door and left it open as he joined Kit in the chamber. He set the tray down on her cushion and fussed over it, rearranging dishes and muttering to himself.

Kit stood and looked back and forth from the dwarf to the open cell door to the elves who were still going out of their way to ignore her.

This must be my chance to break out.

As the dwarf kept fussing, Kit grabbed a branch meant to feed her fire, and quietly approached him. She bit her lip, feeling a little sorry, then activated her skill. "Violent outburst!" She slammed the branch down on the dwarf's bald head. He crumpled over her tray with a groan.

Kit gleefully tossed the branch aside and waltzed out of her cell, brushing bark grit off her palms. She confidently strolled up the walkway, almost missing the way the two elves glared at her. She rested her hand on the iron ring of the door. "Do you want to come?" She asked.

Gold Lashes sniffed through her nose and looked away, but Silky Hair continued to glare at her.

Kit shrugged. "I thought it would be the neighborly thing to offer. Whatever—crabby cakes." She opened the door with a grunt, set foot in the hallway, and the two elves erupted in shouts behind her.

"Escaped prisoner! An elf prisoner has escaped!"

"In the dungeons! Hurry, a prisoner has escaped the dungeons!"

Kit wanted to turn around and give the elves a piece of her mind, but the adrenaline kicked in, and instead, she sprinted down the hallway. She didn't get far before dwarf guards poured out of an inlet and captured her. Again.

The tattletale elves shouted until the dwarves marched Kit back into the dungeon. The guards removed the stunned dwarf from her cell and locked her in.

"That was your lucky break," one dwarf told her. "For no one escapes from a dwarf-made cell." He shook a thick finger at her, although he did frown and wrinkled his brow curiously at the two traitor elves as he strolled past their dungeon cell.

In no time at all, Kit was left alone again with only Gold Lashes and Silky Hair to keep her company. "What the heck was that?" she asked

Gold Lashes sniffed and stuck her nose up in the air. "I don't know to what you are referring."

"I was almost out of here, and you called to the guards!"

"You were loyal-less and planned to leave us behind," Silky Hair said.

"I asked you if you wanted to come with me!"

"Save your words, Whispryo. She is not a true elf. She has betrayed the elegance and honor of our people and is a *dancer.*" Gold Lashes sneered, making her beautiful face look pinched.

Silky Hair nodded sagely. "Indeed. That is why you cannot be allowed to escape," he told her.

Never before had Kit wished she could violently kill an NPC. "Well done. So you two are tattletales *and* snobs! Want a caramel for your prize?" She accented her sentence by flinging one of her burnt caramels at the elves, popping Gold Lashes on the nose.

"Why, you!" The female elf stood, her face stiff with fury.

"Let it pass; she is not worthy of your attention," Silky Hair soothed.

Kit stuck her tongue out at his back and considered unwrapping one of her gooey caramels and lodging it into his perfect hair.

A breeze brushed the back of her neck again as the party channel activated.

"Kit, what's up?" Riko asked.

"I don't think I've ever been so infuriated in my life!" Kit snarled.

"Are the dwarves treating you that poorly?" Riko asked.

"No, it's the elves!"

The conversation fell silent for a moment. Then Prowl spoke. "You mean they're not helping you?"

"No. They're actively working against me."

More silence.

"That's...unexpected," Riko finally said.

"What do you mean by that?" Kit dug through her character panel until she found the candy recipes again.

"Those elves are supposed to help you escape. Prowl and I finally remembered that when we first entered the White Needles Mountains with our main characters, there was an elf in our party. She was taken captive, just as you have been, and two elf NPCs who were in the dungeons helped her escape."

Kit tapped her fingers on a caramel-crusted pot. "So basically, you are telling me that Bryce messing with my character's reputation and making me an elf dancer has screwed me over even more than we thought."

"Sort of," Riko said.

"That's fantastic." Kit sighed. "Are you sure Prowl and Cookie just can't come down here and beat them up?"

"Kit," Riko scolded.

"You have no idea how annoying they are!" Kit complained.

"Try to hold steady for now," Riko said. "We'll keep trying to talk to the king."

"Because it's been working so well already," Prowl said.

"Don't worry. We won't leave you in there, Kit," Riko said. "Prowl will gladly volunteer to go kill a fire demon solo to intimidate the dwarves into doing as we ask."

"When did I say that?!"

Kit smiled. "Thanks, guys. I appreciate the help."

"That's what party members do; we support each other. Oh —the king has returned. Talk to you soon! Bye-byeee!"

After Riko said her farewells, the party channel went silent once again.

Kit rubbed the back of her neck and eyed her candy recipes. "If I've got nothing better to do, I guess peppermint sticks it is."

———

Hours passed, and Kit made several more attempts at escaping. Like clockwork, every hour a dwarf would come in with a tray of food for her, and Kit would slip out of her cell. The moment she opened the dungeon door, Gold Lashes and Silky Hair would shout their heads off, alerting the guards. She tried everything to get around their fury—from slipping out the door as best she could to smacking them with branches as she passed by—which seemed to only infuriate them more.

In the end, she decided to bide her time and see if the two elves would ever sleep—which would probably be her best opportunity.

Still, she did not waste the ample time she had on her hands, and passed the hours cooking candy. It bothered her, though, for in the back of her mind she knew time was a precious commodity, and she didn't know how much of it they had. To be sitting in a cell—even if she was leveling her candy-making skills—was ineffective and perhaps even dangerous.

Kit was still musing over this when a dwarf came in with

another dinner tray and found her lounging on her surprisingly comfortable cot, gnawing on a chunk of toffee.

"Hey there," she said, flicking her character panel away—she had been staring at the dimmed community tab with dread.

A dwarf—the poor dwarf who had thus far been responsible for all her dinner trays and had received multiple whacks on the head in reward—eyed her warily. "Are you going to try to escape this time?"

"Nope. I've given up for now. Unless I can create a caramel that will glue an elf's mouth shut, I'm stuck. I do feel bad about smacking you, though. You want some candy? I have peppermint sticks, caramels, and some toffee that will chip your teeth if you're not careful." Kit spread out the goodies on the tray when the dwarf set it down on her cushion. "I recommend the peppermint sticks. But if you'd maybe be so generous as to bring some milk down here, I could then try my new fudge recipe I got for leveling my candy-making skills."

The dwarf looked curiously back and forth between Kit and the two tattletales in the other cell. "You do not get along with your fellow elves?"

"She is not a true elf!" Gold Lashes stated loudly.

Kit rolled her eyes. "Do you think you could maybe try to expand your repertoire of insults? You could at least make fun of my pink hair."

The dwarf scratched his grizzled beard. "What does she mean, not a true elf?"

"I insult their idea of elvish honor because I'm a dancer."

"She is a disgrace!" Silky Hair chimed in.

The dwarf picked up a peppermint stick. "Then you mean to say all elves dislike you?"

Thinking of the many elf players in Retha, Kit said, "Not all of them, but a vast majority, yes."

"If you are an outcast from even some of your fellow elves,

you may as well say that you are not an elf at all." The dwarf started nibbling on the peppermint stick.

Kit winced. "When you say it that way, it makes me sound like I'm some kind of disease."

The dwarf laughed—a jolly sound that came from deep within his chest. "Not at all! It is quite the reverse, actually. It implies you are probably a good egg."

"A good what?"

The dwarf kicked the cell door open and stepped out of the cell. "Aren't you coming?"

"I thought the point of being imprisoned means that I stay in prison?" Kit said.

"If you're the kind of elf that your finicky relatives can't stand, there's a good chance you'll get along great with us dwarves. So, there's no need to keep you imprisoned."

Kit scrambled to her feet. "You mean that?"

The dwarf released another belly laugh. "Of course! Come, I will reunite you with your companions."

Kit snatched up the various candy-making implements she had left out and shoved them into her inventory. She scrambled out of her cell, hurrying after the dwarf. The elves watched her with raised eyebrows; Kit winked at them.

She hurried to catch up with her jailer-turned-savior, who opened the dungeon door with a creak. "What's your name?" She asked.

"Drust, son of Harvik. And you are?"

"Kitten Lovemuch. It is my pleasure to make your acquaintance."

Drust acknowledged her with the wave of his peppermint stick as he marched on. "I must apologize, Kitten, for detaining you for so long."

She followed him up a spiral staircase. "I'm merely thrilled to be out of prison. How is the peppermint stick?"

"Quite good, actually. You should speak to some of our cooking staff. They make colored, edible crystals that are quite delicious. I'm sure they would be willing to share the recipe."

"You mean rock candy?"

"We call it crystal candy, but I would not be surprised if the rumor spread that they are actual rocks." Drust huffed out another belly laugh as they exited the seemingly endless staircase and marched into an open cavern. "It is probably why so many believe we actually eat rocks. This way. Your companions are feasting with King Brasil."

"Thank you," Kit barely remembered to speak as she gazed around the cavern, hit by another wave of nostalgia.

The dwarf city of Brunascar had been carved into the hollowed innards of a mountain. The buildings seemed to sprout out of the mountain itself and were an elaborate mixture of stone bricks and steeply pitched ceilings. Geometric shapes and jagged lines were carved into every surface, and everything from the ground to the bridges twinkled with unmined gems and ores. Crystals lit the immense cavern, and a rickety mine car track zig-zagged everywhere.

She followed Drust across a bridge that spanned a chasm so deep she couldn't see the bottom. By then her rusty recollection of the area had returned, and she realized Drust was taking her to the feasting hall, a giant stone structure that was sturdy and squat—probably, Kit suspected, because it needed to be unshakeable thanks to all the wild parties the White Needles dwarves threw.

When they reached the feasting hall, Drust nodded to the soldiers standing guard outside, then flung the doors open.

Sure enough, inside, Riko, Prowl, Cookie, Vic, Gil, and Axel were seated around a large rectangular table with King Brasil at the head. Other players were there as well—laughing over the food and talking with each other and some of the NPCs.

Cookie leaped to her feet when she saw Kit. "Kit! You're free!"

Vic leaned around her friend to peer in Kit's direction, as did Gil. "Welcome!" The Crusader said, saluting Kit with a goblet of wine.

King Brasil, however, did not share her friends' enthusiasm. He leaned back in his chair, and between the way his grizzled gray hair erupted around him and his bushy eyebrows, he closely resembled a storm cloud. "Drust, why do you sully our halls with the presence of an elf?"

"I am pleased to say, King Brasil, that Kitten Lovemuch is not a true elf."

"Oh? How can this be?"

"She's been rejected by her own people. The elves we hold in our dungeon for trespassing scorned her and declared she is not fit to be considered one of them."

"You know, it's a really good thing I have strong self-confidence, or this would be really insulting," Kit said.

She was properly ignored.

"And you believe, Drust son of Harvik, that this reject of elvish stock is a suitable companion?"

Drust shrugged. "I thought she couldn't be all that bad, for I've never seen anyone annoy an elf even half as much as she does."

King Brasil nodded slowly and finally addressed Kit directly. "Tell me, reject, why have your people scorned you?"

Kit glanced from Drust to King Brasil. *I think I'm more on trial than I thought. If I give the wrong answer, King Brasil might tell Drust to march me back down to the dungeon.*

She cleared her throat, rolled her shoulders back, and lifted her hands, palms up, in an appeasing manner. "I am afraid, great King Brasil, that my people have abandoned me due to my passion of dance." She took two tiny steps forward, making the bells on her anklets jingle. "It is the elvish way to be demure and quiet—even in one's joy. I find I cannot do this; instead, I rather enjoy wild and passionate dances—which my people find distasteful."

"They reject you over small things such as dancing?" King Brasil frowned.

Kit squirmed uncomfortably for a moment. "And quite possibly for the way I dress. But I have to say that I absolutely would wear something else if I could only find an outfit that I could dance in that covered my stomach. That would be a dream come true."

"I see." King Brasil obviously did not see it at all as he continued to peer at Kit the way a child peered at animals in a zoo. "Well, Mistress Riko and Master Prowl have been yammering away about how wonderful you are and what a close companion of theirs you are, so we may as well take them at their word.... Please, Kitten Lovemuch, join us in this feast." He motioned for Kit to take one of the empty chairs, and then returned his attention to the drumstick on which he'd been gnawing.

Kit slumped into the chair, relieved she was finally out of the dungeons and hopeful they would soon be able to continue the quest.

"Well done, Miss Kit," Gil said.

"Yeah, that was rather ingenious," Cookie piped in.

"I'm surprised it worked," Vic said.

Prowl yawned. "Yeah, well done and all of that."

Riko leaned across the table and squeezed Kit's hand. "I'm sorry we weren't able to help you get out."

"It's fine. I'm out, and that's all that matters. So, have we made any progress on the seals?"

"No, but I suspect your absence is what held us back." Riko gazed around the feasting hall, her tawny skin glowing in the flickering torchlight. "I think now if we approach Brasil when he is alone, he will be willing to discuss them."

Kit took the pewter plate Cookie offered her and nodded. "That sounds about right." She stared at the feast, not really hungry since the dwarves had practically stuffed food down her gullet while she was in jail. She joined Riko in looking around the room, sifting through the deep scents that swirled around her. There was the faint smell of must and mold—which most cavern cities possessed—but there was also the clean, crisp scent of snow beneath it, as well as the metallic odor of molten metals.

Even in the feasting hall, she could hear the faint tap of the dwarven smiths honing their craft.

She cleared her throat and returned her attention to Riko. "Do you think we should approach him as a party—like we did with the old guy?"

Riko shook her head. "No, I don't think it's necessary. As long as you're there, as the party leader, I think only a few of us should go."

"You of course—you're the best with manipulating NPCs," Kit said. "But who else?"

Vic, who had been glaring at Axel as he wolfed down butter-smeared rolls, clasped her hands together. "I'll pass."

Cookie nodded. "Then I will as well. Oh—we could go see Tremblebach Falls again while everyone else is busy!"

Kit picked up a goblet of wine and swirled it as she stretched her memory. "Tremblebach Falls...that's the biggest underground waterfall in this zone, right?" The falls were a thing of beauty—all white and frothy. They gushed at the far end of the cavern that housed Brunascar and provided fresh water for the dwarves year-round.

"Yeah, and they're so impressive. I've never seen a waterfall like that in the real world," Cookie said.

Axel shoved another roll in his mouth. "If you're going to Tremblebach again, I'm gonna train."

Riko winked at the warrior. "Actually, I want you and Prowl to come with us when we talk to King Brasil."

Axel choked on his roll. "Seriously?"

"Yep!"

"No way, I don't wanna," Axel declared.

Prowl snorted into his goblet. "Give it up, kid. When Riko's got her old-lady claws in you, there's no escape."

"If that is the case, may I accompany you—Miss Cookie and Miss Victoria—to Tremblebach Falls?" Gil asked. "Unless...do you need me to come as well, Miss Riko?"

"Nah, I only have two elbows to place handsome young men at, so you go have fun with the girls. Next time I need some muscle-arm-candy, it will be your turn, though."

Gil bowed his head in acknowledgement.

Kit scratched her misplaced cheekbone tattoo, her ears twitching as she started to pick up on some of the conversations the other players in the area were holding.

A short female fae was going from player to player, panhandling for cash. "Can you give me money? I'm so poor and broke."

A dwarf player waved her off, but the fae was not dissuaded. "Someone give me money!"

She paused near a couple—a male human and a female dryad whose skin had a faint blue sheen to it. "Hi, would you give me money, plz?"

The couple ignored her and blew kisses to each other from across the table.

The fae moved in closer to them. "Hey. *Hey!*"

The dryad giggled at her boyfriend, then winked at him. He smiled at her like a sap. Obviously, they were too wrapped up in each other to acknowledge the demanding fae player.

Kit heard a warrior by the fire sigh and the smack of the dryad's lips as she blew her beau another kiss. Though she wanted to roll her eyes, she kept her expression bland. *I need to practice using my elf traits more. It seems like whenever I could really use the positive physical attributes an elf possesses, my mind gets in the way and keeps me from optimizing them.*

The fae gave up on the amorous couple and wandered in their party's direction, stopping next to Riko. "Hi. Could you plz give me money? I'm poor, and I can't use the teleportation gate."

Riko glanced at the fae's nameplate above her head. "You're a level twenty-two hunter. Go kill something in the tunnels and make some money if you're that strapped for funds."

"But I need to get back to Luminos now," the fae said.

"Then you better hurry," Riko said.

The fae frowned at her, then shifted her attention to Prowl and Axel. "Hi. Give me money, plz."

Axel eyed the pushy player and inched down the bench. Prowl draped himself over the table like a cat. "Nobody here is going to fall for your tricks. Get lost."

"But I just started. I need help," the fae said.

Prowl planted his chin on his fist. "You're barking up the wrong tree: I'm playing with a bunch of players at a lower level than you."

The fae stared at the party for several long moments—probably trying to sniff out the weakest of them. Her eyes skipped over Kit and Vic, then landed on Cookie. The night stalker bit her lip as she studied the fae—perilously close to breaking and giving in to her demand.

The fae smiled, then moved in for the kill.... Until Prowl picked her up by the back of her cloak. "That's it. Beat it pipsqueak, or I'll kill you right here." He deposited her away from their table.

She screwed her face up. "I'll report you as a player killer!"

Prowl smiled darkly and squatted down so he could lean into her face. "Do you really think a little thing like that would scare me?" He started to slide a dagger out of his belt.

The fae yipped and scurried away.

Prowl snorted and plopped back down on the bench.

"Thanks, Prowl," Kit said.

He shrugged.

Axel scratched his head. "She was annoying, but was it really necessary to scare her like that?"

"It seemed a little brusque," Gil added.

"It's fine," Kit said. "There's a lot of players like her who go around asking for money. You have to be rude to get them to leave you alone, or they'll add your name to their friends list and start pestering you for cash whenever you log on."

Axel squinted but said nothing more.

Vic tapped her spoon on the rim of her plate. "Interesting. I never pegged you as a softy, Man-Bun."

Axel scowled at the nickname but leaned back on the bench. "I just don't like pushing around anyone smaller than me. It feels dishonorable or something."

"Just pretend it's like PVP," Kit said.

"I don't like PVP," Axel said.

Vic snorted. "*You,* Mister-I'm-the-strongest-stand-behind-me-girls, *you* don't like PVP?"

Axel glared at her. "Yeah, what of it?"

"PVP isn't for everyone," Riko acknowledged. "Many players are more interested in raids and killing difficult monsters than PVP."

Axel pointed to Riko. "Yeah! What she said!"

Prowl shrugged and popped a mint leaf in his mouth. "You're missing out, man. It's pretty satisfying to sink a blade into an enemy's back and win the game for your team."

Axel sucked his neck into his shoulders. "I don't like killing kids and women—even if it is just a game."

"Are you sure you shouldn't have signed up for the knight class?" Vic joked.

"I think it's neat. It just shows he sticks by his values," Cookie said.

Kit studied Axel with narrowed eyes. *I think I'm starting to understand him: he values strength but doesn't want to misuse it. He would never do well with a thief class. He seems overly honest and honorable, which an enemy could use to their advantage, though.*

Axel caught her stare. "What?" he barked.

"Just thinking." Kit smiled sweetly at him, though her thoughts were still clinical. *It brings up an interesting thought... how can I use his quirks to the team's advantage?*

Kit, Riko, Prowl, and Axel cornered King Brasil in Brunascar's library—a huge building that had shelves stacked with scrolls nearly as big as the dwarves themselves.

The king was squinting over a scroll spread out on a great wooden desk when they approached him.

"Why if it isn't Mistress Riko, Master Prowl, and some of their friends. Please, sit with me." King Brasil motioned for them to sit on the stools that lined the desk. "Take some refreshments if you like."

Prowl eyed the square tea set that was set out. "You drink tea?"

King Brasil snorted. "My wife loves it—it's a citrus blend from the east. I prefer ale and mead, but last time I tried to bring that here, the head librarian threw me out."

"We thank you for your hospitality," Riko said as she took a seat.

Axel sat as well, his legs bunched up ridiculously on the small stool as he took a square tea cup that sat comfortably in one hand. "Why am *I* here?" he whispered.

"Because we need to present a strong image," Kit whispered back. "Dwarves respect strength."

Axel looked from his flowery-scented tea to the small stools. "Then I think we chose the wrong place to make our move."

Prowl half-grinned, then pulled his goggles down so they covered his eyes.

Kit caught Riko's eye and nodded.

The druid took a breath and placed a professional smile on her lips. "King Brasil," she said, drawing his attention from his tea. "We would like to discuss the legendary seals with you."

"Ah, yes. I had forgotten the lot of you were after the legendary seals." King Brasil wiped his mouth off on his arm.

"Yes. Would you grant us the great honor of giving us the dwarven seal?" Riko asked.

The dwarf king tapped his thick fingers on the scratched table surface. "I will..."

Kit's heart leapt. She didn't think it would be this easy! *Dwarves have become my new favorite race in this entire game!*

Unfortunately, King Brasil wasn't finished. "But you will have to earn it."

"Of course." Riko kept her expression serene. "It would only be fair."

Kit was not nearly so understanding. "What would you want us to do?"

"It is not so much that you will do something for me, as much as it is that you must display your courage," he said.

Riko glanced at Prowl, cuing the Saboteur to make his move.

He leaned forward and smiled wolfishly. "Cut to the chase, King. What do you want us to do?"

King Brasil laughed heartily. "I admire a lad who knows his mind! Very well. You can have the seal, but your test of courage will be retrieving it."

A sneaking suspicion started to poke the back of Kit's mind. "And where is the seal?" she asked.

"It is in a cavern that has long been abandoned by my people," King Brasil said.

Prowl frowned. "You mean you lost it?"

"Not precisely. It is more that we were...unexpectedly forced to abandon that location."

"Why?" Kit asked, hoping it was only in some far-off area that had experienced a cave-in. That was better than the alternative.

"We were having some trouble," King Brasil said, "with dragons."

Kit forced her expression to stay bland. "Oh? Dragons, you say?"

"The seal is located in one of our smaller treasure chambers," King Brasil said. "Unfortunately, some years ago, there was a dragon infestation in the White Needles mountains. While most of the dragons remain on the exterior of the mountains, a nest of dragons took over that particular treasure room."

"Let me guess," Prowl said. "The seal is located at the very back of that treasure room, behind all the dragons?"

"Yes, presuming none of the dragons ate it." King Brasil said. "How did you know?"

Axel kept his mouth shut as he looked from his companions to King Brasil and sipped his tea with obvious discomfort.

Kit's thoughts raced as she struggled to comprehend the immensity of the task they faced. Normally, fighting dragons would've been a blast. But fighting dragons with four severely under-leveled characters and no healer? *We may as well strip off our armor and do the salsa through the chamber; we'll get killed just as quickly if we don't.*

"That is not all," the dwarvish king added.

"Ahaha—of course it's not," Kit said in her dead voice.

"We always have some guards posted to keep an eye on the dragons—for both safety reasons and in the hopes that one day we might be able to reclaim the treasure room. Recently, there have been some disturbing reports."

"Disturbing in what way?" Riko asked respectfully.

"The guards claim to see shadows—not the regular ones caused by light, but thick tarry masses that move unnaturally." King Brasil thoughtfully planted his chin on his fist. "It would seem you are not the only ones after the seals. Truth be told, it is why I am so willing to give it to you, for I would rather that heroes take possession of it instead of some force of darkness."

"Do you think it is some mindless monster?" Axel asked almost hopefully as his hand strayed to the hilt of his sword.

He shook his head. "No. I believe it is one of Malignus's minions."

Kit stood and smiled at the King. "Thank you for your transparency in the situation. We will do our best to retrieve the seal, for we would also hate to see it fall into the hands of darkness. Before we leave for the chamber, can we take inventory of our stocks and purchase any necessary goods?"

"Of course!" King Brasil stood as well. "In fact, I shall outfit you as I would outfit my best warriors!"

Riko perked up and clasped her hands together. "Really? Free of charge?" She asked hopefully.

"Yes. Drust! Forget about that last scroll I asked you to find. Send for the armorsmiths instead!"

"What about the weaponsmiths?" Drust asked.

"Them, too!"

As Drust trundled down the library aisle, King Brasil walked after him. "Tell them it's for our honored guests!" He bellowed.

Riko stood when the king did, then leaned against the desk with a happy sigh after he left. "There's nothing better than free upgrades!"

"How are we going to break this to the rest of the party?" Kit asked.

"We? There is no we—that's your responsibility, party leader," Prowl snorted.

Axel had managed to maneuver himself so he looked fractionally more comfortable as he sat on the too-small stool and sipped tea from his square cup. "They'll accept it. It's not like we've got much of a choice. We'll have to do it," he said grimly.

Kit sighed. "Axel is right. There's no other way to get out of the game without collecting the seals."

The warrior blinked. "I wasn't talking about that."

"Then what did you mean?" Riko asked.

"The dragons. Taking them down will be hard, but there's no better way to gauge our strength," Axel said.

Prowl turned to Kit. "This is why *you'll* have to be the one to tell everyone. Come on. They're still eating, I think."

Kit flicked her fans open—just to hear the reassuring sound. "Coming."

10

GEARING UP

KIT CLEARED her throat as she once again sat down with her fellow party members in the feasting hall. "So...we have to fight dragons."

Vic stood. "I'm out. There's no way we can fight dragons."

Cookie grabbed her friend by the shoulder and yanked her back into the chair. Vic glared at her, but she stilled when Gil gave her a reassuring smile.

"The seal is located in a treasure chamber that is guarded by dragons—and possibly haunted by one of Malignus's minions." Kit tapped her finger on the table—which looked like someone had once taken a pickaxe to it.

Vic gave Prowl an accusing look. "You knew about this, didn't you?"

"Knew what?" the saboteur lazily asked.

"You knew we were going to face dragons!"

Prowl shrugged. "Not really, actually. While I completed this quest on my main, I worked on it at the same time as four other epic quests that also involved a lot of globe-trotting. I vaguely remember the different feats I had to accomplish, but I can't clearly recall which events belonged with each quest."

Vic pursed her lips.

"Fighting dragons isn't the worst thing I did in Brunascar." Prowl's smile turned sly. "At one point, I also had to take a tumble over Tremblebach Falls. Would you rather do that?"

"Prowl, be an adult please and don't bait the cuties," Riko said.

Vic looked like she still wanted to rip into him, but Cookie— ever the peacemaker—intervened. "It's not surprising that we're facing a difficult task. Usually quest objectives are hidden behind difficult dungeons."

"I don't think the dragons are inherently the problem," Gil said. "It seems our level is more what holds us back."

Prowl nodded. "Exactly. Which brings up the idea—are we sure we want to do this without trying to grind out a few more levels?"

Riko frowned. "What do you mean?"

"We're about to go face dragons," Prowl said. "Unless you have a huge party, you're not really supposed to attack them until you are at least level twenty-five. Riko and I might be above their level, but we can't take the whole cave on with just the two of us."

"We don't have a choice," Kit said. "Besides, if we die, it's not that big of an issue. We just respawn, regroup, and try again."

"We'll lose experience," Prowl said. "Every time we die, it eats one percent of our experience bar."

"Yeah," Axel echoed.

Kit waited until they were both looking at her. "I would rather sacrifice a little experience if it means we're one step closer to getting out of this game. Retha is wild and fun, but we can't play by the rules right now. This isn't just about our characters but about our lives. Because if we don't log off, and if EC can't figure out a way to get the corrupted server fixed..." She trailed off.

"I will follow you, Miss Kit," Gil said.

"Me, too," Riko added.

Cookie opened her mouth, then hesitated and turned to Vic.

The wizard rolled her eyes. "Oh, all right. I've almost been killed by rabid wolves; I may as well become dragon fodder."

"Prowl, Axel?" Riko asked.

Prowl sighed. "Of course, I'm in," he said. "It's just...I don't want it to be like this. *Chronicles of Retha* is a game. It's supposed to be an escape. Not a danger."

"It can still be that," Axel said. "If we think about the danger too much, it'll drive us crazy." He gave the party a wolfish grin. "So instead, think about how awesome it's going to be to take on dragons!"

Vic groaned. "You are not doing a great job at selling this."

"I'm excited," Cookie said. She stood and clapped her hands. "Come on guys! Let's go fight some dragons!"

Riko laughed at Cookie's exhilaration, Gil smiled, and Vic continued to berate her as the tension that had been cast over the party evaporated.

Kit allowed herself to relax and tried to banish the worry that clawed at her throat.

How much time do we have left? When will this gameplay become less a thing of preventative care, and more of our last chance?

"Kit, are you coming?" Cookie asked from the feasting hall doorway.

Kit shook herself from her thoughts. "Where are we going?"

"Riko said King Brasil called for the armorsmiths, and they want to take our measurements for new gear."

Kit was at the door in an instant. "Then absolutely! With

luck, the dwarves will have a much more suitable armor set for me!"

———

Kit was peering over her newly acquired "crystal candy" recipe and was almost run over when Cookie marched out of the makeshift dressing room they had created.

"Ta-da!" The night stalker posed with her hands on her hips and her chest puffed up. Her new armor set was even more sleek and dark, accented with patches of black fur and elaborately forged pieces of metal.

"It looks very warm," Kit said.

"I like it! It's soft, and the stats are much better than my starter outfit." Cookie jerked her thumb to point over her shoulder. "The outfit the tailor picked out for you is on the bench."

Kit eagerly flicked her screens away and slipped past the cloth curtain that marked off the dressing area from the rest of the weapon shop.

A small package wrapped with gunmetal gray fabric waited for her on the little wooden bench set in front of the full-length mirror. Kit hurriedly opened it and slipped into her new armor with high hopes.

Dwarves are a logical sort of people. I bet they won't leave a huge patch bare on my belly...

Her hopes were dashed when she put on the last piece and turned to look in the mirror, flashing her bare mid-drift that still lacked any sort of armor.

Kit's shoulders slumped, but instead of being filled with bitterness, she was mostly apathetic. "Ahh, yes. If I check my expectations, perhaps I will achieve inner peace regarding the poor armor options for dancers."

Thankfully, the dwarves had not entirely failed her as they

had given her blue trousers that cut off at the knee and puffed slightly so she resembled a truffle, and a set of leather slippers to replace her stupid sandals. The shirt cut off at her rib cage and covered her chest; it also encircled her neck with a metal collar that actually reassured Kit, as it did a decent job of protecting her throat. The sleeves had a slit over the shoulders, so they were bared as well, but where they cut off at the elbows, the tailor had sewn elaborate metal pieces to keep the shirt in place and also to offer extra protection. The headgear was a metal band that helped push Kit's hair out of her face, though she had to gather it in a high ponytail to make it comfortable.

Kit stared at her reflection and sighed. She knew she should be grateful as the armor offered superior vitality and dexterity bonuses, but it was still disheartening to traipse around in front of monsters with her belly button showing.

Vic wrenched the curtain open, poked her head in, and sighed. "What's taking you so long to change? Even Axel moved faster than you, and he spent quite a long time preening at the mirror."

Kit laughed dryly like one who had lost all hope. "I am attempting to reach inner contentment instead of falling into depression."

Vic rolled her eyes. "Whatever. Come on, everyone's waiting for you." She removed her head from the dressing area and marched across the room.

Kit sighed at her reflection, then followed the wizard. A dwarf weaponsmith was waiting for her. "I am afraid we don't have many weapon options for dancers, Mistress Kit. However, I took the liberty and made a few upgrades to your...fans," the dwarf said dryly.

He offered Kit the newly remade weapons, and nonchalantly put out a spark from the forge that had landed on some papers and started to flame up.

Kit took her fans and snapped them open, delighted to see that the edges were now covered in razor-sharp steel. The weaponsmith had also reinforced the wooden sticks of the fan with metal, making it much harder to break.

The improvements added to the (insignificant) damage the weapon doled, but most importantly, it greatly increased the durability of the fans so Kit didn't have to worry about them breaking halfway through the treasure chamber.

"Thank you! This will be extremely helpful." She smiled at the dwarf, who raised his bushy eyebrows.

"I'm not so sure about that if you are facing dragons," he muttered.

Before Kit could agree with him, there was a deafening blast on ram horns as King Brasil strolled up to their party.

"Thank you, King Brasil, for your generous gifts," Riko said with a professional smile. She and Prowl hadn't received new armor, but the dwarves had upgraded their weapons instead.

"Of course! What kind of dwarves would we be if we cared not for our guests' armor?" King Brasil boomed. "Now, are you ready to make your way to the treasure chamber?"

Everyone turned to face Kit. She awkwardly folded her hands in front of her belly and smiled serenely. "I believe we are."

"As expected of heroes! The treasure chambers are rather isolated, and the path to get there is quite winding, so I shall send you off in dwarvish style with mine carts!" He gestured to several mine carts that rolled up behind him on the rickety track. Each mine cart was already occupied by a stone-faced dwarf at the wheel and clanked loudly. "Of course, we are providing guides as well. They will take you as close as they dare without raising the dragons' ire. The rest will depend upon your skills as heroes!"

"Oh, gee golly," Prowl said. "We're so thrilled."

Riko smacked him hard between the shoulder blades. "We will not fail. We shall reclaim the seal and return once our task is finished."

"If we're not turned into barbecue," Prowl added.

Riko whacked him again.

"May the hammers of luck guard your path," King Brasil said.

The ram horn trumpets blasted again, which Kit took as their dismissal. She started for the mine carts. "Riko is very good at influencing NPCs," she said abruptly.

Gil, who was closest to her, nodded. "She certainly knew how to best appease King Brasil."

Kit adjusted her metal headband. *Perhaps Riko really ought to be our party—*

"Which is why it is perfect that she is something of our diplomat and banker, while you remain our leader," Gil continued.

They reached the mine carts, and Kit rested a hand on the edge of one of them while she peered curiously at the crusader. "What do you mean?"

"Charisma might be a requirement for leadership success in the business world, but we are in a fantasy game. The ability to see the big picture and how all the different pieces interact in addition to properly managing battles is most important for a party leader." Gil smiled guilelessly. "Which is why we are very fortunate to have you."

Kit laughed and hopped into the mine cart, stiffening when it teetered back and forth on the track. "You are a smooth operator, Gil!"

"Thank you, Miss Kit."

Once the party was settled into the three available mine carts, the dwarf in the front cart announced, "We're leavin'!"

Cookie almost bounced in place. "This is going to be fun. It's like a go-cart ride!"

Vic watched Kit as she hunkered as deeply as possible into the mine cart, then shifted her gaze to Prowl and Riko—who had death grips on their chairs. "I'm not so sure about that."

"Hold on!" Kit turned around to smile at the girls as the mine carts creaked along the track, following a bend in the path. "It can be a pretty wild—Hyaaa—" She was cut off with a grunt when the road abruptly dropped, and the cart careened wildly down the track.

Vic's screams were almost covered up by Axel's wild laughter.

The carts popped up and down as the track alternated from abruptly heaving up to falling off in near dead drops. It felt like a roller coaster—an especially frightening one given that occasionally the tracks nearly threw the carts free, and that Kit and her companions were frequently tossed into the air, with only their grip on the carts to keep them from flying off.

They moved so fast, the wind blurred Kit's eyes, and the lit pathways were little more than blurs.

The dwarf driver of her cart shouted, "Duck!"

Kit lifted her chin. "What?"

The dwarf hunkered down, narrowly missing a bat that smacked Kit right in the face, knocking her back into Vic. The strike took a good fourth of her health and left her dazed, so she almost slid out of the cart when they skidded around an especially tight corner.

The mine carts screeched to an abrupt halt, leaving Kit, Vic, and Cookie a tangled mess of limbs with the bat that hit Kit sitting rather dazed on her lap.

"That was better than a roller coaster!" Axel declared as he leaped from his cart.

Vic covered her mouth. "I think I'm going to be sick."

Gil laughed as he also exited his cart, then assisted Vic. "It was a rather refreshing ride."

"For an old guy, you must have a stomach of iron," Vic grumbled. When Kit finally stood, the bat had recovered and flew off. She staggered from the cart and straightened her clothes that had billowed wildly during the ride.

"Nature's Blessing," Riko held her palm out to Kit, applying a heal to her. "Playing Retha with you, Kit, has opened my eyes to all the possibilities in this game. After all, I don't think I've ever seen anyone take a bat to the face."

Kit rubbed her forehead. "Always happy to be of service."

"The entrance to the abandoned treasure room lies at the end of this passageway," the driver of Kit's mine cart said. He pointed up the empty tunnel, which grew darker as fewer torches were posted on the walls. "We shall wait here with the guards for your return."

The other two drivers had already gotten out of their mine carts and begun chatting with five well-armed guards lined up neatly with their backs to the wall.

"Thank you for your help," Kit said. "Hopefully we won't take too long."

The dwarf nodded. "If you take more than a few hours, we shall assume you have met your end."

"Gee, your confidence in us is astounding," Prowl said.

The dwarf bowed to them. "May the light of King Brasil shine upon your weapons and guard your feet." He scuttled away before Kit could respond, joining his brethren farther back in the passageway.

Kit adjusted her hair tie and discreetly checked her inventory one last time.

"All right! Who's ready to face some dragons?" Axel hefted his unnecessarily giant sword above his head and wolf whistled.

Prowl glared at him, but it was Gil who mildly said, "Perhaps it would be best if we quietly approached the dragons so we do not alert them to our presence?"

"You've got it, Gil," Kit said. "We don't want to face more than one dragon at a time, or we'll be completely overwhelmed."

"Even though Prowl and Riko are a much higher level?" Vic asked.

"Yes. Although monsters in Retha have levels, like us players, they also have different ranks. The ranks affect how difficult they are to beat. So normal monsters are easy, while on the other side of the spectrum there are bosses, which are much more difficult," Kit explained. "Dragons aren't bosses themselves, but as they are considered epic creatures, they are about as hard to kill as a mini-boss."

"Of course, more confusing level-ranking. I should have known," Vic said dryly.

"The same is true for players, isn't it?" Cookie asked. "I mean, until you reach the level cap, you're just normal. But once you reach the max level, isn't it possible to continue to improve your character? I read about that when I was reading up on Retha."

"You are right," Riko said. "Players—or heroes—can go on to become 'legendary heroes,' which basically means you've cleared a lot of the content whether it be raids, quests, or PVP battles. When that happens, your character class can become specialized. Solus Miles is a perfect example. Before he became a legendary hero, he was just a plain knight like many other players. But now, due to his excellence, his class expanded so he's a Royal Knight."

Kit scratched her scalp. "How is that going, by the way? They were starting to roll that out right before Milk Crown disbanded, but none of us ever tried to get it even though we were at the level cap at the time."

"It certainly makes it far more interesting for players who

reach the level cap," Riko said. "Unfortunately, neither Prowl nor I have characters at that level, so we have not experienced it firsthand."

"Tough Beard is a legendary hero," Prowl said. "It definitely has made him a lot more badass."

"That's great and all, but what about the dragons? Are we going to go fight them?" Axel popped up and down on the balls of his feet and wore a wolfish grin as he peered down the tunnel.

"I can't decide if you're bloodthirsty, an idiot, or a blood-thirsty idiot," Prowl said.

"Blood thirst brings you extra courage," Axel said confidently.

"Is that what it is called?" Vic asked. "I was going to say it brings being downright stupid—"

"Let's move out, team!" Kit bounded down the hallway, her bell anklets jingling with every step.

"Aye aye, leader!" Cookie saluted, then marched after her. The others paused only momentarily before joining them, striding down the tunnel as it pitched deeper and deeper into the earth. There were a few tunnels that peeled off from the main passageway, but judging by the cobwebs that hung from the frames, they hadn't been disturbed in years. (Either that, or those tunnels were connected to the giant spider nest that was located somewhere in the area, if Kit remembered correctly.)

Kit knew they had reached the treasure chamber when the main passageway abruptly ended with a narrow opening. The smell of sulfur and the metallic scent of tarnished gold wafted from the next chamber, though they couldn't see much through the small entrance.

"Cookie, would you go in first using some of your stealth skills and check it out?" Kit asked.

"You got it." Cookie activated her "Cloak of Shadows" skill as she stepped into a shadow and disappeared.

Kit's tapered elf ears twitched as she listened for the night stalker, who padded into the treasure chamber with the agility of a cat. The rest of the party crowded around the opening, peering into the dimly-lit cavern.

The treasure room was dimly lit by glowing blue and gold crystals that jutted out of the walls. Their muted light made the mounds of gold coins and stacks of priceless treasures twinkle. Deep in the cavern, a dragon roared, and the ground shuddered beneath Kit's feet.

Riko speculatively stroked her chin. "I wonder if King Brasil would mind if we happen to help ourselves to some of the gold while we pass through."

"I kind of doubt they would let us keep it," Kit said.

"That would be so stingy of them!" Riko said.

"That's really ironic coming from you," Prowl said.

"Won't the dragons have good drops?" Gil asked.

Axel snorted. "Who cares about drops? It's all about the experience!"

Vic wrinkled her forehead. "Is Cookie going to be okay out there?"

Cookie abruptly popped into view when she stepped out of the shadows. "Aw, Vic, you were worried about me!" Before the wizard could object, Cookie turned to Kit and saluted her. "There's one purple-colored, level-twenty dragon around this first bend of the cave. After that, the treasure room opens up into a rather large cavern. There're a lot more dragons there."

Kit repositioned one of the metal cuffs of her sleeves. "A huge cavern isn't ideal. Attacking out in the open like that would bring several dragons on our head at once. But maybe after we defeat this first one, we could drag the others back into the smaller part of the room?"

Riko nodded. "That's probably our best tactic with this size and level of group."

"So the purple dragon first." Prowl slipped into the treasure room, his eyes warily scanning the treasure.

Kit and the others slowly joined him, with Axel striding happily to the front. Kit dawdled behind the others, unable to shake the feeling that something was wrong as the hair on the back of her neck prickled. Cautiously, she looked to the front of their party, where Riko had taken charge of Axel and was holding him back from running around the bend and straight into the purple dragon.

Kit risked wasting a moment to turn around and peer in the direction from which they had come. The small opening seemed dark, and as Kit watched it, the shadows that screened it warped and bubbled. She flicked her fans open and prepared to shout for the rest of the party, but when she blinked, the strange shadows were gone. She frowned, recalling a similar sight when she had left the alleyway where they had found the old man. She took a step back toward the entrance, intending to investigate it, when a crash interrupted her thoughts.

Axel, who had scaled a wall of the chamber in an attempt to get a height advantage, had accidentally dislodged one of the massive glowing crystals, which crashed to the ground and shattered into hundreds of pieces.

There was a moment of stunned silence.

"Axel!" Kit hissed when it became apparent the dragon hadn't heard.

"Oops!" Axel said.

Instantly, a purple dragon lumbered around the bend.

11

ENTER THE DRAGONS' DEN

IT WAS APPROXIMATELY as big as an African elephant, and though its eyes glowed red, its scales were as dingy and tarnished as the gold it guarded. It roared, shaking the entire passageway, then spun around and slammed its tail like a club, narrowly missing Vic.

The wizard fell and emitted a loud scream when the ground buckled beneath her.

The dragon swiped its tail across the smooth stone floor, slamming it into Vic.

Vic was sent flying head over heels into a heap of coins.

The dragon, its wings pressed flat against its back, advance toward her with its mouth gaping open, revealing rows of silver teeth.

Cookie darted between its legs and slammed a dagger into the leathery flesh at the base of its claws.

The attack was barely more than a pinprick of the creature's health bar, but it roared in anger, lashed out with its forepaw, and slammed her into the wall.

"Nature's Blessing!" Riko shouted, slowly healing Cookie.

"We have to fall back and group up," Kit said.

She either hadn't been loud enough, or firm enough, for Axel raised his sword over his head and charged in. "Gut Buster!" He stabbed his sword at the dragon's underbelly and scored a minor hit. He laughed wildly, until the dragon sat down on his head.

"Nature's Blessing!"

Riko's spell barely reached the warrior in time, before the last of his health leaked away.

Thankfully, the dragon lost interest in Axel and instead turned back to Vic.

"Fireball!" The wizard launched the fire attack at the dragon. The beast snorted when the fireball burst harmlessly against its plated scales, doing no damage.

The dragon tilted its head back, its mouth gaping open as its throat started to glow with the telltale sign of fire.

Vic tried to hide behind a set of gold armor, but Gil stepped in front of her with his shield raised. "Shield Wall!" His shield glowed as he braced himself for impact.

The dragon lurched forward, belching a stream of fire at the Crusader. Gil's skill cut much of the damage, but the strike left him with barely a sliver of health.

"I can't heal him!" Riko shouted. "All my healing spells are on cooldown!"

"Gil, take a potion," Kit shouted.

The crusader nodded and quickly popped a red health potion, restoring most of his health points.

As the dragon exhaled a smoke ring, Kit took the opportunity to say, "We should fall back and have Prowl trap it with a stun trap. That'll give everybody time to reset their skills."

It seemed no one heard her over the din of battle, for Axel launched another Gut Buster—at least this time he was smart enough to move after the attack. Cookie jumped from the shadows of the wall, landing on the dragon's back. "Backstab!"

She sliced her dagger down the row of scales, doing a little more damage this time.

Kit gaped at the dragon's daunting health bar that hovered above its head. In spite of all the attacks, they had only lowered his health by a sixth. Maybe even less.

We've got to change our tactic!

Wildly attacking the dragon was doing more harm than help, and Riko, instead of attacking (despite the fact she had the highest attack power due to her level), was frantically healing. "Nature's Blessing!" The druid pointed to Cookie, restoring some of her health.

"Don't just stand there, party leader. Tell them what to do!" Prowl growled.

"I've tried!"

"Yeah, well you haven't been loud enough to get their attention. They're going to get themselves killed at this rate, and they'll take Riko down with them!"

Kit leaped to the side, barely avoiding the dragon's tail when it swung it at her. "This is why I shouldn't be the party leader. I can't do it!"

"Stop making excuses," Prowl said. "I've seen you in action —you know tactics better than anybody here thanks to your main character! We need that right now, so grow a spine, and do your job!"

Kit gritted her teeth, angry because she knew the saboteur was right. Unfortunately, the realization came too late as the dragon had divided the team with Vic, Gil, and Riko on one side of the monster, and Axel, Cookie, Kit, and Prowl on the other. There was no way for everyone to retreat and group up. Kit chewed on her lip as she thought. "Do you have any item that will stun it, like your pepper grit?"

"Here." Prowl tossed her a small packet. "You'll have to get it in its eyes though. Sorry."

"I don't mind. After spending this much time as this character, I'm used to crummy jobs by now," Kit said dryly. Clenching the powder tight in her fist, she ran straight for the dragon. She ducked, barely avoiding it when it smashed its tail into a wall— dislodging some crystals and rocks that pelted her like hail.

With its attention stuck on Vic and Gil, Kit ran up its front right leg, exhilarated when she felt her elf race traits kick in and give her an extra burst of agility. The dragon didn't notice her until she climbed all the way up its neck and began to use some of the ridges on its forehead as handholds to climb down its face.

It shook its head, jarring Kit and slamming her against its sharp scales. The scales made slices on her legs, arms, and of course her unprotected stomach.

Kit hissed at the sharp pain but kept climbing. When she was close enough to its right eyeball, she clung to its scales— bloodying her hands—and tried to rip open the packet with her teeth. She almost lost her grip on the thing due to her slippery, bloodied hands, but she was able to pour the packet into its open eye before it managed to dislodge her. It tossed her up over its head so she landed on the spines of its back with a painful crack.

Kit coughed, the air thrust out of her, though she was aware of the fact that the dragon had frozen and was no longer moving. She switched to the party channel and desperately sucked in air so she could shout. "Stop attacking! Prowl, lay traps in layers to hold the dragon back so it keeps triggering them every time it moves forward. Everyone else, fallback to the entrance of the treasure chamber, or Riko will no longer heal you!"

Kit rolled off the dragon, her back aching horrifically from the impact, and joined Vic in running to the door.

Prowl wasted no time in making the pathway between the dragon and the door a sea of traps.

"Those aren't gonna hold him long," he warned as the

dragon crashed through the first line of traps and was held in place.

Kit flicked her fans open. "They don't have to. We just need enough time to reorganize ourselves." She launched into her only skill—Battlefield March—twisting and twirling in a confined space near the party. The music that accompanied her skill twined around the group, improving their physical attack and defense skills.

As she danced, she continued to speak. "Vic, focus your fire on its face—particularly its eyes and its mouth. Bubble Barrage uses less mana, right?"

"Yes. And it's instantaneous—no casting time. But it's not very strong."

"If you use it on the right part of the target it will be. So *only* use Bubble Barrage. Fireball won't do much damage to the dragon anyway. Don't hit him with everything you have, instead aim for slow and steady so you don't drain your mana too quickly. Once he breaks free of those traps, Cookie, Axel, and Prowl, you three need to launch your highest damage-dealing attacks. Gil, while they do that, use your taunt skill and try to keep the dragon's attention on you. It won't hold with the amount of fire power being thrown around, but it will distract him and make him keep switching targets. If that doesn't work, use your hammer strike skill on him. Finally, Riko."

"You want me to heal, right?"

"No. I want you to get your Earthen Pit skill ready and then use it on the dragon when it reaches the last of the traps, before everyone else attacks. Then *immediately* use Nature's Bindings and tie him up with vines, but call it out when you do!"

"He's to the last line of traps," Prowl said.

"Riko, start casting Earthen Pit!" Kit spun around to face the incoming dragon. "Here we go!"

Just as the dragon lurched free of the traps, Riko hit it with

Earthen Pit, opening a hole under it. The skill was unable to swallow him up—as it had with the nether wolf—but the sides of the pit closed in, crushing the dragon and causing massive damage.

As it roared, Vic kept up a steady stream of bubbles. Though her knees shook, her aim was good, and she hit its eyes, blinding it.

Gil, running with Cookie, Axel, and Prowl, hit it with a taunt, making the dragon weave its head back and forth between himself, Riko, and Vic.

Axel stabbed the dragon in the throat, which did more damage than all of his previous attacks combined—although he barely avoided getting crushed when the dragon smashed its head down on him. Unfortunately, when Axel rolled out of the way, he smacked into one of the treasure piles, causing a rather large chest to fall on top of him.

Prowl ran past the fallen warrior and slapped what appeared to be a wad of clay on the dragon's snout. He must have been using some kind of aggression-lowering skill, as the dragon didn't even glance at him.

Cookie seized the opportunity to stab the dragon in the eye, inflicting a bleeding wound on it that slowly carved away at its health.

The dragon thrashed wildly, squirming out of the pit Riko had trapped it in. It flung Axel to the side and would have scooped Cookie away from the rest of the party with its tail if not for Gil. The crusader raised his Shield Wall, which absorbed some of the damage and instead sent both him and Cookie sprawling backwards.

Prowl nimbly avoided the dragon's thrashing and slapped something on its underbelly.

"Casting Nature's Bindings," Riko shouted.

"Cookie, Gil, Axel, and Prowl—get out of there until he's

tied up again." Kit—who had forced herself to fight her instinct to hang back and instead danced near the dragon so the stat boost from her dance could cover the entire party—zipped back to Riko's side.

"Hold off! I need one more second." Prowl completed his circuit around the dragon and slapped another wad of clay on its side.

"Nature's Bindings," Riko said. Vines sprouted out of the ground and wrapped around the dragon, holding him in place.

Kit stopped dancing—there were no attacks being launched at the moment anyway—to give her mana a few moments to recover. "Start casting Earthen Pit again, Riko. What are you doing, Prowl?"

The Saboteur crouched down and flipped a dagger out of his boot. He ran his thumb across the blade and murmured a few words, making the droplet of blood that now coated the dagger glow. "You wanted my biggest attack? This is it. It's got a mega long cooldown before I can use it again, though, so this is our only shot."

The dragon chewed at the vines, snapping them and freeing his front legs.

"Wait until I cast Earthen Pit again, then I can hold him for you," Riko said.

Kit's heart shuddered when the dragon tilted its head back and roared, and she could see the smallest flicker of light gather at its throat. "No, cast it now, Prowl."

"But Earthen Pit—"

"The dragon is about to use a fire attack—he's head-on, and there's no way he can miss us so we *have* to interrupt him instead. Cast it, Prowl!"

Prowl whipped his dagger out in front of him and ran at the enraged beast. "Mangle!"

The wads of clay Prowl had stuck to the dragon shot out

lines of dark blue light, forming a triangle. Black fog blasted around the beast, and it suddenly began to move slower—as if it were stuck in tar.

The attack had laid a powerful de-buff on the dragon that greatly stripped away his agility and defense.

Cookie whistled. "Now *that* is what I call a de-buff."

"Yeah, but that's not the attack," Kit said.

Red tendrils of light shot out of the clay masses and convened to one spot on the dragon's throat—right where Axel had stabbed him in the previous run. Prowl skidded to a stop just below the dragon's head even as the monster's mouth began to sputter with flames. He threw his dagger, which bit deep into the dragon's hide and shed red sparks.

Bolts of lightning zipped from the dagger to the wads of clay, before the red magic that swirled around the weapon erupted with a flash of light and a loud boom.

Its attack interrupted, the dragon swallowed its fire and roared with pain as its health plummeted.

Kit sprinted for the dragon. "Riko—use Earthen Pit. Everyone else, attack!"

The druid released her spell—which had been building during Prowl's attack—and the cavern floor fell out from underneath the dragon again and pinned it in place while further crushing it.

Bubbles filled the air as Vic attacked, and Kit leaped into her dance just before Axel, Cookie, and Gil reached the dragon and started pounding on it.

The dragon started to squirm loose of the crater Riko held him in, but he had only a bit of health left. He freed one leg and started to unfurl his wings—which smashed into the ceiling and dropped chunks of rock down on them.

Both of its eyes started to glow, and jagged lines of fire traveled down its spine and encircled its claws.

It's going to launch a final attack. It will kill us!

"Attack him with everything you have—take him down!" Kit shouted.

"Gut Buster!"

"Hammer Strike!"

Cookie, unlike the others, crouched low to the cave floor and stared up at the dragon with narrowed eyes. The dragon roared and began to launch a fire attack accompanied with a shock-wave that sent everyone sprawling. Flames flooded the area, roasting them with such blistering heat and pain, Kit and the others were paralyzed...except for Cookie. She flicked two daggers, nailing the dragon in the roof of the mouth.

Her assault chiseled away at the last little bit of the dragon's health. Its eyes turned vacant, and it cut off its attack before collapsing on the ground and shaking the tunnel.

Kit—her clothes smoldering and ashy even though her pink hair was as perfect as ever—collapsed to her knees with only a few points of health left. "We did it."

Rainbow-colored lights flashed around her while musical notes bumped her burned skin. The familiar "LEVEL UP" message flashed above her head, welcoming her to level twelve. A glance at the rest of the party revealed everyone except for Riko and Prowl had leveled-up as well.

Her character panel automatically popped up.

Congratulations! You have learned the dancer skill: The Luck-Luck Dance
Your sheer luck allows you to live dangerously—or foolishly!
Effect: Increases party members' luck and critical hits. Can be interrupted.

Kit scratched her nose and considered the skill—which wasn't bad despite its ridiculous name. She was a little surprised, though, as dancers were known to have de-buff skills to cast on enemies, and it seemed strange to get two buff skills in a row. *Unless, maybe the de-buff skills became less used when the raid-build dancers fell out of favor....* "If only this skill worked outside of battle. Maybe then I wouldn't take a bat to the face."

Vic and Riko plopped to the ground next to her, their mana completely drained. "I can't believe we survived that," Vic said.

Riko turned a suspicious eye on Prowl. "Mangle is that attack of yours that uses soul shards, doesn't it?"

Prowl adjusted his goggles and swept ash from his hair. "Yeah."

Riko's left eyebrow twitched. "Are you crazy?! Three of those shards cost as much as a good weapon!"

"Do you think we could have beaten that thing if I hadn't used Mangle?" Prowl asked.

Riko scowled at him, but she got up and stood long enough to cast a healing spell on herself before sitting down again.

Gil limped over to the group. "That was more difficult than I imagined it would be."

"I told you dragons were tough," Axel said.

"Then why were you the one who got the dragon's attention and launched the first attack?" Vic asked.

"That was an accident," Axel insisted.

Kit studied her fans' paper surface, looking for damage from the dragon's final attack. "We're going to have to re-think our strategy for snagging the seal."

Prowl snorted. "No kidding."

"I think we could defeat another dragon," Cookie said. "My concern, though, is that it will be impossibly difficult to pull just *one*. In this case, we faced a single dragon because there was only one in this tunnel. When it opens up into the bigger cavern, there's no place to hide or withdraw, so it's pretty much a given we'll have at least two charging us at once."

"I don't believe we can fight two dragons at the same time," Gil said.

"My mana won't last through two," Vic volunteered.

"I won't be able to use Mangle for a few hours," Prowl said.

Riko stood and this time cast a healing spell on Prowl and Kit, then sat down again to boost her mana recovery. "Plus that skill costs thousands of gold."

"Cash isn't really a concern right now," Prowl said.

"Cash is *always* a concern," Riko corrected.

"So what do we do?" Axel asked. "Try to catch one dragon at a time and lure them back to this tunnel?"

"No," Kit said. "We're going to sneak our way through."

Everyone in the party swung his or her gaze to her.

"...what?" Prowl finally asked.

"You're all correct. We haven't a hope that we can fight our way through when we're this low-leveled," Kit said. "However, if we can avoid detection, grab the seal, and then split, I think we can make it."

"But what about the dragons?" Gil asked.

"The dragons don't matter. The quest, remember, is to reclaim the seal. Technically, we don't have to kill any. We just have to get the seal and get out in one piece." Kit stretched her arms out in front of her as Riko's heal settled into her bones, restoring her to full health.

"Wouldn't that be even more dangerous?" Vic asked. "We might accidentally pull multiple dragons at once."

Riko tapped her fingers on the cave floor. "The answer is both yes and no. While the actual plan itself might be more dangerous while we're in the process of pulling it off, it's still far more doable than trying to kill every single dragon in this cave."

She stood up again, and cast her heal on Vic, Cookie, Gil, and Axel before sitting pretzel style on the ground once more.

"Plus it will take a lot less time," Cookie said.

"I don't like it," Axel announced. "Sneaking around isn't my style."

"That's why you'll stay here, along with Vic and Gil," Kit said.

"I approve," Vic chirped.

"Why do you wish for us to stay behind?" Gil asked.

"Cookie has a skill that lets her walk-through shadows without being seen. As Prowl is also one of the thief classes, I'm assuming he has one as well, right?" Kit looked inquiringly at the saboteur, who nodded.

"But Riko doesn't have any such skill," Gil said.

"You're right, but she's much higher leveled, and she has a heal skill. If we are spotted, it will be necessary for her to heal whatever party member is carrying the seal."

Axel snorted. "Then why are you going? You can't tell me you'll be useful for anything."

Kit shrugged, not at all offended by the truth in his words. "I'm not. So I'm going along as bait. If we're caught, hopefully I'll be able to distract the dragons long enough to give the rest of the party a head start."

"Wouldn't it be better if I went along to act as bait?" Gil asked. "I have my taunt skills and more health points than you do."

"Yeah, but it's pretty much guaranteed that the bait is going to become crispy fried chicken and will respawn back in Brunascar," Kit said.

"And you'll lose experience," Axel was quick to add.

Kit adjusted the collar of her shirt. "In any case, there's no point in making you go through it when the dragons can just as easily fry me. Does everyone agree that this is our best course of action?"

"It will certainly be far faster than attacking each dragon individually," Riko said.

"You might all die," Vic pointed out pessimistically.

Prowl shrugged. "If we wipe, we'll just come back and give it another go."

"Listen to you, mister optimistic," Riko said.

The saboteur stood and adjusted his dagger belt. "I don't think we'll all die, except for Kit, that is. She's definitely a goner."

Kit flicked her pink bangs out of her eyes. "And with that cheerful prediction, let's get ready."

———

Kits eyes were so narrowed in concentration, they were little slits she could barely see out of as she pressed herself against the cavern wall and slowly waddled along, doing her best to remain in the shadows.

"You are aware that just because your eyes are closed and you can't see the dragons doesn't mean that they won't be able to see you, right?" Prowl drawled quietly. He, like Cookie, had cloaked himself with the shadows and was invisible.

Riko must've had some kind of Prowl-radar, though. When she lashed out with a foot, she connected with Prowl's invisible shins.

"Ouch!" the saboteur hissed.

"If you can't say something nice, don't say anything at all," Riko chastised in a whisper.

"But then I would never talk," Prowl murmured.

A drop of sweat trickled down Kit's back. "Would both of you just be quiet?" She spoke a little louder than she meant to, and one of the five dragons that roamed the cavern—the orange one which was closest to them—turned in their direction. Its eyes glowed in the dim light, and a growl rumbled deep in its throat.

Kit bit her tongue and stopped moving. She even stopped breathing.

The dragon raised its snout and tasted the air with a flick of its tongue. After what felt like an eternity, it turned away and nosed a pile of gleaming jewels.

Kit released the puff of air she'd been holding in.

"That was frightening," Cookie whispered just off Kit's left side.

The wall curved inward, and Kit dropped to her knees and scurried along to avoid any more draconian attention. "Can either of you see the seal, Prowl, Cookie?"

"I think I see it," Cookie said. "Or at least where it's being kept."

"That inlet at the very back of the room? Yeah, I'd bet Riko's last gold coin that it's in that little hovel."

"Which reminds me, do you think the dwarves would mind if we grabbed some of their extra treasure?" Riko whispered as she and Kit skittered past a gold statue.

Kit paused momentarily to pull up the collar of her shirt, which was steadily traveling south as she inched along. "You already asked that, and there's no way we're risking you making a noise when you start grabbing handfuls of coins."

"A girl can dream."

"I'd say you should just marry one of the rich dude players," Prowl said. "But I don't think any of them would want you."

Riko snarled. "You mushroom-faced brat!"

"You can get married in *Chronicles of Retha*?" Cookie asked.

Kit frowned when she crawled around three stacked treasure chests and came to a huge pile of coins that was as big as a small house. She had seen it from the entrance of the room and thought there was a space between it and the wall. Now she could see it was flush against the cavern. They would either have to climb over it or crawl around it, which would veer them dangerously close to a red dragon, who was curled up like a cat and kneading its claws into two different sets of gold armor.

"It's not really marriage, per se." Riko used the momentary pause to adjust the hood of her robes. "In the game, it's referred to as 'pledged,' which is really just a fancy way of saying engaged."

"Oh revered party leader, are we going to get moving anytime soon?" Prowl asked.

"As long as you're invisible, you are incredibly cocky and absolutely insufferable," Riko whispered.

Kit, having made the decision to creep around the pile of gold rather than climb it—as she feared they would loosen some of the coins and send cascades of them falling down, alerting the dragons to their presence—started to army-crawl alongside the mini-mountain of gold. "Retha doesn't offer marriage because it wants to minimize the possibility of legal action. There're lots of cases in which couples got married in other games, and then eventually separated, which made going through their joint character bank accounts and belongings a legal nightmare. With the whole pledged thing, characters never combine belongings, so any kind of break up is very cut and dry."

"Oh," Cookie said. "That's a fun thing to include."

Though Kit couldn't see the red dragon over the piles of treasure, she heard the alarming noise of its claws crushing armor. The creature had to be only a gold stack or two away. Kit pressed herself so close to the floor she was almost slithering around like a snake as she edged along the mountain of gold coins.

When she almost reached the safety of the cave wall, she

exhaled with thankfulness and even dared to push herself up onto her hands and knees. She scurried forward about two feet before she was blasted with hot, sulfur-scented air.

A dragon.

Kit, barely daring to breathe, glanced over her shoulder. Only Riko was there, blinking curiously at her. "Kit?"

Kit's heart pounded in her throat, and another blast of acidic air hit her. Dread boiled in her stomach, and Kit slowly turned to stare at the pile of gold coins.

Barely visible under the show of wealth, a gold dragon snout poked out from under the mountain of coins.

Kit swallowed her exhale and carefully pointed out the dragon.

A sharp intake of breath that came from behind her told Kit Riko saw the beast as well. Together, they slowly crawled away from the pile of money, sweating profusely whenever the creature breathed on them.

When they were finally far enough away from the sleeping dragon that Kit could inhale without fear of waking it, Cookie whispered, "I'm sorry. I should have scouted ahead and noticed that dragon. That was my failing."

"Not at all, Cookie," Riko said out of a corner of her mouth. "Useless Prowl could have found out that much as well."

"The important thing is we made it." Kit's heart sputtered as they closed in on the little inlet. They were almost there! "We'll just have to make sure we don't go back that way."

"I'll check ahead and make sure the seal is really here," Prowl said.

Kit, Cookie, and Riko were silent as they inched along, weaving their way through priceless treasures in order to reach the seal.

When Kit and Riko dared to stand, Prowl threw off his cloak skill and flickered into view. "It's here." He pointed to a rather unassuming burnished gold disc that was the size of a saucer. A couple of runes were carved into its surface. Otherwise, there was nothing remarkable about it. It sat on a little wooden stand on a gold table that was probably far more valuable.

Kit swallowed thickly and held her breath as she picked up the seal—which was heavier than she expected. She froze for a moment, waiting for some kind of outcry from the dragons, but nothing happened. A quest certification, however, popped up.

You have obtained: The Dwarvish Seal.
The Elvish Seal, Human Seal, and Fae Seal remain for you
to claim.

"Well done," Gil praised over the party channel. "We received the notification that you successfully retrieved the seal. We shall continue to wait for you at the cavern entrance."

"Great, thanks guys." Kit turned on her heels and peered into the darkness. "Cookie?"

"Here." The night stalker stepped out of the shadows, revealing herself.

Kit passed her the seal. "Remember, if we are attacked, you have to get out. Just keep running, even if the rest of us stop to fight. Do you understand?"

Cookie gave her a businesslike nod. "I'll get this out of the treasure chamber. I swear it."

Kit smiled and squeezed her shoulder. "Just do your best."

Cookie slipped the seal in her inventory, then stepped back into the shadows and disappeared again.

With the seal safely stowed, Kit turned her mind to the

increasingly difficult task of picking a way to exit the cave. "There's no helping it," she said. "I think we'll have to edge past the gold dragon again. If we follow the opposite wall, it will put us smack dab in the path of the green dragon, and he roams."

"Don't sweat it," Riko said. "We already got past the gold dragon once. As long as we don't stop to tickle his nostrils, I think we will be fine."

Kit pressed her lips together. "I still don't like getting that close to a dragon. But I don't think we have another option."

Prowl, having also cloaked his character, spoke somewhere to Riko's left. "You could always strut up to a dragon, kick it, get one-shotted, and then respawn back in the city."

"Once again, your helpfulness is positively astounding," Riko said.

"It's a legitimate tactic," Prowl said.

"It is, but quest lines can be tricky," Kit said. "There's no way to tell how fussy it is— and if anyone dies if it will still count. So I would at least like to attempt to make it out of the treasure chamber in one piece."

"The gold dragon it is," Cookie said.

Kit nodded and again got down on her hands and knees with Riko copying her. Together, they inched along the cavern wall, pushing themselves as close to the ground as possible whenever one of the dragons happened to glance in their direction with its glowing eyes.

Though the chamber air was cool, sweat glistened on Kit's brow as she edged past the gold dragon's protruding nostril. (Glistening, Kit knew, because elf characters—even elves who were disliked by their fellow elves—would never resemble a sweaty pig.)

She was starting to feel optimistic about their chances of survival after navigating around almost the entire mound of coins that were piled on top of the sleeping dragon. She could almost reach out and touch the cave wall when there was a scrape of metal being dragged across the ground. It was barely louder than a pin falling, but all the dragons in the room turned and looked at them.

Kit turned around to look at Riko, who was wide-eyed and clutching a coin in her hands. "Sorry?" the druid said.

The previously sleeping but now enraged gold dragon shot out of the gold pile, sending coins flying through the air like metallic bits of hail. The coins hit Prowl and Cookie, interrupting their cloaking skills and revealing them to the room.

Kit scrambled to her feet as the dragon roared with enough force to shake the chamber. "Run!" She shouted. "Cookie, stick to the wall. Riko, Prowl, split up!" Kit fought every part of her mind that screamed at her to make a beeline for the exit, and instead turned sharply to run into the middle of the room.

The red dragon swatted at her with its tail, and she barely managed to fling herself out of the way before it crushed her. She immediately rolled to her feet and kept running, making good use of her swear-proficiently skill when a white dragon spat a ball of lightning at her.

"Maggots, mobs, and malarkey! I hate dragons!" she yelled. The crimson-orange dragon swiped a claw at her, and it was so close, it cut through the puffy fabric of her pants, but only nicked her leg. "We have zero luck. Zero!"

"This is all Riko's fault, with her greed and lack of self-control." Prowl jumped onto a dragon's back and slid down its side. "The dragons are just following their nature."

"Shut the front door, Prowl!" Kit thundered as she jumped a treasure chest and continued to weave her way toward the smaller passageway.

"Yeah, Prowl." Riko darted behind a gold statue to avoid a dragon, which cut straight through the thing with one of its claws. "Now is not the time to point fingers!"

"Oh, would you rather review your stupidity in a post-battle tactics discussion?" Prowl yelled.

Kit glanced back and saw the gold dragon unfurl its wings—revealing five pony-sized mini dragons that zoomed around it. "Great, we've got a mini-boss on deck."

"Do you want us to come help?" Gil asked over the party chat.

"A dragon mini-boss? I bet it has amazing drops!" Axel enthusiastically added.

"No!" Riko shouted.

"In fact, get out of the cavern. We're coming in hot!" Kit said.

"I'm in the passageway!" Cookie reported.

"Keep running!" Kit said. "Don't stop until you're out of the treasure chamber."

When the gold dragon reared back and its throat and mouth started to glow with white hot flames, Kit was inspired to new speeds and zipped under the belly of the green dragon—which stood between her and the tunnel.

She was trying to hustle around its clawed paws without getting herself impaled, when trumpets sounded, sparks fizzled around her, and a pop-up window loaded in front of her face, blocking her view.

Congratulations! You have learned the life skill: Cowardly Leader
Due to your cowardly ways, you have learned how to flee faster! Skill effect: If you are leading a party, all party members receive a speed boost when fleeing engaged enemies. PASSIVE SKILL

"Worst! Timing! Ever!" Kit shouted as she tried to dismiss the screen.

"Oh, Kit! Did you just get a new skill? That is a nice speed boost," Cookie said.

"Yeah, but what's the name again?" Vic asked.

Kit didn't answer and concentrated on hustling the remaining distance to the smaller cave.

Why does everybody in this party turn into a peanut gallery in the most dangerous moments?

"I'm in the hallway," Riko said.

"Me, too," Prowl said.

The ground shook again when the gold dragon heaved its head down, flames crackling in its mouth.

"Yikes!" Kit yipped as she made it into the passageway and turned the corner just before the dragon spat out its fire. Flames exploded just outside the passageway opening and shattered several of the crystals that dotted the walls with its heat.

"Kit, are you okay?" Riko asked.

"Yeah, I'm fine. Is everyone out?"

"Gil, Axel, and I are out in the main hallway," Vic said.

There was a pause, then Cookie added, "Exiting the treasure chamber now."

Kit followed the passageway as it snaked, making a sharp ninety-degree turn. The angle let her see back into the large cavern, where two dragons slithered into the passageway after her. "Two dragons are following me in," she announced. After she turned the corner, she could see Riko running just ahead of her, her blue robes streaming behind her like a puffy cloud. "I'm just behind you, Riko."

"Great! We're almost there."

The dragons that had followed Kit into the tunnel picked up their speed. One of them was the white dragon, which spat another ball of lightning at Kit.

"Incoming!" Kit shouted. She dropped to the ground so the lightning sailed harmlessly over her head. As soon as it passed, she leaped to her feet and sprinted down the tunnel, encouraged by the sight of the treasure chamber entrance.

"Look out, Prowl." Riko darted to the side, also avoiding the lightning.

"I see it." The saboteur spun around to face the attack and threw some kind of powder at it.

The lightning froze for a moment, then sizzled and exploded with a deafening thunder.

"What was that?" Axel stuck his head into the treasure chamber, his red hair and man bun making him stick out like a sore thumb.

"I said stay out!" Kit roared as the other dragon, the red one, closed in on her.

Axel sucked his head back out of the room like a mouse retreating to its hole. "Geez, you don't have to be so cranky about it."

The red dragon lunged forward, its jaws gaping open, and barely missed snapping Kit up in its mouth. "I have two rampaging dragons who are close enough behind me to snap off my neck. I'll be crabby if I want!" she shouted as she started running in serpentines.

"I'm out," Prowl announced.

"Me, too," Riko added after a moment or two.

Kit tried to put on another burst of speed as she aimed for the small dark entryway. She heard the white dragon inhale deeply, then spit out another ball of lightning.

If I try to avoid it, the red dragon will be on me in an instant. I'll just have to gun it.

Her heart hammering in her throat, Kit sprinted for the entryway. The lightning crackled just behind her, bearing down on her like a missile. She threw herself forward and flew through the small entryway, barely avoiding getting struck by the attack.

She rolled into the main passageway, flying head over heels, and smacked into a boulder parked in the middle of the path. "I hate dragons," she said.

A trumpet sounded.

Congratulations! Your life skill, "Cowardly Leader," has risen to level two!

"We made it!" Cookie laughed. She jumped for joy, then squeezed Vic into a hug.

The wizard, for once, did not resist and instead suffered through the sign of friendship. "Just barely."

"It is still worth celebrating," Gil said. He was far calmer than the rest of the party members. "They managed to escape five—no, six—dragons, one of them being a mini-boss."

Riko wiped sweat off her forehead with the sleeve of her robe. "It was a little more excitement than I bargained for."

Prowl shrugged, though he couldn't disguise his happy grin. "It's one of the main quest lines; of course they will make it difficult. Not to mention you all were under-leveled. And Riko is a greedy git."

"I wish I could've been there," Axel sighed. "I got a new skill with my last level. I want to see how effective it is against dragons!"

"With your level? Not very," Vic predicted.

Kit had not untangled herself from the heap she sat in at the base of the boulder, and instead concentrated on regaining her nerve.

Cookie glided up to her and leaned against the rock with a

smile. "Thank you for entrusting me with the seal. Do you want it back?" She held out the large disk, which seemed to glow under the light shed by the crystals and sputtering torches.

"No!" Kit shivered and rolled onto her side so Cookie no longer appeared to be upside down. "Heck no. It still is best for the party if you keep carrying it."

Cookie reluctantly hefted it. "If you say so..." She put it back in her inventory.

"I do." She glanced at the entryway as she started to scrape herself off the ground, then froze. "Everyone get back!"

Standing at the entrance to the treasure chamber was a bony creature that was clothed in a sickly green-black cloak. Its head was that of a cow skeleton, with horns that jutted out on either side, and it held a warped, black sickle that was larger than it was, and its eye sockets glowed poison green.

It took Kit a moment to identify the creature as a shadow reaper—one of Malignus's minions that usually popped up in important quest lines. They were always a bugger to kill, but a quick glance at this one revealed it was only level twenty-one. It outleveled them, but Kit had faced shadow reapers as high as level ninety-nine. *This one should be easy in comparison.*

The reaper laughed, a hissing noise that made all of its bones clatter. "Heroes," it said in a slithering voice.

Cookie retreated to stand with Vic and Riko while Axel unsheathed his sword, and Gil adjusted his grip on his shield.

The shadow reaper tilted its head in a putrid imitation of human curiosity. "Always parading around, completely ignorant of the glorious kingdom that is about to return to this land."

"What are you talking about?" Axel demanded.

"Why, the kingdom of Lord Valdis Moarte. Malignus stands on the threshold of returning Lord Valdis to his rightful throne, and when he succeeds, chaos and darkness shall descend upon Retha, and all heroes shall be slaughtered."

A whimper slipped out of Vic; it was so quiet, Kit would've missed it if not for her elf ears. Riko patted the young wizard reassuringly on her shoulder. "It's okay," she murmured.

"What do we do, leader?" Prowl asked, his eyes hooked on the creature.

Kit narrowed her eyes. *It's okay. It's just a game. As frightening as this shadow reaper is, I can't afford to surrender to fear, or I'll lose sight of the real enemy: time.* "Gil, cover Vic and Riko. Axel, Cookie, Prowl, attack from three different directions," she murmured into the party chat. Even though the creature couldn't hear her in the private channel, her voice wouldn't let her speak above a whisper.

"Got it," Gil murmured.

The shadow reaper looked up and down the line in which their party stood. "You have recovered the dwarves' seal. Give it to me."

Kit snorted. When it looked at her with its eerie glowing eyes, she shrugged. "What? You thought just because you asked nicely we would hand it over? Here. Have a caramel!" Kit threw one of her burnt caramels, which popped the shadow reaper on the eye socket and fell straight through the hole.

The creature was frozen for a moment, then snarled. "So you will not surrender? Very well. I will recover the seal from your dead bodies." It extended its scythe, muttering darkly, then slammed the weapon into the ground. Five shadow snakes erupted from the blade of the weapon and launched themselves at Kit and her crew.

Gil stepped between two of the shadowy reptiles and Vic and Riko. He grunted when the snakes slammed into his shield, and his health dropped by at least 20%, but Riko was on him in an instant, healing his fallen health bar.

"Axel, Prowl, Cookie, attack one snake together," Kit yelled as she started her Battlefield March skill. "Vic, Riko, attack one of the snakes Gil is tanking for you."

As Kit moved to join the wizard and druid behind Gil, the shadow reaper appeared between her and her friends.

"As for you," the shadow reaper said as he pointed a finger at her. "You shall know the wrath of Malignus!" It swung its scythe, slicing straight into Kit before she had the chance to flee. The weapon curved around her back and sent sizzling black bolts of magic up and down her spine.

Her health bar dropped, crawling all the way toward zero. Stunned, she dropped to her knees as pain spread through her body before being replaced with the numbness that signaled death. "You one-shotted me! You puss-eating—"

Before she could finish, the world grew black.

12

STATUS AILMENT: CURSE

KIT SNAPPED AWAKE JUST outside the feasting hall—the designated respawn spot for all the areas around Brunascar. She sat pretzel legged and pursed her lips at her health bar. "I don't mind being fragile—or I would've never played as an echo on my main character. But couldn't I at least get some kind of kickass skill to go with being so easily killed? Or at least some kind of skill that makes me feel better about all these high-health/high-level monsters that kill me? Like...the ability to put bunny ears on them or something?"

She sighed and raked a hand through her hair, upsetting her perfect locks. She was tempted to talk in the party chat, but she didn't want to distract everyone else while they were in the middle of the battle. A handful of dwarves passed by, peering at her from under furrowed foreheads. She managed to pawn off peppermint sticks on all but one of them, when Vic abruptly joined her, respawning next to her.

"It's absolutely unfair that getting hit hurts way more than dying does," Vic announced as she brushed off her cloak.

Kit offered the wizard one of the few pieces of toffee she

had made that had turned out halfway decent. "Did a snake get you, or was it the shadow reaper?"

"A snake." Vic took the proffered treat and chewed it angrily. "The shadow reaper left after killing you."

"Ahh. That figures. Here I was hoping Prowl would have another sneaky and powerful skill to blow him up with."

Kit heard a hissing noise; when she peered over her shoulder, though, there was nothing there. She was about to ask Vic if she had heard anything when all the air was abruptly squeezed out of Kit's lungs.

She coughed, trying to regain her breath, but nothing worked. She could hear her blood pounding in her ears, and knife-sharp pain spread to her heart.

"Kit?" Vic asked. She crouched down next to her. "Are you okay?"

Kit shook her head and tried to speak, her lungs burning with the need for air. The hissing stopped, and as abruptly as the pain had come, it left. Relieved, Kit took in great gulps of air. As soon as she recovered enough, she snapped upright and glared at her health bar.

She hadn't noticed it before, but there was a little icon of a cow skull beneath her health and mana bars. "Fa la la la la—I'm cursed," she groaned.

"Cursed?" Vic asked.

Kit stared gloomily at the icon. "Cursed. It's a high-level de-buff that can give you some pretty serious status ailments depending on the kind that's cast on you. Unfortunately, they affect elves the worst—something to do with the darkness being extra effective against their pure natures. Unlike most de-buffs, however, curses won't come off if you're killed—or even if enough time passes."

"How do you get rid of it then?"

"It has to be removed. Some player classes—like priest or

priestess—can do it. Otherwise, you have to go to a cathedral to get blessed, which will cancel it."

"Do they have cathedrals here?"

Kit lay flat on the ground, her limbs sprawled out so she resembled a stick person. "No. They're only found in human cities."

Vic thoughtfully narrowed her eyes. "Won't that make it hard for you as both Imperials and Court of the Rogue allies hate you?"

"Yep," Kit said in the dead voice.

"We defeated all the shadows snakes," Riko said via the party chat. "We're just about to meet up with the dwarves and hitch a ride back in the mine carts. We'll meet you at the feasting hall."

"Yeah, that will work," Kit said. "We can talk to King Brasil and head off on our merry way."

"Roger that!" Cookie cheerfully chirped.

"At least this time we won't have to ride all the way to the Lèas," Prowl said. "We can take a transportation gate to Luminos and ride from there."

"About that," Kit said. "I'll need to take a little side trip."

"Why?" Axel asked.

"She's cursed," Vic piped in.

Prowl whistled. "You have the worst luck, don't you?"

"Where will you get it removed?" Riko asked. "The cathedral in the capital is guarded by Imperial soldiers. There's no way you can get past them without being spotted."

Kit finally peeled herself off the ground and popped up into a standing position. "I was hoping maybe I could ask other players for help in the capital."

"You do that and the Court of the Rogue NPCs will hear about it and come for you," Prowl said.

"Couldn't she go to the White Veil Nunnery?" Gil asked.

"The what?" Axel asked blankly.

"The White Veil Nunnery! I'd forgotten about it! It's the biggest cathedral in all of Retha, and it's also where all priests, healers, and priestesses have to go for their character class side quests. It's located just a bit north of Luminos. You're right, Gil. That's probably my best bet," Kit said.

"How did you know about the White Veil Nunnery?" Riko asked.

"I also have a character class quest that sends me to the nunnery to retrieve a blessed item."

Kit, feeling much more cheerful about her future prospects, clapped her hands. "Perfect! Gil and I can head to the nunnery, and you guys can prep for our trip to the elf lands."

"Sounds good," Riko said. "We'll see you in a minute; then, we can chat with King Brasil and get on our way!"

———

The party was reunited just outside the feasting hall. Cookie launched herself at Vic with a cry. "I'm so sorry, bestie! I failed you. I can't believe I let you die!"

Vic tried to dodge her, but Cookie was too fast and had her in a chokehold-hug within the blink of an eye.

"Sorry you died, Kit, and I'm really sorry about the curse. I wish I could do something about it" Riko said, her eyes flickering to the skull icon below Kit's name.

Kit shrugged. "It's probably better that he killed me and hit me with this de-buff as everyone else is about ten times more useful."

Riko winced. "I think you're being overly harsh on yourself."

"No." Prowl, chewing on a mint leaf, shook his head. "You're totally not."

"So what are we waiting for?" Axel reached for the iron handles of the feasting hall doors. "Let's go inside—whoa!"

The doors were abruptly thrown open, nearly nailing Axel in the face. "Welcome back, heroes! Congratulations on your successful quest," King Brasil thundered.

Behind him, Drust clapped politely, and the rest of the feasting hall was stuffed with dwarves and players roaring with laughter and raising their mugs in toasts.

"At least, I assume you successfully retrieved the seal?" King Brasil asked.

Riko was all smiles, having made the switch to her diplomatic mode. "Indeed, we did. Thank you for providing transportation for us."

"'Twas the least I can do," King Brasil said. "And how did your battle against the dragons go?"

"We only killed one," Kit said.

King Brasil squinted at her. "Just one?"

"Indeed. We successfully snuck past the rest," Riko said.

"That's using your head, I guess." King Brasil scratched his grizzled beard. "But I would be lying if I said I wasn't hoping for you to kill the dragons so we could reclaim that chamber. But, no matter! You retrieved the seal which was your most important task...I suppose."

"Oh yeah, I still have the seal." Cookie once again plucked the seal from her inventory and held it out.

"If you don't want to carry it, Riko is probably the wisest choice," Kit said.

Cookie studied Kit with her wide eyes. "Shouldn't you take it as our leader?"

Kit laughed dryly. "With my luck? Absolutely not." As if on cue, Kit heard a hissing noise she was quickly coming to hate, and just like the previous time, all air squeezed out of her lungs. With a strangled urk, she fell to her knees and tried to calmly ride out the curse as it pried at her chest and shot through her heart.

King Brasil frowned down at her. "What is wrong with our not-a-real-elf-elf-friend?"

Riko bit her lip in worry as Kit struggled—and failed—to breathe. "After sneaking the seal out of the treasure chamber, we were attacked by a shadow reaper."

King Brasil puffed up in anger. "A shadow reaper? In my halls?" He whipped a battle axe off his belt and turned to the feasting hall, clearly intending to rouse his fellow dwarves.

"It's already gone!" Kit managed to choke out. The curse ran its course and slowly left her. She panted on the ground for a few moments before recovering enough to stand again.

"You defeated it, then?" King Brasil asked.

"Nah," Prowl said. "It ran off."

King Brasil raised his battle axe with renewed vigor, and Riko was quick to add, "We're certain it is gone, though. It is also attempting to gather the seals, so as we have the dwarven one, I doubt it will remain in your domain."

The dwarf king thoughtfully ran his thumb over the sharp edge of his weapon. "You may be right. It does make me glad, though, that you retrieved the seal, or it would bode poorly for the future of Retha."

"Which is why we must set off immediately. May we use the Fibbit services to take a teleportation gate?" Kit asked.

"Of course!" King Brasil thundered. "By all means, do not let us stop you! Though...we had hoped to throw a great feast in your honor."

Vic raised an eyebrow as she looked past the king and into the packed hall. "It appears you already started the feast even though you did not know we had succeeded."

"Yes, well, we thought we would either honor your

successful quest or honor your valiant memory." King Brasil smiled broadly, making it impossible to stay mad at him.

"I'm afraid we'll have to pass this time," Riko said.

"But if we return, I'd like to try a firebrand kegger," Axel said excitedly. When all the members of the party turned to stare at him, he shrugged. "What?"

Vic pinched the bridge of her nose. "You have no sense of urgency."

"I think it is more that he is optimistic," Gil said.

"No, that would accurately describe you. Axel is an idiot," Vic said sharply.

"Hey!"

Kit ignored the squabble and smiled at the dwarven king once more. "We thank you for everything you've done to aid us. And we hope to one day return to this mountain to celebrate our friendship."

"May the forges of prosperity swell for you on your journey," King Brasil said.

"And also for you." Riko bowed deeply. "May the weapons of your enemies shatter, and your health run as thick as your mead."

Instead of grinning broadly, as Kit expected, the dwarf king's expression grew serious. "Mind your back. The shadow reaper only proves my previous warning. Dangerous times have come, but we need your help, heroes. Fight well, and with great courage."

The rest of the party murmured various goodbyes, then together they set out for the Fibbit service stall—which was located on the other side of the city near the Silver Pickaxe Inn.

King Brasil stood outside the feast hall, watching them until they turned up a street, and he disappeared from view.

"So that's one down and three to go." Axel folded his arms

behind his head. "After Kit gets rid of her curse and we replenish our supplies, where are we going?"

"To the elves," Kit said decidedly.

"You mean we're going to see Lèas?" Cookie asked excitedly.

"Yep."

Cookie skipped ahead. "I can't wait! I love the elves! They are so beautiful, and elegant, and stately. Just like you, Kit. They're pretty enough to be princesses!"

Vic frowned. "If you love elves so much, why did you choose a human character?"

"Because I knew you wanted a wizard character, so I was better off choosing a thief character to counter you," Cookie said.

"That was quite thoughtful of you," Gil said.

Axel, who marched next to Kit, glanced at her. "You don't look too thrilled with our next destination."

"I'm a little nervous," Kit admitted. "I'm worried they might hold my character class against the entire party and give us a more difficult quest on purpose."

"I wouldn't be too worried," Riko said. "You are still an elf. They might be snotty about you, but everyone knows elves have the most race pride in all of Retha. It will be fine."

Kit tilted her chin up to peer at the Fibbit services stall at the far end of the street, making her bell earrings jingle. "I hope you're right..."

Even with Riko's encouragement, Kit couldn't shrug off the unease that plagued her.

I hope it's just the curse. It must be the curse. Or else getting this next seal is going to be impossible without help.

———

After days of failing to find the mysterious Milk Crown member in Luminos, Solus Miles was ready to banish himself from any settlements that contained other players and roam the wild parts of Retha until EC restored log off capabilities.

He hadn't been able to find a single whiff of the Milk Crown player—he didn't even know what character class she played as, on her main *or* on the secondary character.

Moreover, Miles was always a man of few friends, but the few players he was comfortable with were all offline. This ratcheted Luminos up from being merely annoying with its great mass of eager players to downright intolerable.

He stood on the roof of the tallest tower in Luminos and stared down at the glittering city.

Where can I go that will be quiet, less populated, and where I can still continue my unfinished quests? Miles opened up his quest log and skimmed over the options. *I could work on the questline the Sword of Deceit expansion brought...but no, I need to visit the City of Wizards for that, and that place will be almost as bad as Luminos. Where else?*

His eyes stopped when he reached a questline that took him to Fione Forest—the dominion of the elves. If there was a sanctuary in Retha, it was Fione.

Miles nodded, his mind made up. *Then I shall set my course for Fione and leave this city filled with babblers.*

He turned so he looked out at the Aridus Plains and called his pet. "Sinistre. Come."

When darkness had settled over Luminos, the creature had settled down outside the city walls. It perked up when it heard Miles speak—as far away as he was—and was visible only by its copper-colored eyes.

Though Sinistre couldn't talk, Miles could feel his curiosity. "We're leaving Luminos," Miles said.

Sinistre's copper eyes disappeared in the darkness of the night.

Miles waited until he heard the steady beat of Sinistre's wings, then leaped off the edge of the tower, landing on the back of his dragon. He positioned himself behind the beast's black shoulder blades and held onto plate-sized scales. "Fly," he said, "for Fione."

13

ELVEN REPUTATION

TO GET to the White Veil Nunnery, Kit and Gil took a transportation gate to Vippa, the satellite city near Luminos. From there, it was a short ride north along the river.

"We're almost there," Kit said. The forest trees began to thin out as Chester tried to snag a snack of leaves.

Gil, steering his horse with one hand, glanced at her in surprise. "You recognize this area?"

"Nope," Kit said. "I've only been to the White Veil Nunnery a handful of times. It's just that I can hear the bells in the distance."

They popped out of the forest and halted their horses where the Aridus Plains opened up before them. The White Veil Nunnery was located in the middle of a lake formed by a dam in the river. The nunnery was white with accents of royal blue and gold, and it was reminiscent of European cathedrals with impossibly tall spires topped with star steeples, flying buttresses, and a domed ceiling. The sunlight made it and the clear blue lake that surrounded it sparkle and glitter.

"It's beautiful," Gil said.

"More importantly, it's holy." Kit nudged Chester forward,

and the plump pony swished his white tail as he ambled toward the cathedral.

It didn't take long to pass through the giant nunnery gates and trot down the long, white stone bridge. They had to pause when the curse kicked Kit in the chest, and she fell off Chester, but she recovered in record time and hauled herself back onto the pony, determined to rid herself of the painful de-buffs.

When they entered the cathedral courtyard, they dismounted and dismissed their horses.

Gil fondly patted his horse's neck before it faded away. "To complete my quest I must seek out Vicar Dominique. But first, I believe we should take you inside."

Kit snatched her hair out of Chester's mouth before the pony left her. "No, it's fine. I'm totally capable of getting inside the cathedral on my own. I've been in it before, and I know what to do to get this curse off me."

Gil eyed her. "Are you certain?"

Kit nodded as she watched two priestesses and a buccaneer exit the cathedral. "Yes. I want to take as little time here as possible, so separating is the most efficient thing to do. Go get your quest. I'll be waiting for you when you get back."

Gil nodded and strolled away, heading for one of the tall spires. Kit turned her attention to the cathedral and made a beeline for it. Players entered and exited it in a slow trickle, creating a quiet hum of conversation and footsteps.

Kit paused outside the large wooden doors, taking a moment to straighten her clothes.

"Oh, my!" A nearby nun wearing a habit placed a fist over her mouth in horror.

"Um, hello," Kit said.

"My dear, we must take you inside immediately!" The woman grabbed her by her hand and patted her consolingly before she opened the large doors with ease and dragged Kit inside.

The interior of the cathedral was just as impressive as the exterior. Just about every surface glittered, the air was lightly scented with frankincense, and a choir hummed quietly in the background.

The moment Kit crossed the threshold of the cathedral, a white light gathered at her feet, and the skull icon below her name faded away. A bell tolled in the highest bell tower, and Kit could feel the de-buff dissipate. "Wow." She blinked. "I don't believe it. I didn't even have to be blessed to get that curse off me."

The nun smiled piously at her. "Indeed, I should expect so —though for your moral benefit, I do recommend you are blessed before you leave here."

"What do you mean 'expect so?'" Kit asked.

The nun stopped towing her forward when they reached the front pew. "The White Veil Nunnery is the most holy place in all of Retha," she said. "Even setting foot in it will fill your body with holy light."

Kit, who had been watching nuns slowly circle the perimeter of the vestibule, glanced at her name. Sure enough, a shining star icon that represented a holy status bonus shone beneath her name. "I see. That's amazing." She absentmindedly played with her bell bracelets, wondering how she could use it to her advantage.

When she played as Azarel, cursed status ailments hadn't meant much to her. To begin with, curses didn't affect humans as badly as they did elves, and a holy status bonus hadn't done much for her either.

It's interesting. I thought Retha was the same no matter what kind of character you played. But playing as an elf compared to a human has been a radically different experience...dancer class notwithstanding.

"So how do I get a blessing?" she asked.

The nun beamed. "I would be delighted to bless you, my child."

Unbidden, a novice nun holding a piggy bank-sized wooden chest popped up at the nun's elbow. "Do you need any help, Sister Miriam?"

The nun smiled at the novice. "No child, unless you have your own prayers to add."

The novice shook her head, though she glanced curiously at Kit, her eyes lingering on Kit's bare belly before she rolled her eyes.

You and me both, Kit longed to tell her.

Before she could speak, the nun began. "May the light of heaven shine upon you, brightest of the elves. May it guide your actions and keep you safe as you venture into the darkest of battles."

Lights from one of the skylights fell on Kit like stardust, making her hair glow pink.

The nun beamed and clasped her hands. "There. You shall be protected now."

"Thank you," Kit said. "Do I owe you anything for your services?"

The novice nodded and rattled her piggy-bank coffer, but the nun shook her head. "No, child of light. Here at the White Veil Nunnery, we offer our protection and services to any who need them. Furthermore, as you are a child of the light, it was my delight to aid you this time."

"Though we would appreciate funds for a new roof," the novice whispered.

The nun shook a finger at the novice. "We do not shake down those who seek the light, for it is our honor to aid them."

When she turned her back to the novice to face Kit again, the novice pressed her lips together, stared at Kit, and pointed to her coffer.

"If you ever have need to restore yourself in the light again, please return," the nun said to Kit.

"Thank you," Kit said genuinely. "I will."

The nun bowed her head, then glided away, the robes of her black habit swirling around her.

The novice stayed behind for a moment longer and shook her coffer.

Stifling a snicker—for she had never before met such a logical NPC—Kit dropped a few bronze coins through the opening of the coffer.

The novice nodded her head in thanks, then hurried after the nun, her coffer jingling.

Kit smiled as she glided back down the cathedral aisle and slipped out the doors, emerging into the warm sunlight.

A breeze touched the back of Kit's neck, signaling the activation of the party channel.

"Hey, Kit," Riko said. "Besides more health potions, are there any supplies you need?"

"Are you at the general store?" Kit asked.

"Prowl and I are," Riko said.

"Vic, Axel, and I are on Retailer Row. Do you need something special?" Cookie chirped.

Thinking of her candy, Kit said, "If you wouldn't mind picking up some goat milk and butter, I'd be forever grateful."

"Sure," Cookie said.

"How much you need?" Vic asked.

"Probably fifty of each."

"What?" Vic hissed.

"I'll pay you back. Oh, and there's something I've been

meaning to give you, Vic," Kit said. "Now that you're a high enough level, I can give it to you when we meet up again."

"This had better be worth it," Vic muttered.

Kit laughed. "I think you'll like it."

"How much longer are you going to take?" Prowl asked.

"I've been cleared of my curse, but I think Gil is still working on his quest. We shouldn't be much longer, though. Meet you at the market soon."

"I think I'm going to buy face paint," Axel announced.

"Why?" Vic asked.

"To make it harder for those sneaky elves to see me in their forest."

"It won't do you any good," Vic said pessimistically. "You open your big mouth all too much to go unnoticed."

Kit laughed as she walked around the cathedral courtyard, the bounce back in her steps. "Play nice, guys. We'll be there soon."

The chattering on the party chat continued as Kit glanced at her character panel, purring over her holy status bonus and absence of the curse. Her eyes lingered on the still dimmed community tab.

It still hasn't been that long. I have to remember that. Time passes much faster here in Retha...but how much longer will this go on?

———

Kit and her party took the Fibbit teleportation gates as far as they could, but once they reached Fione Forest—the largest domain of the elves—they were forced to ride in the rest of the way to the elven city of Lèas.

"So, I don't get it," Vic said. "Aren't there a lot of elf settlements that will let everyone inside?"

"Yes," Cookie said.

Vic picked up her calico cat, the gift Kit had alluded to, from where it sat perched on the front of her saddle and tickled it under its chin. "But in these woods, once you reach a certain distance from Lèas, you can only enter in if you are an elf ally or an elf?"

"Correct," Riko said. "While there are a number of elvish cities scattered around Retha, there are only two areas the elves technically have dominion over: these woods, and an area to the far east. The Eastern elves are much more relaxed and let just about anyone in. But Fìone Forest is considered the homeland for elves, so they're pretty picky about whom they let into Lèas."

"And that is why we must rely on Miss Kit," Gil said. "Because as an elf, she should have access to the city, yes?"

"Right," Riko said.

"I'm still not sure about that," Kit said. "The two elves I met in the dwarf dungeons hated me. Like, a lot. I kind of doubt they are going to let me into Lèas since I'm pretty disliked."

"Even if they hate you, it's still a basic race trait that as an elf you are allowed into all elvish strongholds," Prowl pointed out.

Kit shrugged a little but said nothing more and busied herself with peering around the woods. It was an area she was well acquainted with, as she had played as Azarel in Fìone Forest to get the highest reputation level with the elves. Even so, the area still inspired awe as many of the trees were thick enough to drive a car through and sported leaves as big as Kit's head.

The forest was alive with wildlife, and thankfully there were very few monsters. There was an unfortunate number of bobokins scattered in the woods, but they usually congregated around camps and moved at night, making the woods one of the safest areas to troop through even though the party was still horribly under-leveled. (They had done their best to snag a few levels on their way to the forest, but Kit and Vic were still the lowest in the party and were only level sixteen.)

Kit would have preferred to level a little more, particularly as it was only going to get worse in terms of needing levels to retrieve seals, but they were trying to finish the quest line as quickly as possible; level grinding was not high on the priority list.

"Is that a wall?" Axel asked, pointing straight ahead of them.

Living trees that were planted so closely together their trunks brushed and branches intertwined created a solid wall, barring them from going any farther.

"Yeah, this must be the beginning of the city limits," Prowl said.

"How are we supposed to get in?" Cookie asked.

"There should be a guard station somewhere nearby," Riko said.

"I see it," Kit turned Chester, directing the portly pony to a gap in the natural wall, which was guarded by six elven warriors. The party rearranged themselves and set out for the gap.

Vic petted her cat. "So because Kit is an elf, she should be able to get us inside as well?"

"Maybe," Riko said. "Once players with elf characters get to a certain level, they are allowed to shuttle party members in and out of Lèas. Problem is, I don't remember what the required level is."

"It'll be easy enough to find out," Prowl said. "All she has to do is ask if she can bring us inside."

Axel scratched his chin as his horse tossed its head. "Unless because she's hated, everyone associated with her is also automatically hated?"

Kit snorted. "Just for that I'm not giving you any fudge, Axel!"

"There is some risk to it," Prowl said. "But it won't have long-lasting effects."

"I am not a communicable disease," Kit said.

"We're almost there," Riko said. "Are you ready, Kit?"

Kit squared her shoulders, and Chester tossed his head. "Yep. Here goes nothing." Kit nudged Chester so he trotted forward, separating from the rest of the party. Kit put on her most cheerful smile as they approached the cloaked guards. "Good morning, brethren. I seek entrance to—"

Before she could go on, one of the guards fitted an arrow to his bow and shot her in the heart.

Kit toppled off Chester, but the blow was so powerful she felt no pain and only the numbness of death. She coughed and scowled at the guard. "I hope you go bald," she managed to say before the last of her health faded and everything turned black.

———

When Kit woke up in the respawn area of Fione Forest—a cute little meadow filled with wildflowers and edged by a pond—she scowled. "I can get that they don't like me and would maybe even forbid me to enter, but shooting me on sight? Really? Talk about overreacting!"

"Another one-shot death, and this time by an elf!" Axel snickered over the party channel. "You should make a video montage of all the stupid ways you've gotten yourself killed."

"Shut up and ride," Riko barked.

Kit glanced at the party screen, taking in everyone's damaged health bars. "What happened?"

"After they killed you, they started firing at us," Prowl growled.

"Thankfully, it seems they did not want to kill us as they did with you," Gil added. "They didn't aim for our vitals."

"I don't understand." Kit pulled up her character panel with a frown. "I know my reputation is low with them, but as an elf I should still be able to get away with this. It's usually only high-standing dwarves that they shoot at if they haven't already become kindred with them..." Kit trailed off when she looked at her skill and trait list.

Each race available to play in Retha had several unique skills assigned to it and checks to keep it in balance—like Kit's superior elf senses had the check of being extra susceptible to curse status ailments and darkness.

These traits were always clearly listed on the character profile.

Elven Senses: Grants player superior physical and spiritual senses
Pure in Spirit: Players have affinity for holy status, but are especially susceptible to darkness
Perfect Hair: Player's hair is always perfect—never disheveled or dirty
Elf Heritage: Player is granted automatic max reputation with elves and elf allies and entrance to all elven strongholds: ***VOID DUE TO SELECTED CHARACTER CLASS***

Kit stared blankly at the list. "This is so ridiculous, I'm not even upset," she said.

"What is it?" Riko asked.

"My Elf Heritage skill is canceled due to my dancer class," Kit said.

"Huh. Your cousin was really doing his best to whack you out of balance, wasn't he?" Prowl asked.

"I thought Retha's algorithms were so sophisticated they would counter-balance for something like this," Cookie said.

"In the actual game, sure," Prowl said. "But it's possible the algorithms are not designed to make allowances for anyone stupid enough to screw themselves over during the character design process."

Kit didn't respond to Prowl's sharp remarks; she just stared at her character panel. This most recent blow was almost freeing. *It's a relief to know there's not a single redeemable thing about this character.* "At least I have perfect hair," she said dazedly.

Prowl snorted. "Yeah, 'cause looking awesome while you're getting slaughtered should be a top priority."

"If you were kickass, it would be useful," Axel said. "You could take video and be extra epic."

"Why would you want to record video *now*, in the middle of a crisis?" Vic asked.

"You mean you're not?" Axel asked.

"...Do you seriously mean to tell me that while we are in a possible fight for our lives, you've been *recording this?*" Vic asked.

"Yeah."

There were a few moments of silence, then Cookie said quickly, "Vic, you can't kill him. That will get you labeled as a PK."

"A what?"

"A player killer—someone who kills other players in a non-PVP zone."

"I think it would be worth it," Vic said.

Though Kit could only hear Vic over the party chat—not see her—she could imagine the wizard's look of disdain.

"Pah! As if you could ever kill me," Axel snorted. "You're just a toothpick wizard. You can't do anything."

"My spells are far more powerful than your melee attacks," Vic said.

"So? I'll kill you before you get a skill loaded."

"Not if I'm holding you down," Cookie said in a voice that was much darker than her usual sunshine tones.

"What happened to player killers being a bad thing?" Riko asked.

"He insulted Vic."

"So he must die?" Riko asked.

"Naturally."

"Miss Kit, I believe your calming presence here would be greatly appreciated," Gil said.

Kit laughed and summoned Chester with a whistle. "I'm on my way." She swung up onto the little pony and brought up her mini-map, looking at the dots that marked where her companions were before she nudged Chester forward.

"We need to plan our next move," Riko said. "We have to get inside Lèas to move the quest forward."

"Could we sneak in?" Cookie asked.

"It's been done before, but only by extremely high-level rogue characters," Prowl said.

"But it won't help us anyway. We *need* the elves to like us so they will give us the seal. If we go in without a max reputation level with them, they'll just shoot us on sight," Riko said.

"How will that be any different than it is now?" Axel asked. "Oh, wait, they only shot at us 'cause we were with Kit. Got it."

"Axel!" Cookie scolded. "She can't help it!"

Kit had to tug on her reins to keep Chester from veering off toward a patch of clover. "No, he's got a point. I should definitely *not* attempt to enter Lèas with whoever we send in. It will just get us shot again."

"But how can we send anyone in if no one has the required reputation level?" Vic asked.

"We'll have to earn the reputation," Riko said. "It's easy enough to gather. You can either complete quests and raise your reputation in the area, or farm—kill monsters for drops that grant you reputation items."

"But getting the max reputation level for all of us is going to take forever," Prowl said.

"Prowl, Riko, do either of you have any base reputation with the elves already?" Kit asked.

"Yes," Riko said. "I'm 'respected.'"

"I'm 'tolerated,'" Prowl said. "Why, do you have a plan?"

"Possibly. Hold up, I'm almost to you guys." Kit squeezed Chester into a canter. He loped past shrubberies that were bigger than him without batting an eye and quickly joined up with the rest of the party—who were still mounted and spread in a ring.

"Alright, sorry about that." Kit maneuvered Chester to join the circle, slipping in the space between Vic and Riko.

"No problem at all," Riko smiled.

Vic leaned precariously out of her saddle—upsetting her cat —to pat Chester's thick neck.

"So, what's your idea?" Prowl asked. "Hit us with it."

Kit uneasily shifted in her saddle as the rest of the party looked at her expectantly. *It still feels weird to be the party leader. I always feel like I'm one step away from massively screwing up.* She cleared her throat and put on a brisk smile. "I believe the best plan of attack would be for all of us to farm reputation items so Riko and Prowl can enter the elf city together."

Vic boosted her cat onto her shoulder. "And reputation items are?"

"Specific items you can give NPCs to increase your reputation with their race or faction," Riko explained. "You receive them as drops from monsters or as rewards for quests."

"It makes sense, to me anyway, that Riko and Prowl should be the ones to go," Cookie said. "They have higher reputation than us, so it would be faster than starting from zero."

"But do they both have to go?" Vic asked. "Wouldn't it be faster to send just one of them in?"

"It would be faster." Kit thoughtfully rubbed her face tattoo. "But as this is the party quest, I suspect more than one of the party members must be present in order for it to count. That's what the rules used to be, anyway."

"It still is for most quests," Riko said.

"I'm not opposed to it." Prowl rubbed a tripwire between his fingers. "But how do we manage it?"

"The bobokins that camp in the outskirts of Fione Forest drop reputation items. We can kill them and get experience, and you guys can take whatever reputation drops they leave," Kit said.

"The bobokins are level 30 at least," Prowl said.

"So, we'll have to hunt them in a party," Cookie said.

"I assume the bobokins will be easier to kill than the dragons?" Gil asked.

"They are," Riko assured him. "They'll come down fast. It should be great experience for you guys, so you'll get a couple levels pretty quickly."

"But in the meantime, won't we inflict next-to-no damage?" Vic asked.

Riko shrugged. "It's hard to say, but with Prowl's and my level, it shouldn't be a problem."

Kit sighed. "If I had a defense de-buff that would make things easier—and as a support character I *should* have one by this time, stupid algorithms. But it doesn't matter. You should at least be able to do some damage, Vic."

Vic frowned. "Why me?"

"Bobokins are notoriously susceptible to fire, so Fireball will naturally deal more damage on them. Plus, you have your cat now," Kit said.

Vic blinked and looked down at her cat. "What does my pet have to do with it?"

"In Retha, pets aren't just for decoration," Prowl said. "Each pet has something they specialize in. Cats enhance magical power; dogs can search for hidden treasure and will often join their masters in fighting; hawks can scout out maps and find enemies, and there's a few warhorses that can be used to fight."

Axel whistled. "I didn't know that! I need to get me a dog and a horse!"

"You can't," Kit said. "In Retha, you can only have one pet per character. It's how they keep the system from being gamed."

"That's also why a lot of people don't have pets," Riko added. "There's a huge variety of pets, but there's also a bunch of rare ones. Some people hold out buying pets in hopes that they will get something better. For instance, phoenixes are a relatively rare type of pet, and they're highly sought after for healer character classes as they automatically resurrect their owner."

Vic petted her cat's silky head. "I have to say, *Chronicles of Retha* really is like living out an epic fantasy story. They have thought of everything."

Cookie beamed. "I'm so glad to hear that, bestie! I'm sure we'll have lots of fun memories in Retha—once we're not stuck in here, that is."

Vic sniffed. "I never said I enjoyed living out an epic fantasy, only that for a game it is well made."

"Great, let's all join hands and sing camp songs," Prowl drawled. "Party leader, could you please move on with your little plan?"

Kit shrugged. "There isn't much more to it than the idea that we should get you and Riko up to maximum reputation level."

"And earn levels!" Axel gave the group a thumbs up. "I don't care if the monsters are way over-leveled for me. I'm fighting them!"

Gil raised his hand to cover his eyes as he squinted across the circle, looking beyond Kit and Riko.

Vic scoffed. "You are such a barbarian."

"No, I'm warrior," Axel corrected.

In one smooth motion, Gil unhooked his shield from his horse's rump and brandished it in front of him. "Look out!"

Kit turned to look over her shoulder. "Hmmm?" She moved just in time to see the three elvish scouts before they shot her in the shoulder, once again draining her health bar. Kit slumped off Chester and fell, again. She didn't even have time to speak before everything turned black.

———

When Kit woke up in the respawn zone, she scowled. "I forgot about the scouts."

"Kit, are you okay? Did you respawn?" Riko asked over party chat.

Kit stood and brushed off her puffy dwarven pants. "Yeah. That's what I get for idle conversation, I guess. What happened to you guys?"

"We managed to run off before they did too much damage," Riko said.

"Great. Why don't we start with the northern-most bobokin and goblin camps so I don't have to backtrack to meet up with you guys?"

"I don't know if that's a great idea," Riko said.

Kit scratched one of her tapered ears. "What do you mean? It's one of the smaller camps. I thought it would be easier to attack with all of us working together."

"Yeah, about that..."

The druid hesitated too long, so Prowl jumped in. "Whenever we get shot at by the elves, it dings our reputation with them. In other words, hanging around you is only harming our mission."

Kit rubbed her eyes. "I should've expected that. Fine, I'm assuming you guys want me to stay far away then?"

"Sorry, Kit," Riko said.

"If we were higher leveled, I would join Kit so I could test my sword against an elf scout!" Axel said.

"NPCs are nearly impossible to kill, particularly elves," Riko said.

"So?" Axel asked.

"Will you be all right alone, Miss Kit?" Gil asked.

"Yeah. I used to play this zone a lot as Azarel. There're a couple of quests I can do that will have me running around the woods. I can still stay away from the bobokins and goblins while getting reputation items as rewards. I'll work on those while you guys clear out the baddies," Kit said.

"They added some more quests with the *Gray Wraith* expansion pack," Riko said. "A few of them are even appropriate for your level—they tacked them on so lower-level elves who visited Lèas for quest purposes had a way to get experience. Some of them give you pretty high-leveled rewards too."

"Thanks for the intel," Kit said. "At least I'll be able to do something useful instead of sitting around waiting for you all to finish."

"Are you sure about this, Kit?" Cookie asked. "I could always come with you; I can cloak myself so the elves won't see me."

"Or I could come. As a tank, I can take a little more damage," Gil offered.

"The only reason why the elves haven't one-shotted any of you is because they haven't been serious about killing anyone besides me," Kit said. "But if it's just two of us, they might not be quite so lenient. Don't worry about it; I'll be fine. Getting Prowl and Riko reputation is our main goal right now. It doesn't matter if I die a couple times in this area while soloing."

"It will probably be more than a couple," Prowl muttered.

"I'm going to change the status of our party," Kit said.

"You're not going to leave it, are you?" Vic asked with a hint of worry in her voice.

"No. But I'm going to make it into a raid—even though we don't have nearly enough players—and then divide it into two parties. That way, if we need to communicate, we can use the raid chat, but you guys can use the party chat to talk tactics." Kit opened up her character panel and accessed the party information. She transformed it into a raid, calling it *Desperation*, then broke it into two sub-parties. She made Riko the leader of the reputation party, which she gave the name of *Bobokin Hunters*. She titled her own party, *Please Don't Kill Me*.

"Is everyone set?" she asked in the raid chat.

"We're all good here," Riko said.

"Excellent. Good luck, you guys; call me if you need me."

"Same here," Riko said.

"Thanks," Kit said before she switched off raid chat. She studied the mini-map, wracking her memory for the location of the quests she knew about. She mentally marked off the ones that took her too close to Lèas, which still left her with a handful. Her course marked out, she summoned Chester with a whistle and mounted up. "Here goes nothing."

14

THE HERMIT OF LOVE

KIT CAUTIOUSLY POKED her head out from behind a tree and studied the crest of the hill with narrowed eyes.

It had been three days (in game time) since she last saw everyone, and in that short time span, she had been killed no less than twelve times—with the majority of those times being at the bow of an elf. As such, she now did not meander through the woods, but tip-toed.

It's surprising I have not learned some kind of creeper skill after all this practice. She slowly edged around the tree trunk, then once again consulted her mini-map. She was searching out ingredients as part of a quest from a wizard. He kept sending her out on a wild goose chase to look for supplies for both his dinner and a potion. (It was one of the new quests meant for lower-leveled players that Riko had recommended, so Kit had never done it before.) He richly rewarded her for all the ingredients she brought back—already he had given her a new armor set and earrings, in addition to reputation items. However, the quests were very convoluted and sent her running back and forth across Fione Forest a lot.

For instance, her latest job was to find a merchant who sold salt and fools' gold. She had found the merchant; however, he refused to sell her anything until she passed a message along to an old hermit who lived in the area. So now she was on the hunt for a hermit, who apparently had the same cloaking skill as Cookie, for Kit had been wandering around the hill for the better part of an hour and still hadn't been able to locate him in spite of his location marker on her mini-map.

She circled the hill, keeping track of the invisible hermit's marker on her mini-map as she looked for anything suspicious. *There must be something I'm missing.... Do I have to do a quest to find the hermit first? That would stink.*

"Oh, look, Halbryt! It's the dancer who pretends to be an NPC."

Kit whirled around and choked on a groan as she saw the smiling pirate who had hit on her in the Griffin Hill Armory and his beast-tamer friend.

The pirate trotted toward her on foot, but the beast tamer rode a furry black cat with white spots that was as big as a small car.

"Greetings, fair maiden!" the pirate beamed. "Are you lost?"

Kit made her posture stiff. "May the light shine upon you, son of man."

The pirate laughed. "I'm sorry, but your NPC act isn't at all convincing out here. So now you have no choice but to talk to me! Are you on a quest? I could help you out, 'cause baby, you're the Renaissance to my Dark Ages! What do you say, beautiful?"

Kit was wondering if she should either scream and hope an elf NPC was around to kill her or try to kindly turn the pirate down, when his friend intervened.

The beast tamer frowned as he stared at the ground—probably tracking something with his cat's help. "Egelthas," he said, "don't be that guy."

"What?" the pirate complained. "I'm hitting on her, but I'm not being *lewd* or a *creep*."

"Then pay attention to her nonverbal cues: she looks like she wants to disappear or punch you in the face."

The pirate rolled his eyes. "I'm pretty sure you're projecting your feelings onto her."

Kit cracked a smile at the interaction.

"Ah-hah! You smiled! You find me funny—which is a very attractive trait, isn't it? Come with us, and I'll have you laughing all night!" The pirate smiled slyly and wriggled his eyebrows.

"No, thank you," Kit said, opting to ditch her NPC act. "I'm already in a party."

"But you're alone," the pirate pointed out.

"Um," Kit said.

Just behind the pirate, the beast tamer stroked his cat, making the giant creature purr. "You're making her uncomfortable," he said.

"You shush!" the pirate hissed.

The beast tamer shrugged. "Okay, but did it ever occur to you that she might be so un-talkative because she's a *girl*?"

"Because she's female?"

"No. A *girl*. G. I. R. L.: guy in real life."

The pirate scowled. "You suggested that about the last two female players I approached."

"I'm just trying to give you a reasonable out."

"What do you mean by that?"

"You suck at trying to communicate with females and come off as a weird guy in an alley."

The pirate rolled his eyes. "Because you are so much smoother?"

"At least I haven't set off a girl's creepy meter so badly she pretended to be an NPC." The beast tamer turned his cat, who started to stalk off. "Come on. Little Neck picked up on the scent—we have to go this way."

"Fine—wait for me!" The pirate started to chase after his friend, but paused long enough to wave at Kit. "Farewell, beautiful angel! I'll see you again—I'm sure!"

A ghost of a smile settled on Kit's lips for a moment as she watched the odd pair disappear into the trees. *Retha is filled with good people.*

She sighed and eyed the hilltop one more time where the hermit was supposed to be. *Okay. One last look, and then I'll give up.* She chewed on her lip, then slowly trekked her way to the top. The hilltop was one of the few sunny spots in the woods as it poked above the treeline and only sported a few birch trees. The rest of it was covered with silvery ferns and white flowers that sparkled like stars.

She systematically searched the hilltop in a grid pattern, and was just about to give up when a branch broke on one of the birch trees, and a man fell from the sky with a splat.

The man sat up and rubbed his head. "Well, that will teach me to try and rob acorns from a squirrel's nest." He laughed sheepishly, then smiled at Kit. "Greetings, fair one!"

Kit studied him, taking in his nameplate that marked him as an NPC. "Are you Habakkuk the Hermit?" She asked skeptically.

He stood, only to bow deeply. "I am he!"

Kit's forehead puckered. "Really? You look awfully young for a hermit."

Habakkuk, who appeared to be maybe in his early 20s and sported an X-shaped scar on his cheek, grinned. "I am an unusual hermit. Now, how can I help you?"

Kit was about to relay the message from the merchant when a twig cracked. Kit dropped to the ground on instinct, making her a harder target to hit, and scooted around until she faced the source of the noise.

Solus Miles, the top player on the server, exited the treeline and strode toward Kit and Habakkuk the Hermit.

"Welcome, hero!" Habakkuk said to Solus.

Solus only nodded and glanced at Kit, who was still splayed out in the dirt, with a raised eyebrow.

Slightly disgruntled, Kit brushed herself off and stood. *Of course I would meet Solus in my* new *armor.*

The armor set she had received from the merchant was slightly belittling, as it stuffed Kit in a blue silk skirt that was accented with long strips of white gauze material edged with gold embroidery. As it seemed a full shirt went against Retha's moral code, she was still in a belly shirt—this one a blue that matched her skirt—that was edged with gold tassels. Her new sandals strapped all the way to her knees, and for headgear, she had been given a white veil that trailed behind her and seemed to work as a target marker for elvish scouts.

The ridiculous armor set, though possessing better stats, did not precisely fill Kit with confidence (particularly as she had been shot in the stomach at least three times now) and did not make her feel any better about facing down Solus Miles AKA Intimidating Eyebrows.

Kit flatly stared at Solus Miles—or at least at his eyebrows that were slightly hitched in judgment.

Fantastic. The one time I'm in a foul mood, I happen to act slightly snarky to the best player on the server...and now I'm alone in a forest with him. She picked a leaf out of one of the many tassels her armor set boasted before flipping her veil over her shoulder. *But if he's such a big deal, chances are he probably doesn't remember me, particularly given how newb-ish my character looks. Yep, I think I'm safe.*

As Solus continued to stride toward her and the hermit, Kit

sucked a breath of air in and focused on emitting a serene feeling. *I am a still lake,* she told herself. *Intimidating Eyebrows cannot stir me.* She shuffled until she faced Habakkuk the Hermit again and smiled.

Habakkuk looked back and forth between her and Solus. "How lovely! Are the two of you together?" He pulled a bouquet of red flowers from the sleeves of his robe.

Kit's eyebrow twitched against her will, but she forced her smile even as Solus joined her. "We are no—" she paused, and she realized Solus was staring down at her, one of his thick black eyebrows arching sarcastically. Kit made her smile so wide she was afraid it might break her face. "Can I help you?" she asked with falsified sincerity.

"You shouldn't be here," Solus said.

"How perfect. It's been a while since I've had a pair approach me," Habakkuk said. He continued to rattle on, but Kit and Solus ignored him.

Kit's smile turned brittle as she stared up at Solus. "I beg your pardon?"

"You should not be in these woods. You are severely underleveled."

Kit fidgeted with one of her gold charm bracelets. "I assure you I wouldn't be here if I didn't have to be."

Intimidating Eyebrow's other eyebrow joined its twin in looking judgmentally down at her. "You cannot have a valid reason for coming into an area over twenty levels above you, alone."

Yep. He totally thinks I'm a newbie. Not that I blame him. "As it happens, I am not alone. My party and I are here to retrieve one of the four seals that locks Malignus's castle."

Habakkuk droned on in the background as Solus shifted slightly, revealing the metallic glint of his armor when he brushed his cloak aside. "If that is your aim, it will only end in failure."

Kit's mask of serenity cracked. "You must have a lot of people beating down your door trying to be your friend."

"I only speak the truth." Solus gazed out at the silvery ferns that swayed in the breeze. "A shadow reaper will attack you every time you retrieve a new seal. If he ever beats you, he will steal the seal, and each time you tackle a new part of the quest, his level is drastically increased."

Kit stared at Solus' chestplate in shock. She knew retrieving the seals would be difficult, and they would probably wipe several times when tackling the quest...but she had never added the shadow reaper and its possible complications into her plan.

"If you agree, Solus Miles, give your agreements," Habakkuk said.

Solus gave Kit a slight nod—which Kit couldn't help but read as being high-handed—then began to turn back to Habakkuk.

Kit interrupted him before he could speak. "Thanks for sharing about the shadow reaper, but I still have to say it really is no business of yours what I do or even why I'm in the area."

"I beg to differ," Solus said as Habakkuk launched into another monologue in the background. "Under-leveled characters roaming an area always impact it—whether it be through upsetting monsters' spawns by dragging an abnormal amount of mobs after them, or just by generally causing a scene."

"I may be under-leveled, but you know nothing about my party."

"I don't, but I can make many inferences based on your character type and appearance, and I assume that anyone with a higher-level character is not likely to associate with you."

Kit's jaw dropped. *This guy! I hope his eyebrows fall off!*

"And you, Kitten Lovemuch," Habakkuk said. "If you take Solus Miles to be your pledged, give your agreement."

"Yeah, yeah." Kit froze, then spun toward the hermit. "Wait, what?"

The young hermit beamed and threw a handful of rice in the air, then gave Kit the bouquet as a bell tolled.

"Then it is my pleasure to bless your pledge. May you be forever intertwined!"

Kit looked from the flowers to the hermit with horror and was immediately barraged with multiple game messages.

Congratulations! You have pledged yourself to: Solus Miles!
May your love last forever.

Congratulations! You have received the skill: Love's Call.
Your heart can cry out leagues away to summon your sweet
honey to your side.
Skill effect: Summon your pledged

Congratulations! You have received the skill: Love's Blessing.
Your fierce love for your pledged lends them your strength!
Skill effect: Grants your pledged a quarter of your status points.

Kit stared at the announcements—too stunned to read the rest of the new skills she had acquired with this unexpected relationship. "What just happened?"

"It seems we have become pledged," Solus Miles said.

"Obviously!" Kit snarled. "But how? You can only receive the blessing to become pledged at cathedrals by priests!"

"Normally, yes!" Habakkuk said brightly. "But I happen to be the Hermit of Love. As my heart is moved by the affection heroes have for each other, I freely give the blessing to become pledged to anyone who seeks me out!"

Solus still looked at Kit with narrowed eyes, but now they were more questioning than judgmental. "He was the elopement hermit they added with the *Gray Wraith* expansion. Some players were unable to pay the fee cathedral pledge ceremonies require, so EC added him with the caveat that there was no official ceremony or party afterwards, so the vast majority still go to cathedrals. He is used in several other questlines, as well."

Stunned, Kit could only stare blankly ahead. *This never would have happened five years ago. I didn't think things had changed much...but all the old classes have fallen out of favor, and now this? I was horribly wrong.* Kit tried to breathe deeply. *Enough. I have to stop being dramatic. This isn't that bad. It's nothing that can't be broken off, and I think Solus wants to associate with me even less than I want to associate with him. Think on the bright side: at least I haven't been shot by an elf scout recently.*

Feeling a smidge calmer, Kit was better able to sift through the facts. "But don't you need rings to exchange the pledge promise?" She gestured at Habakkuk with her left hand, then froze when she realized a gold band was fitted over her ring finger.

Silence stretched out in the clearing for several long, uncomfortable moments. "Solus Miles. Please don't tell me you just randomly carry a set of gold rings around," Kit said. "Because I sure as chicken feathers did not have any rings on me!"

Solus flattened his lips and looked away.

"Seriously?" Kit groaned. "Why would you carry rings around? What quest could possibly require them?"

Solus ignored her and spoke to the hermit. "We wish to break our pledge off."

Habakkuk scratched the back of his neck. "Already? That's unfortunate. But it makes no difference. I'm sorry, but I can't help you."

Kit moved in until she was approximately three inches away from the man. "Why not?"

"I'm the Hermit of Love," Habakkuk said brightly. "It goes against my nature."

Solus pinched the bridge of his nose. "So, we'll have to visit a cathedral to submit our breakup."

"No, I'm afraid that won't work either," Habakkuk said. "It's as you said, as the Hermit of Love, I usually only give my blessing to heroes who have fewer funds on them, and while your pledge will be recognized by the church, it isn't exactly pleased that I bless couples without requiring the usual fee, so they refused to notify the break ups."

Kit felt her eyes bulge in their sockets. "This is permanent?"

"No, you just have to search out my associate: Jehoshaphat, the Hermit of Singleness."

"Sometimes Retha has a twisted sense of humor," Kit grumbled.

"Where is Jehoshaphat?" Solus asked.

Habakkuk grinned and shook a finger at Solus. "Nope! Not going to tell you. The two of you can search him out, and perhaps by the time you find him, you will have repaired your relationship and discovered true love!" He knitted his fingers together and smiled happily.

"The Hermit of Singleness? He'll be easy to find if we just look him up in the community tab...Or not..." Kit trailed off as she recalled that the reason why she was stuck as a dancer was because of the corrupted server.

"Kit, are you alive?" Vic asked via the raid chat.

Kit quickly switched to the raid channel so she could respond. "Yeah, give me a moment. I'm in the middle of something." She scrunched her eyes together, weighing out the guilt of being borderline rude and continuing with the seal quest against delaying the quest to sort this mess out. *Sorry, Solus. This quest is looking more and more like a life-or-death matter, so breaking up an accidental relationship takes the back seat.* "Look. I've got to go. If you go find Jehoshaphat and summon me once you track him down, I will happily agree to break up."

Intimidating Eyebrows was back to disdainfully judging her. "You believe I should be the one to track him down?"

"Yeah, I don't have very much time right now."

"And you believe your time is more valuable than mine?"

"I wasn't the one walking around the forest with rings in my inventory.... Unless," Kit froze. Solus Miles was the best player on the server. It was very likely he actually did have girls beating down his door trying to get hitched to his character...which made it very unlikely that he had just happened to be carrying the rings. "Were you coming here to get the blessing for a pledge with someone else? Do I have to be concerned about a jealous girlfriend?"

Down came the eyebrows. "No."

Kit relaxed fractionally. "Thank goodness. The last thing I need is to be killed due to some misunderstanding. But yeah, I have some seals to find. So, if you would track down Jehoshaphat, that would be great."

"I don't know that it will be possible to find Jehoshaphat with the community tab down."

"Go to Luminos and ask in the global player channel. Someone has to know," Kit said.

"Do you know who I am?"

Kit scratched the top of her head. "Sort of."

"I'm not going to raise server speculation by asking where the Hermit of Singleness is."

Kit squinted. "I guess I do see your point. Well, then just deal with it. I've got things to do, and I need to run. Habakkuk, here's a message for you from a merchant." She passed him an envelope. "Thank you for teaching me the importance of attentively listening. Though I wish you could have taught it to me with a less drastic outcome."

Habakkuk took the envelope from Kit. "I am always pleased to be of service!"

"Uh-huh. Thanks." Kit waved to Habakkuk, nodded to Solus, and then trotted down the hillside. *Wow. Kitten Lovemuch is pledged. That's something I never accomplished as Azarel.* She winced slightly. *I do have to say I feel sorry for Solus. Having a character like his tied to my elf dancer? But once we're out of here, I'll never be logging back on as her again, which means he will be able to file for separation with the Hermit of Singleness once I've been off the game for two weeks.*

"Is everything okay?" Riko asked over the raid chat.

"Yeah, there's just an unexpected issue that popped up. How's everything going for you guys?" Kit asked.

"Good!" Cookie chirped.

"If we add in the reputation items you received from your quests, we believe we have enough items for both Riko and Prowl to have kindred," Vic announced.

"That's great! Wow, you work faster than I thought you would."

"Axel died a lot in the beginning because he kept pulling too many bobokins, but the cat does strengthen my magic. Thank you for giving it to me," Vic said.

"I'm glad you find it useful! So how about we meet up near the city outskirts so I can give Riko and Prowl the items?"

"That will work for us," Riko said. "I think we're maybe five to ten minutes away from it. We'll see you there?"

"Yep! You betcha." Kit switched out of the raid chat and glanced up at her character name. Two inter-joined rings appeared by her name, notating that she was now pledged. She shook her head in disbelief. *Yep, sorry Solus. It might be humiliating, but I have bigger monsters to chase.*

15

THE ULTIMATE SACRIFICE

BY THE TIME Kit made her way to the wall surrounding Lèas, the rest of the party was waiting for her.

She looked cautiously around for any elf scouts, then slipped out of the underbrush. "Hi everyone!"

"Hello, Kit," Cookie greeted.

Vic peered around Kit. "Where's Chester?"

"I haven't been using him," Kit said.

Prowl scratched his chin and leaned against his horse. "You walked here?"

"Yeah. Chester whinnied when we were going past a scout outpost and got me shot. I wanted to be safe rather than sorry this time. Here—I have the reputation items."

Kit initiated a trade with Prowl and handed over her cache of items.

Gil clipped his shield to his horse's rump. "Do you think they'll send you, Miss Riko, outside of the city to retrieve the seal, like the dwarves did?"

Riko—mounted on her beautiful palomino mare that had an elaborate fire-bird blanket and little ribbons woven into her hair —furrowed her brow. "I'm not certain. I would say it is likely, but I also don't believe the elves would misplace the seal or keep it anywhere unsafe. Do you remember what you had to do, Prowl, to earn the seal?"

Prowl shook his head. "I can't recall the details, but I remember you stay inside the city to snag it. The elves are fussy, so I doubt they would keep it anyplace besides in a guarded library."

"I would say they're more *careful* and have a higher appreciation for history," Riko said.

Cookie gazed reflectively at the sky. "If they kept it in the city and you could locate it, would it be possible to steal?"

Prowl gave her a half-grin. "There's always one way to find out."

"We have not grinded our reputation for days just to bring their wrath down on our heads by attempted thievery," Riko said sharply.

Vic frowned slightly. "You say that, but you were the one who drew the dragons' attention by swiping a coin."

"That was different," Riko protested. "We hadn't spent days gathering items to make friends with the dragons!"

"Uh-huh," Vic said, clearly unconvinced.

Cookie batted her long eyelashes at Riko. "What if there is no other way?"

"Yeah, Riko," Prowl said. "What if there is no other way?"

Riko scowled at her guildmate, then turned to Kit. "Could you try and talk some sense into them?"

"Stealing will not be necessary." Kit said. "As Riko and Prowl now have the max reputation level, the elves will be extremely welcoming. But they'll still have to sit through several meetings about the seal, I'm sure, so we'll be kicking up our heels while we wait for them."

"Was that a high-handed hint that we should get moving?" Prowl asked.

Axel's eyes were bright as he threw himself on his horse. "We could level while they're busy!"

"Aren't we too low-leveled to do anything by ourselves?" Vic asked as she cradled her cat.

"If we fight one bobokin or goblin at a time, I don't believe so," Gil said. "We've gotten several more levels between fighting our way here and then grinding drops. Plus, Miss Kit will be on hand to lead us."

"...And now you're ignoring me?" Prowl said.

Riko nodded at the entryway—the very one where Kit had been shot. "We should get going."

Prowl sighed and rubbed his face. "Right. Time to face the tree-huggers."

"Good luck," Cookie said with a bright smile.

Prowl nodded to her, but Vic grabbed her by the sleeve. "Come on. Let's get going," the wizard said.

"You mean you actually want to level? Vic...I'm so touched!" Cookie sniffled and let Vic lead her to the horses.

Kit flicked her eyes back and forth between Cookie, Prowl, and Vic, noting the new party dynamics as Riko and Prowl started to meander toward the entry point.

"Take care," Riko called.

"You, too! We look forward to hearing what our next task is." Kit whistled, summoning Chester, then mounted the stocky pony. "Okay, is there a particular camp you guys think we should pull our targets from?" Kit's spine stiffened when she heard the velvet sound of an arrow being pulled from a quiver.

Reacting on instinct, she kneed Chester—who lurched into a canter just in time to avoid the arrow one of the elf guards had shot at her.

She wove the pony around to make her a harder target, and spied Riko and Prowl passing through the entryway—unmolested by the guards who were scowling at her.

"We're right behind you," Cookie shouted.

Kit leaned closer to Chester's neck and wove her fingers through his thick mane. "Great. Let's get out of here."

Days later found Kit sprinting through the forest with a bobokin hot on her trail.

The blue-skinned creature—which was similar to a goblin though it had more of a pig snout and bigger ears—released a bloodcurdling cry and threw a wooden spear at her.

Kit dodged it by zooming around a tree. *I think I finally am getting the hang of elvish athleticism!* Her triumphant thought came too soon, for as she made a sharp turn to sprint up a dry creek bed, she almost overshot the turn and barely avoided running into a tree.

She veered back into the creek bed, where the bobokin grabbed her by her veil and yanked her backwards. Kit flicked one of her fans open and swept its metal edge across the goblin's face, slicing it.

The bobokin let her go and grabbed its pig-snout-nose with an angry howl.

Kit righted herself and again started up the creek bed. She glanced over her shoulder to see if the beastly creature was following, and kicked her speed up an extra notch when she saw it was not only following her, but it had removed its short sword from its leather belt and had somehow lit it on fire.

I can't believe this, even with my cowardly leader agility boost, this thing is just as fast as I am! Kit swallowed the gob of spit that threatened to choke her as she fought to breathe. "I'm coming in hot...very hot."

"We're ready for you," Gil said.

Pebbles and silt crunched under Kit's sandals as she ran,

jumping the occasional large boulder that dotted the dry creek bed. She skidded to a stop only when she reached a dead end, where a massive boulder taller than she was had once created a waterfall.

Cornered, Kit turned around and pressed herself against the boulder, her throat closing as the bobokin jumped at her with its flaming short sword.

Kit winced, but at the apex of the bobokin's jump, Gil leaped out of the bushes and slammed into the creature with his huge shield.

The creature hit the ground and rolled, swiftly popping back to its feet with a growl.

"Cry of Challenge!" Gil pointed his spear at the bobokin and shouted. The magic behind the skill slammed into the fallen bobokin, pummeling it back into the ground again.

Gil crouched in a defensive stance, his shield held out in front of him, as the creature crawled to its feet. It jumped at Gil, slamming his shield with its broadsword, landing a small hit to the crusader.

"Axel, Cookie, whenever you like," Kit said.

Axel needed no more prodding and jumped from the lower branches of a nearby tree with a shout. "Blade of fury!" His gigantic sword glowed white hot as he held it above his head, then swung it down, smashing it into the bobokin's skull.

Gil scooted back several feet. "Going up, Miss Kit?"

"Yeah, thanks." Kit took the hand the Crusader offered her. She climbed onto his back and jumped to the top of the giant boulder, joining Vic in the out-of-the-way location.

Vic already held a glowing ball of fire in her hands. "Can I get started?"

"Just give me a sec to get my dance up and boost your critical hit stat," Kit said.

Vic nodded and glanced down at her cat, which twined around her ankles.

Kit took a deep breath, then balanced on one foot and twirled, beginning the sequence for her skill, the Luck-Luck Dance.

Though the name is slightly dopey and the dance sequence makes me feel like a bobbing chicken, it is a pretty nice stat boost.

"The buff is up," Kit announced.

Vic raised her hands to throw the fireball, but it was Cookie who attacked first.

The night stalker stepped out of the shadows directly behind the bobokin—which was getting passed back and forth between Gil and Axel. Cookie's usually bright and expressive face was a chilling mask of cold apathy as she crouched behind the bobokin, who had just delivered a good jab to Axel's side and taken the warrior's health bar down by at least 40%. When the bobokin staggered backwards after Axel threw him off, Cookie struck with her daggers.

"Savage," she said.

Black flames danced around her blades as she cut into the bobokin's back.

"Fireball!" Vic shouted seconds later, releasing the magic attack she'd been holding onto.

The bobokin howled as it hopped back and forth on its feet, on fire and sporting a bleeding de-buff from Cookie. It had only a sliver of health left.

"He's mine!" Axel shouted. He rushed forward and stabbed the creature in the gut.

The bobokin screamed and babbled, then flopped to the ground and disappeared.

The familiar rainbow-colored lights and white musical notes poured down on Kit as big, beveled, golden letters formed over her head. "LEVEL UP."

No notification of a new skill popped up, to Kit's disappointment. (Though it wasn't a surprise as at level twenty she—along with every other player—received the Safe Haven skill that let her set a save spot and teleport there when desired. That was going to be extremely useful in the future!)

"Congrats on level twenty-one!" Cookie said.

Kit smiled and glanced at the night stalker before she began sifting through the items the bobokin left behind. "Thank you."

"I would've thought you would catch up to us faster," Vic said. (When they had separated to grind reputation items, Vic, Cookie, Gil, and Axel had gotten a few levels ahead of Kit. Now Vic was level twenty-three, Cookie twenty-four, and Axel and Gil twenty-five.)

"Now that we're partying together, we're all getting the same amount of experience though," Kit pointed out. "So technically it's impossible for me to catch up as long as we party together. Plus, I've been dying a lot, and every time I respawn I lose one percent of my experience bar."

Vic picked up her cat and peered over the edge of the boulder. "I see."

"Would you like assistance down, Miss Victoria?" Gil asked, holding out an arm.

Vic nodded and sat on the boulder before scooting over the edge, letting the crusader catch her and her feline.

"We're really starting to get a system down now!" Axel said enthusiastically. "Kit hasn't died once during the last five battles!"

"Our measure of success is slightly broken," Kit said, "as normally we would only be dying in very dire circumstances."

"Such is life when we're attacking monsters that are so much higher-leveled than we are," Cookie said as she sheathed her daggers. "Speaking of higher-leveled, I wonder how much longer Riko and Prowl are going to take."

"Should we private message them?" Axel suggested.

"No, we have no idea what they're doing and might contact them at a very bad time," Kit said. Using her elf agility, she leaped from the boulder and landed gracefully in the creek bed. She adjusted the hem of her skirt, which was riding perilously high, and gazed into the forest, which was turning purple with twilight.

How long have we been playing.... Not just since Riko and Prowl left, but since we were transferred to the corrupt backup server?

Time was a tricky thing in the Chronicles of Retha. Days passed in mere hours of real life, but to those playing, it still felt like a normal twenty-four-hour day—sort of how dreams often felt.

Though they had been in-game for days, possibly weeks, it had likely only been several hours of real life.

"You know, Kit, even though you try to make Riko the party leader whenever you get the chance, you're really good at tactics," Vic said as she cradled her cat. "We never did anything half as fancy or worked nearly as well as your idea to drag the bobokin to us when we were item grinding."

Kit shrugged. "When I played as an echo of arcane, it was my job to take out the biggest threat first. So, I had to learn how to read a battle and take appropriate counter-measures. Any good echo would operate the same way."

"Uh-huh." Vic rolled her eyes. "You're horrible with compliments."

Kit was saved from responding when a trumpet sounded, and an information screen popped up in front of her.

Congratulations! You have received: The Seal of the Elves.
The Human Seal and the Fae Seal remain for you to claim.

Axel whooped. "Pay dirt! Now we're halfway through the questline!"

Kit grinned and switched to party chat. "Way to go! You guys got it with just the two of you! What on earth did you have to do?"

"We don't want to talk about it," Prowl said. His voice was extra flat and dead.

Kit twirled one of her fans by its wrist strap. "Oh, okay. Should we meet up with you guys at the entryway you entered Lèas through?"

"We'll be there," Riko said, sounding scarcely more alive than Prowl.

Gil raised his eyebrows. "I hope they did not have to suffer horribly for the seal."

"Their health bars never dipped down," Vic pointed out.

"We'll find out soon." Kit whistled, and Chester appeared with a happy nicker and a mouthful of ferns. "Let's go meet them!"

———

Chester was in the process of yanking Kit's arms out of their sockets so he could stretch his neck long enough to reach a white flower when Riko and Prowl staggered out of the city limits and passed the elf guards standing outside the wall.

"Woah," Vic said. "The elves must've really put them through the wringer."

The pair teetered along with rumpled clothes, mussed hair, and dark circles under their eyes.

Kit bit her lip, but she didn't dare slip off of Chester and veer into the elves' sights. "Are you two okay?" she asked when they finally wobbled up to the party.

Riko blinked slowly, then scrubbed her face with her hands. "That was awful."

"What did they make you do?" Axel asked with a frown. "Face a goblin army?"

"Worse," Prowl croaked. "We had to listen to them tell stories about the seal for three nights and three days."

Kit winced in sympathy. "Yikes."

"I think I will hear the elf lyre playing in the background for the rest of my life," Riko said.

Prowl gingerly nodded. "I think I didn't remember it because it was so traumatizing—and boring."

"Sounds like torture," Axel said.

Vic rolled her eyes.

Riko waved off their concern. "The first day wasn't so bad. The elves are always gracious hosts and offer plenty of refreshments. And their voices and stories are beautiful, but halfway through day two...let's just say it's like listening to the song that never ends."

"I'm sorry it was so difficult," Cookie said as she peered at Prowl in worry. "But I thank you for this great service you have done our party."

The praise put a little iron in Prowl's spine, and he rolled his shoulders back and nodded. "We have the elf seal, and that's what matters."

Riko snorted. "That's not what you said this morning."

He ignored her and opened up his inventory. "Here it is." He held up the seal, which resembled the dwarven one in that it was a saucer-size disk. The elf seal, however, was forged out of a platinum-like metal, and instead of bearing runes, it was covered with a curling script.

Kit absentmindedly patted Chester while the pony

scratched his front right knee. "I think you should hold on to it, Prowl," she said, recalling Solus' Miles warning about the shadow reaper.

That's right. The shadow reaper!

Kit abruptly turned Chester and nudged him away from Lèas. "I think we need to get out of this area."

"What's the hurry?" Axel asked.

"Are you thinking of the shadow reaper?" Gil asked.

"Yes. I suspect he'll attack us soon, given that Riko and Prowl just got us another seal. I'd rather not battle near the wall where the elf guards might come and put an arrow through me."

Riko groaned. "You are right, but I'm so exhausted. And those stingy elves didn't even give us a single coin! Ugh."

In spite of their groans, both Riko and Prowl whistled, calling their horses. In no time, their party quietly navigated their way through the woods, making a beeline for the transportation gate that was just outside the forest.

Kit carefully combed the forest with her eyes, whipping around at every tree branch that snapped and any bird that took off flying. The hair on the back of her neck prickled again, and she could feel something dark draw near.

It's coming!

Axel suddenly leapt off his horse and unsheathed his sword. "There it is!"

Kit looked to where the warrior was pointing just in time to see the shadow reaper step out of the gloom.

16

FINAL BATTLE

THE SHADOW REAPER cocked its head and laughed, a grating sound that made Kit shiver. "I see you managed to convince the elves to give you their seal, *heroes*. Well done. It would've been a difficult task to secure it for myself, so I praise your efforts. Now. Hand it over."

Riko snorted. "After what we went through to get it? Never!"

The shadow reaper screeched in fury and swung its scythe in a crescent shape. The blade seemed to slice through their reality, opening a gap in the air from which black fire poured through. The fire spread faster than lightning, and hit them all in an area attack. It burned, but it also felt like talons clawing into Kit's skull as it encircled her.

The fire ate away at roughly 45% of Kit's health bar. A glance at the other party members confirmed they all sported high damages as well—though hers was definitely the worst as she was also the lowest leveled.

"I will not repeat myself, heroes. Hand over the seal, or face certain destruction!" The shadow reaper glided closer to them, its bare skull gleaming in the moonlight.

Axel laughed and wiped a smudge of blood off his chin. "Destruction? How can you say that with a straight face when you told us you would kill us last time, too? You should probably think of changing your tactics as they don't really seem to work."

The shadow reaper screamed with rage, and Kit used the few moments to review the situation.

The shadow reaper was now a level thirty-two, so Solus Miles had been right. With each seal, it seemed that the shadow reaper's power and level would grow.

Unless we want to spend a lot of time grinding levels, we won't be able to finish this quest without him wiping us out at some point, which means we would lose the seals.

"He's doing something suspicious again!" Vic announced.

The shadow reaper raised its scythe again, and this time swung it in a vertical line. Seven spindly limbed creatures wriggled out of the gash he created. They were made entirely of shadows and were so skinny their leg bones were probably as thick as Kit's wrist. Though they were tall, they crouched close to the ground, their clawed hands almost dragging through the dirt. They were ink black with no visible eyes, making them hard to see in the dim moonlight that managed to pierce through the tree canopy.

Kit shivered as the creatures, unnaturally silent, crawled toward them. She had faced many of this particular monster with Azarel, and had died by their hands more times than she cared to remember as their speed was especially dangerous for an echo of arcane. "That's an umbra-nox," she said. "They're fast and brutal."

"Any other words of advice?" Gil asked as he hefted his shield.

Kit grimly flicked her fans open. "Don't let them get behind you—their favorite move is to yank up your head and slash at your throat."

As if they could understand, one of the umbra-noxes zipped forward like quicksilver, sliding behind Gil with ease. It reached for his head with its talons, but Vic had already started sketching a symbol in the air.

"Fireball!" The wizard shouted. She launched the glob of fire, hitting the creature in the back.

It screamed like a dying rabbit and retreated, rejoining the others.

"Your orders, party leader?" Prowl pointedly asked.

Kit tensed. She knew this was the moment in which she should be barking out orders, but her nerves were too frayed. *This is a dangerous situation. I don't mind getting myself killed, but if one move is wrong, the entire party could wipe, and we'll lose both seals!*

Another one of the umbra-noxes slunk close to the ground and ran at them. Axel, who'd been waiting with enough energy to power a lightning storm, smashed his sword down on the creature's back legs.

The umbra-nox whirled around, a clawed skeletal hand grasping for his face, but Riko was ready for it. "Nature's Bindings!" Vines shot out of the ground and wrapped around the umbra-nox, holding it in place.

"What do we do, party leader?" Cookie asked.

Kit was frozen by her fear of failure and the nagging feeling that her place was *not* giving orders in the center of the battle, but hanging back like she always had. *I'm not right for this—I'm not good enough!*

Unsure, Vic backed up while Axel veered dangerously near the six monsters that stood in a clutch.

"Kit!" Prowl snapped. "Get out of your freaking head and just breathe! These things should be a breeze for you!"

"What Prowl is trying to say," Riko said with a grunt as she renewed the bindings on the stranded umbra-nox. "Is that you are over-thinking this. You know tactics—just think it through like you would as Azarel and tell us what we need to do."

Kit took a deep breath and followed Riko's advice. She pushed her fears about the corrupted servers out of her mind, and even shed the pesky reminder that she was the party leader and was responsible for the well-being of the quest.

This is Retha, she reminded herself. *It's my world, or at least it used to be, and this fight is just a chess match. I only have to compare the pieces and find a winning strategy.* Her mind skittered over their previous battles, and the things she had learned about her party members, as well as her memories of fighting various umbra-noxes.

"Prowl, is your Mangle skill a single target attack, or is it area of effect?"

Prowl struck out at an umbra-nox that was stalking Cookie. "The de-buffs are area of effect, but the attack itself is for a single target."

"We have to group them up so Prowl can lay that de-buff on them. His de-buff will slow them down and make them much easier to fight. They're pretty breakable if you can actually hit them," Kit said. "Riko, if they concentrate their aggro on Gil, can you keep him alive?"

"If I don't have to heal anyone else, and if he can supplement with potions."

"Gil?" Kit asked.

Gil slipped between Vic and an umbra-nox and took a blow meant for the wizard. He grimaced, but shook the pain off. "I believe I can handle it."

"Make it happen," Kit said.

Axel and Cookie peeled off, slinking into the shadows. The umbra-noxes began slipping after them, until Gil planted his shield in the ground. "Cry of Challenge!" He shouted.

Six of the seven umbra-noxes descended on him, with the seventh still being caught up in Nature's Binding.

"Now, Prowl!" Kit launched into Battlefield March, boosting Gil's defense stats. "Vic, Cookie, Axel. If you have any powerful attacks with load times, start casting them now."

Prowl, visible only because the buckles of his armor stood out on his all-black clothes, stalked around the group of umbra-noxes that were slaughtering Gil. Just as he had with the dragon, he planted the wads of clay and a triangle formation, though this time he set them on the ground.

"Move faster, Prowl," Riko said. "My cooldown on my heals can barely keep up with Gil."

Kit, planted close to Gil to make sure her buff spread to both him and back to Riko, gazed past the umbra-noxes. The shadow reaper was still there, its white skull gleaming hideously in the faint light. It made no move to summon more umbra-noxes—thankfully—but it leered like a specter as it watched the battle play out.

"Look out!" Axel shouted.

Kit realized too late one of the umbra-noxes had been lured away from Gil and launched itself at her. She leaped backwards, but it reached out with one of its irregularly long limbs and manage to slash her across the chest. Gil immediately launched another Cry of Challenge at the creature, dragging it back, but the damage was done.

Kit staggered backwards, her health bar down to 15%. She hissed at the burning, bubbling sensation that tore through her and quickly popped a health potion, restoring her only to about 50%.

"I'm sorry—I can't heal you." Riko motioned furiously, firing off healing spell after healing spell at Gil.

"No, it was my fault." She shook her head, throwing off the

edge of the pain, and launched back into Battlefield March—
this time making sure she stood a little farther away.

"Here we go!" Prowl shouted. "Mangle!"

The wads of clay shot out lines of dark blue light that
connected, and black fog rolled in—looking extra chilling in the
darkness of the forest.

Abruptly, the umbra-noxes started moving slower—more on
the level of "fast" instead of "lightning speed."

Red tendrils of light shot out of the clay masses and convened
on one umbra-nox. Prowl threw his dagger at the creature,
sticking it in the chest. The dagger shed red sparks, and bolts of
lightning zipped from the dagger to the wads of clay before the
center point erupted with a flash of light and a loud boom.

The umbra-nox was thrown back from the impact then
disappeared, defeated.

"One down, six to go!" Axel hooted.

"Launch your casted attacks now," Kit shouted.

Cookie slunk out of the shadows and stabbed an umbra-nox
in the back. Axel used his blade of fury attack again, and sliced
the same umbra-nox. They had done a pretty decent amount of
damage to it, but it was Vic who took it up a notch.

"Heavens Fury!" The wizard pointed a finger to the sky and
then cast it downward. The area where the umbra-noxes were
still congregated begin to glow, and it took Kit a moment to
realize the glow was coming from the sky. Soccer ball-sized
meteors crashed through the tree canopy, bludgeoning the
umbra-noxes and tossing them like rag dolls.

"Holy crap!" Axel shouted. "That is one sick skill!"

"How long have you had that skill?" Cookie asked.

Vic shrugged and charged her fireball spell. "A while, but
the cast time is so long I've never had the chance to use it."

When the meteors stopped falling from the sky, the last rock pummeled the umbra-nox Cookie and Axel had attacked, smashing its last remaining bit of health and killing it.

"Five remaining," Gil counted out.

Kit, her health bar still dangerously at the half-point, chugged another health potion when its cool down time ran out. "Prowl, you work with Axel and Cookie. The three of you need to attack one target to take it out as fast as possible, then move on to the next. Gil, you tank for Vic and Riko."

Everyone split off, moving to their assigned partners.

"Shall I use Heaven's Fury again?" Vic asked when she was safely hidden behind Gil.

Kit started the first few dance moves for her Battlefield March again. "Does it eat up your mana too much?"

"No, it's just the cast time."

"Then cast it one more time. Then use Fireball and attack the target of Riko's choice."

Vic nodded as her cat sank its claws into her clothes to remain on her shoulder. The wizard turned back to the group of umbra-noxes and began sketching symbols in the air.

An umbra-nox glared at Kit from over Gil's shoulders. Kit skittered backwards, but the monster grabbed her by one of the white pieces of linen that hung from her skirt and yanked her. It couldn't reach her torso, but it opened a nasty gash on her leg with its dagger-like claws.

Gil walloped it, not doing very much damage to it but regaining its attention as Kit hobbled backwards, still performing Battlefield March. "I am not irritated with this character class. I'm not irritated with this character," Kit repeated to herself. Her health potion cooldown had not reset yet, so she was forced to continue with Battlefield March, dancing with a very dangerous health bar at less than 20%.

She was glad to see, however, that Prowl, Axel, and Cookie finished one umbra-nox and moved on to the next with ease.

There was a chiming noise, and an unfamiliar male voice filled Kit's ears.

"What are you doing?"

Kit blinked, and it took her a few moments to realize that Solus Miles was sending her a private message. "I'm sorry, what?"

"You've been dying like a fly for the past three days, and now your health bar keeps zigzagging up and down. What are you putting your character through?"

Kit blinked. "You have the pledge notifications on?" As part of being pledged, you received a notification whenever your significant other logged on or off, died, or was gravely injured. Kit had turned off the system about five seconds after leaving Solus Miles with Habakkuk the Hermit of Love, but apparently the royal knight had not done the same. Unless... "You can turn them off in your settings panel, you know."

"I know," came Solus Miles' flat response. *"But what are you doing?"*

"Oh, I was leveling, but right now my party and I are facing down the shadow reaper..." Kit trailed off as she, between twists and twirls, gazed past the now three remaining umbra-noxes.

The shadow reaper was still there, but Kit could tell by the way it held its scythe that it was getting ready to leave. Apparently, if it became obvious you were going to successfully fight off its little mob, the shadow reaper disappeared.

So it only faces you when you're already dead. Coward.

For a moment, the unfairness of the situation made Kit clench her hands into fists. They were in the fight of their lives, literally. She was swiftly losing hope that EC would find a way to fix the corrupted server, making this quest their only chance to get off. And soon it would become an impossible hurdle to jump—particularly as the balance of Retha continued to swing the shadow reaper up in levels.

I hate their blasted balance! It still hasn't balanced out my character—unless you count Solus Miles marrying me, which doesn't necessarily do anything for me, and it was really only a result of a poor attention span.

Which was when it occurred to Kit...if the algorithms allowed her to waltz around as a character that was so poorly balanced, in what other ways could she upset the balance of the game?

"*Kitten?*" Solus Miles asked.

Kit stared at the shadow reaper, which was far across the clearing and swiftly disappearing into the shadows. "Call me Kit..." She trailed off as her thoughts crashed through her mind.

If I'm wrong about this, I might get us all killed. But there's a chance I'm right...

She switched to her party chat. "Gil, let one of the umbra-noxes chase after me for a few seconds, then taunt it and get it back."

"Are you crazy?" Vic asked. "You're almost dead!"

"We have to kill that shadow reaper now," Kit kept her eyes on the shadow reaper as she chugged another health potion. "This is our only chance, or we'll have to go back to Luminos and recruit higher-level players to come back with us, and after our reception last time, I'm not so sure that will go over well. Our best option is to take it down, now."

"Are you sure about this?" Prowl asked.

Kit snapped her fans shut. "No, but it's a calculated risk that might pay off!" She charged straight through the cluster of the remaining umbra-noxes, and sure enough, she proved to be an irresistible target. One of the noxes tried to take a swipe at her, but thankfully it missed and chased her a few feet as she ran toward the shadow reaper.

Her Cowardly Leader buff kicked in, impressively boosting

her speed, and she was halfway across the clearing before Gil could lure the umbra-nox back.

The shadow reaper's cloak started to blend in with the night as he faded, but between her physical elf capabilities and her Cowardly Leader skill, Kit was able to smash into him with a flying tackle before he completely disappeared.

They crashed into a tree. Though Kit was slightly dazed, she quickly disentangled herself from the shadow reaper. Using one of her closed fans, she smashed it in the face. "Violent Outburst!" The feeble attack barely dinged his health bar, but at least he was fully trained on her.

The shadow reaper wasn't going anywhere.

"You," the shadow reaper growled. It kicked her in the gut, sending her sprawling. "You have made a grave mistake."

———

Solus Miles stared at the crest of his horse's white mane. "She's fighting the shadow reaper."

The forest around him responded with silence.

He sighed and looked up at the treetops above him—which were starting to glow pink as the sun slipped above the horizon. *Should I help her? The battle seems to be quite difficult for her given the lowness of her health.*

Normally he wouldn't care. The girl was either a risk-taker or horribly unskilled based on the frequency in which she died, and he had only come across a few players who were ignorant enough to make a miserable character like an *elf dancer*.

But she doesn't talk like an inexperienced player. She knows too much about how everything operates—though she seems to be going off old information. Perhaps she has a friend who used to play who explained everything to her?

He rubbed the gold band, making Kitten Lovemuch's stats

appear. Her health bar was again popping back and forth between near death and a decent amount of health. *She must have a healer in her party—or she's good at timing her health potions.*

Solus Miles' horse shook its head, jostling its blue barding.

He pinched the bridge of his nose. Pledging himself to a player who had named herself *Kitten Lovemuch* was probably going to be the greatest embarrassment of his gaming career. It would be particularly humiliating once word got out what sort of player she was.

He glared at her name and stats—which still hovered in front of him—then shook his head. *No. It's not her fault. Getting pledged is exactly the sort of attention-grabbing move I wanted to avoid, but I only have myself to blame for it.*

After all, if he hadn't been carrying the rings around, the hermit never would have performed the ceremony.

She didn't react the way I thought she would, though.

Kitten Lovemuch had clearly been irritated, but for the most part polite and eager to get away from him. Usually, other players only had two or three reactions to him: adoration, respect, or hatred. Polite disinterest was not something he had encountered in years.

Mulling over the pink-haired dancer, Solus Miles brought up his mini-map. *Just how far away is she?*

———

Kit scrambled to her feet as the shadow reaper stalked toward her. It raised its sickle to attack her, but Cookie appeared behind it, melting out of the shadows. She stabbed it in the back, temporarily drawing its ire.

The shadow reaper whirled around and slammed the butt of its scythe into her chest. Cookie was knocked into a tree and barely avoided an umbra-nox that had wriggled free from Gil's taunts.

"Nature's Bindings!" Riko snapped her vines around the loose umbra-nox, buying Cookie and Kit a little time.

The shadow reaper turned back toward Kit, but Prowl darted in front of her, laying a tripwire as he skidded past on his knees.

The shadow reaper broke through the tripwire easily, too strong for the attack to hinder him.

Prowl cursed under his breath. "Riko, Vic, you want to hurry it up back there?"

The earth groaned, and an umbra-nox screamed.

"One left!" Riko shouted.

"Cookie, Prowl, Axel, jump the reaper all at once! I'll give you luck," Kit shouted. She flicked her fans open and stepped into a twirl, activating the Luck-Luck Dance.

Axel sprinted across the clearing, stopping near Kit. "I'm here. Are we ready?" The warrior had a side wound that was bleeding pretty badly, and his health bar was only 50%, but he grinned like a maniac as he set his sights on the shadow reaper.

Kit barely avoided the shadow reaper when it took a swing for her ankles with its scythe. "Yes, do it now!"

The trio jumped the shadow reaper all at once, ripping into him with their melee attacks. Unfortunately, it seemed to do minimal damage as the shadowy monster lost barely a sliver of his health bar.

A captive umbra-nox broke through the last of the vines holding it in place, and it leaped for Cookie. It landed a blow to her shoulder, but when it tried to pursue her, Prowl threw a trap down in front of it, stopping it in its tracks.

"Riko, Vic, Gil, what's your status?" Kit asked.

"We're coming, but we'll take out the last umbra-nox first," Riko shouted from somewhere behind them.

"Cookie, back off. Throw your daggers at the shadow reaper if you can, but try to avoid getting aggro," Kit instructed.

The night stalker gave her the okay signal and shrank back into the shadows, leaving Prowl and Axel to play with the monster.

Axel tried to attack the creature from the front while Prowl jumped at its back, but the shadow reaper struck the ground with the tip of his scythe, releasing a black shockwave that knocked both Axel and Prowl backwards.

Prowl landed on his feet, but Axel hit a tree and crumpled to the ground, laying there without moving even though his health bar was still a third filled.

Kit, recognizing the signs of a stun—a status ailment that mentally knocked a player out of it. "Toss him a cure!"

Vic unearthed a crystal bottle filled with a blue liquid, and then threw it at Axel so it cracked him in the face and shattered.

"I didn't mean literally!" Kit shouted. "He has to drink the stuff to fix it, not get it spattered across his face."

"I hope those glass shards don't scar him," Cookie joked as she straightened up with a grimace.

Before Vic could toss the warrior another cure, he groaned and sat up. Apparently some of the liquid had drizzled through his open mouth. "While that is a wickedly manly way to take a potion, I think I prefer to have you deliver it a different way, Vic," Axel said, moving slower than usual.

The shadow reaper stalked toward Axel and Vic, but Gil popped up between them, taking a scythe swing at the prime with his shield. He grunted as he was knocked back several feet, but his defense held. "Shield Wall!"

"All umbra-noxes are down. But I'm running low on mana," Riko announced. "And I've already used a mana potion."

Kit kept moving, keeping the Luck-Luck Dance active. "Try using Nature's Bindings on him."

Vines shot out of the ground, entangling the shadow reaper. With one sweep of his sickle, the shadow reaper was free. "You really believe your weak attacks can stop me?" The shadow reaper pointed at Riko with one bony hand and hissed.

Kit, knowing it would be awful to lose their only healer, grabbed a rock and threw it at the shadow reaper, clipping its outstretched finger.

At the last second, the shadow reaper switched its target from Riko to Kit with an angry snarl. "I curse you," it said. "I curse you to darkness—may it eat away at your light!"

Black smoke covered Kit. Though it didn't hurt, it made her eyes water, and it filled her mouth, choking her.

"I can't keep aggro!" Gil shouted.

Kit coughed, still choking on the black smoke, but she glared up at her name where another curse icon had appeared. This new curse was a powerful de-buff that severely cut her stats. She was basically a sitting duck. She staggered out of the cloud, narrowly avoiding being impaled by the shadow reaper's scythe.

"Gut Buster!" Axel jumped at the shadow reaper, but it didn't even turn to look at him as it extended a hand and clenched its fist. Chains of black smoke formed around Axel's throat and yanked him backwards, slamming him to the ground.

Prowl tried throwing daggers at the foul being from the tree-tops, but the shadow reaper followed him with its gaping eye sockets and, using its scythe, cut straight through the branches, toppling the saboteur out of the trees.

"Earthen Pit!" Riko shouted.

A hole opened up below the shadow reaper, but it did not fall into it. Instead it stood on a disk of shadows and sneered at the druid. "Is this truly the best you can do?" It slammed its sickle into the ground, and the same shadow-like chains that had subdued Axel wrapped around Riko.

Kit stopped dancing and turned, intending to move behind a

tree, when hot pain exploded across her lower back as the shadow reaper sliced her.

She collapsed on the ground with a cry, her health bar hovering at about 5% remaining.

I guess I miscalculated. He may be more than we can take on. But what else could we have done?

Kit tried to stand, but the scythe blow had struck her with a slight paralysis, freezing her legs in place. Terrified, Kit swiveled to face the creature head-on. She gulped as it stood before her, its sickle raised high.

"The darkness will greet your soul," it said before swinging.

Kit stiffened herself for a blow...but it never came.

17

PLEDGED PROTECTION

"BELOVED'S GUARD!"

When the shadow reaper's blow struck Kit, it hit an iridescent blue shield. Her health didn't budge an inch.

The shadow reaper straightened. "What?" it hissed. "How can this be?"

Solus Miles, riding a white charger, crashed into the clearing. He dismounted his horse as it galloped past, then pulled his sword from its scabbard in a move as smooth as butter. Holding it in front of him, he stood before Kit, guarding her.

"What. *What*. WHAT?" Riko babbled as the shadow-like chains that had restricted her and Axel faded. "Did he just say beloved?"

Kit gaped at the man standing in front of her, her jaw dangling freely.

"Seriously, people. Did Solus Miles just say Beloved's Guard?" Riko demanded.

The shadow reaper swung its scythe at Solus. The royal knight held firm, his health bar barely dinging from the hit as he remained crouched in front of Kit. "If you want credit for killing this thing," he growled in his deep voice. "I can't kill it for you. Your party will have to."

Kit shook off her shock. "Prowl, Cookie, use daggers and nail the reaper from a distance. Vic, use Fireball. Axel and Gil, use your melee attacks, and Riko hit him with whatever you can!"

"Woo hoo!" Axel darted forward and stabbed the shadow reaper through the gut.

The creature didn't even look at him. It roared in anger and instead kept striking out at Solus Miles, who stood as still as a mountain.

"Why is Solus Miles here? And why did he just say Beloved's Guard?" Riko demanded. Though she seemed distracted, she was surprisingly adept with entangling the shadow reaper's feet with vines as it kept up its fruitless attack.

"Kitten Lovemuch is my pledged," Solus Miles said. (Kit almost laughed as she was still able to hear the barely discernible disbelief in his voice.)

"What!?" Riko shrieked. "How! When! *Why?*" When the shadow reaper turned to take a swipe at Axel, the druid wrapped vines around its neck and dragged them backwards, almost tipping the monster over. "Kit, did you know you are married to the best player on the server?" she asked.

Kit used a tree to climb to her feet, shaking off the worst of the mild paralytic. "Of course I knew, and we're not married, just pledged. We had a bad run-in with Habakkuk the Hermit of Love." She took a few tottering steps like a baby lamb, and then managed to launch into Battlefield March.

"How can you be taking this so calmly? This is Solus Miles!" Riko said. "Do you know how much money he has?"

"And there stands the reason for her shock and awe. Ladies and Gentlemen, the greedy hag." Prowl took a moment from attacking to bow and gesture at Riko.

"Who cares about Kit's new boy toy?" Vic snapped. "We have bigger issues. Like, why isn't this thing dying?"

One of Solus Miles' eyebrows popped up. "Boy toy?" He said in a voice that was dangerously low.

"Vic has a point. This shadow reaper isn't going down fast enough," Cookie shouted. "Even if we aren't taking damage, we're all running low on mana."

"Shadow Reapers have high defense," Solus Miles said.

Kit rummaged through her memories of class traits and skills. "I don't think any of us have any skills that can counter that. Unless—Prowl do you have something?"

Prowl leaped backwards when the shadow reaper took a shot at him. "Not at this level, no."

"Grrr." Kit scratched her ears and shut her eyes in concentration as she mentally replayed boss battles she had taken part of as Azarel. Being so fragile, she was constantly placed a safe distance from the battle, and she was always careful to line up the release of her spells with the de-buffs of support players. Combine that with her sniper role in PVP, and Kit had memorized a ridiculous number of class skills.

She *knew* dancers had a basic de-buff skill. She had seen it used in hundreds of battles. So why didn't she have it?! "It's the one where they dance in reverse. What was it called?"

"I respect that you're our tactical genius and all, but how is muttering to yourself with your eyes squeezed shut helping?" Prowl asked. He threw a fistful of pepper grit at the shadow reaper, but it didn't work.

Kit ignored him. "Prowl, Riko, do you remember that dancer buff skill that worked in reverse and cast a de-buff on enemies?"

"Yeah." Riko frowned as she cast another round of Nature's Bindings on the shadow reaper. "What about it?"

"Was that a learnable skill—one you can teach yourself outside of leveling?" Kit asked.

Riko shook her head. "I don't know... It was one of the basic skills—if a dancer got it they learned it before level thirty."

"Then there's a chance." Most learnable skills had to be forced before level thirty—by then your character build would branch out and become more specialized.

The likelihood that the de-buff was actually learnable wasn't good, but Kit couldn't think of anything else to do. With her heart pounding in her chest, Kit stopped Battlefield March.

Gil glanced in her direction and tilted his head. "Miss Kit?"

Prowl was not so subtle. "What the heck are you doing?" he demanded as he stabbed the shadow reaper in the back.

Kit bit her lip as she mentally worked through the steps of Battlefield March in reverse—which was surprisingly difficult. "Trying a hail-mary pass." She fumbled several times as she tried to get the rhythm and smoothness down.

"I'm no sportsman, but I'm pretty sure that's not what a hail-mary pass is." Vic threw another fireball at the shadow reaper with a grunt.

Prowl pulled his goggles off his forehead so quickly the band snapped audibly. "Trying to force a skill in the middle of a battle is not a winning strategy, Kit. We don't have time for this!" He shouted as Kit was finally able to perform the first few steps of Battlefield March in reverse with a little more elegance.

A trumpet sounded.

Congratulations! You have learned the secret dancer skill:
Counterdance
Your sense of rhythm is so groovy you can dance backwards—just
don't trip!
Skill effect: Casts reverse effect on enemy forces of the last dance
you performed, at the dancer's skill level.

Kit couldn't help it. "HAH!" She snorted as she arrogantly tilted her chin up.

A little icon of a music note appeared under the shadow reaper's name, marking Counterdance's de-buff. As the last dance Kit had performed was Battlefield March, Counterdance —casting the reverse effect—hit the monster with a physical attack and defense de-buff.

YES! I knew dancers had a defense de-buff. With this, it should be easier for everyone to damage the shadow reaper!

"Keep dancing—it's working," Riko said.

Gil was the first to step in and wallop the shadow reaper. "Hammer Strike!"

"Gut Buster," Axel shouted and stabbed the shadow reaper on the other side.

Prowl and Cookie descended on the shadow reaper's back, chiseling away with their daggers.

"Fireball!" Vic shouted. Her attack was powerful enough that it finally set the shadow reaper's ratty cloak on fire.

The shadow reaper howled as the party continued to rain attacks down on him, and Solus Miles kept aggro. When it had only a bit of health left, Riko had built up enough mana. "Earthen Pit!"

The earth once again opened up under the shadow reaper, and this time it fell in and was crushed between the slabs of earth, stealing its last bit of health.

The shadow reaper made a noise like shattering glass. "I have fallen, but you will never defeat my master," it promised as its eye sockets started to glow a putrid poison green. "Malignus will succeed, and Lord Valdis will rise again and devour all in his path!"

Axel snorted. "Whatever. Say your prayers, creep." He

stabbed his sword into the creature's chest cavity. Shadows exploded from the monster before it crumpled like paper and faded.

Instantly, the area was flooded with noises announcing level increases for most of the party, and a list of the drops popped up in Kit's view.

Kit let her legs give out and slumped to the ground. "What the french toast—that was way too close for comfort."

"I'd say so," Prowl snorted.

"What inspired you to attack the shadow reaper in the first place?" Vic asked.

"Ahhh, Solus mentioned that if it successfully killed us, it would steal the seals. And as it will keep growing in levels every time we see it, I thought now was our best shot," Kit said.

All eyes turned to Solus, who ignored them as he sheathed his sword.

"Well, we did it, and that's what matters," Riko said.

"Yes, and now we can rest assured that we won't have to face the reaper in the future," Gil added.

"So we're halfway through the quest, and I assume this means we got the worst battle out of the way?" Cookie asked.

Vic shrugged. "Beats me."

"In all probability, yes," Riko said. "Although I believe the human seal and fae seal will be more difficult to retrieve than the last two."

"Hey, getting that elf seal was the pits," Prowl said. "But yeah, you have to go on some long quests lines to get the last two seals."

Kit chuckled as she listened to her party and sorted through the drops the umbra-noxes and the shadow reaper had dropped. (There was no dancer-appropriate gear, of course.) It had been a tough fight, but they did well. Kit was even pleased with her own class! Counterdance had been a great support skill to have.

Solus stood in front of her, casting a shadow over her. "How did you know about Counterdance?"

Kit startled and looked up. "Sorry, what?"

The royal knight blinked. "How did you know about Counterdance?"

Kit tried to discreetly tug the hem of her skirt down. "Um, it used to be a common skill on certain dancer builds ages ago, and I knew all it involved was reversing a dance order...sooo I gave it a shot."

Solus silently stared at her.

"Thanks, by the way," Kit added after a few uncomfortable moments. "I would have died if you hadn't arrived when you did."

He nodded, ignoring Riko who was rubbing her hands and beaming at him behind his back. Kit glanced guiltily off to the side. *He's a lot nicer and more tolerant than I originally thought. Woops.*

Solus narrowed his eyes slightly, making a striking picture as the morning sun—now strong and warm—lit up the trees behind him, giving him a halo effect. "If you need me, PM me," he said abruptly.

Kit blinked. "T-thanks! I appreciate it—but you don't have to help me as a bribe to get me to break off the pledge, if that's what you're thinking."

Solus shrugged his shoulders, then whistled. His charger—a white stallion who was most likely a rare reward or drop based on its fancy sparkling blue and white tack and armor pieces—strode into the clearing and snorted. It halted next to Solus and pawed at the ground with a black hoof.

Solus climbed up with one hand and twitched his cloak over his horse's back. He glanced at Kit—once again raising an eyebrow that gave his stone expression a slightly disbelieving/disdainful look—then nodded. He nudged his horse forward, and the charger strode off into the trees, disappearing from view.

Kit scratched her head—confused and puzzled by his actions—as she watched him go.

No sooner had his horse's hoofbeats faded from hearing than Riko pounced on Kit.

"How on earth did you get *Solus Miles* to marry you? You played before his time—you can't personally know him!"

Kit sighed. "It wasn't by choice. Habakkuk the Hermit of Love struck."

Riko blinked rapidly. "You two talked to the *elopement* hermit?"

"Yep." Kit turned back to the rest of the party. "Well done, guys. Everyone should have a new piece of armor or a new weapon in their inventory. It was tense for a few minutes there, but I think we did really great considering the circumstances."

Riko scratched the inside of her ear. "Avoiding talking more about your pledge, hmm? That's fine. We can just whistle up your boyfriend whenever we want more information."

"He's not my boyfriend," Kit said through a clenched smile. "Next, I think we should go for the human seal, but we should go back to Luminos first. I need to visit the White Veil Nunnery as I've been cursed. Again."

Cookie winced in sympathy. "I hope it doesn't cause you any pain like the last one?"

"No, but all my stats will be docked until I get it removed, so my buffs won't be as strong." Kit scowled up at the little skull icon below her name, then relaxed. *A little curse like this is nothing compared to the threat the shadow reaper posed.*

She cleared her throat. "While I'm doing that, you guys can get new gear. We've gotten enough levels, and the next area will be difficult enough that we should probably tinker with our characters and raid my loft for higher-leveled gear before we start it."

"I am interested to see what I can do to boost my damage." Vic picked up her cat as it meowed at her feet. "Seeing the damage Heaven's Fury caused was..."

"Overpowering?" Axel suggested.

"Invigorating," Vic said.

"To Luminos it is, then!" Cookie said.

Gil partially bowed. "As you wish."

As the other party members whistled up their horses, Riko gave Kit the stink eye. "You do realize this means you can't trash Kitten Lovemuch after we get out of here, right? You want to talk about having a special character? She's it. No one else can boast of being pledged to Solus Miles."

Kit's ear twitched as she listened. "It's not like he actually likes me." She looked from one side of the clearing to the other— she could have *sworn* she heard the creaking of a bowstring being pulled back. "Do you hear something?"

Riko mounted her horse. "Hear what?"

Kit looked up at the trees, and groaned when she saw an elf guard crouched on a branch with a nocked arrow aimed at her. "Wait—I'm just leaving—"

The elf cut her off before she could say anything more, killing her with one arrow to the heart. Everything went black as the game faded away.

———

Kit woke up in the Fione respawn area with a growl. "*Festering elves!*" she snarled. "I take back what I said—even a saint couldn't like this character! I hate it!" She pounded the earth with a fist for a moment then sighed as her frustration left her.

The wind brushed the back of her neck.

"We successfully evaded the scouts," Riko said. "So, we'll meet you at the respawn area and then head for the teleportation gate?"

Kit pulled a fistful of grass out of the ground, picturing it as the elf guard's perfect hair. "Yeah. See you soon."

"Don't mind it, Kit," Cookie said over the party chat. "One day you'll get back at them."

"Thanks, Cookie."

When the party chat went silent, Kit stood up and brushed herself off. The sun cast golden light through the trees, and the air was alive with the trill of song birds and the scent of dew.

If it's a deathtrap we're playing, it's a beautiful one.

Kit rolled her shoulders back and nodded to herself. *That's right—that's what matters, ending this quest and getting out of here.* She pulled up her character panel and, in spite of her realistic outlook, was still disappointed to see the dimmed community tab.

"We'll get out," Kit promised herself. "And we'll take as many people with us as we can. But for now...we're one step closer. And that will have to be enough."

———

Bryce Napert, one of the community managers of *Chronicles of Retha*, paced in his small office.

The corrupt servers, the inability to disconnect players, all of it had created a PR nightmare that was playing out publicly as time continued to pass. It didn't look good for the company, but what was more terrifying was that they were no closer to solving the horror than they had been when they first realized the backup servers were corrupted hours ago.

However, though Bryce was a loyal EC employee, the company was not his primary worry. It was his cousin, Kit.

Bryce rubbed his chin, scratching his five-o'clock shadow. "Kit's in there...with that joke of a character," his conscience pummeled him, and he grimaced.

He had done this to her. He had used his connections to dump her in Retha as an elf dancer. It was supposed to be funny! But now...it was a matter of grave severity. Perhaps even a life or death situation.

Bryce shook his head. *No, I can't think like that.* "It's Kit." She'll get out—she *has* to. I mean, if anyone can pull it off, it's her. She can't just..."

He limply plopped down in his chair. He woke up his smart phone and hesitated before opening up what had once been an active group message. He paused, then typed in a short text and sent it off before he could regret it.

Milk Crown: Kit is stuck in Retha.

THE END

Sleeping Beauty

Frog Prince

12 Dancing Princesses

Snow White

Three pack (Beauty and the Beast, The Wild Swans, Cinderella and the Colonel)

The Fairy Tale Enchantress:

Apprentice of Magic

Curse of Magic

The Elves of Lessa:

Red Rope of Fate

Royal Magic

King Arthur and Her Knights:

Enthroned

Enchanted

Embittered

Embark

Enlighten

Endeavor

Endings

Three pack 1 (Enthroned, Enchanted, Embittered)

Three pack 2 (Embark, Enlighten, Endeavor)

Robyn Hood:

A Girl's Tale

Fight for Freedom

The Magical Beings' Rehabilitation Center:

Vampires Drink Tomato Juice

Goblins Wear Suits

The Lost Files of the MBRC

Other Novels

Life Reader

Princess Ahira

A Goose Girl

ABOUT THE AUTHOR

Author by day, but a hunter (or very frazzled priestess) by night, A. M. Sohma is a lover of books, video games, and sweet armor sets. She aims to write entertaining stories with relatable characters, and spends her days lurking in libraries or wasting time on the internet.